# SEEKER'S QUEST

## SEEKER'S WORLD, BOOK TWO

## K. A. RILEY

**Disclaimer**

**Cover Design**

www.thebookbrander.com

THE SEEKER'S SERIES

## The *Seeker's* Series

*Seeker's World*
*Seeker's Quest*
*Seeker's Fate*
*...and more, coming soon...*

# SUMMARY

*I was alone with no heroic prince racing to save me, no merciful lord to offer me a stay of execution, and only myself to rely on.*

*I could only hope that this time, I would be enough.*

Vega Sloane's brother and best friend have been taken, and it's up to her to bring them back to the safety of their own world. But what seems like a simple rescue mission quickly turns into something far more perilous than Vega could ever have imagined.

Trapped in a place where nothing is quite as it seems, she can't help but wonder if she'll ever find her way back to the Academy, to the strange new friends she's met...and to the mysterious boy who has captured her heart.

In her first encounter with the Usurper Queen, Vega learns that she's not the only one with family secrets.

Then again, some secrets are best left unsaid.

*Seeker's Quest* is the second book in the *Seeker's World* Series.

*For everyone who's ever thought they weren't good enough.*

# NANA

THE SMALL, white-haired woman standing on the other side of the ancient kitchen table was gazing at me with an expression I'd seen on her face a thousand times over the years.

It was the same reassuring look that soothed me when I was five and a wasp stung me on the elbow. Or when I told her one of the Charmers—the trio of evil teenage girls at Plymouth High School who loved to make my life miserable—put a dead mouse in my locker before sharing a video of my horrified shriek on social media.

It was almost laughable to think of a time when a little rodent or a small posse of snarky girls had been my worst enemies. Especially after I discovered that my *real* arch nemesis was a powerful queen who lived in a dark, terrifying castle in a realm called the Otherwhere.

And I wasn't entirely sure anyone—even my grandmother— could talk me through my growing fear.

"Everything will work out, Vega dear," she cooed. "You'll see."

Nana had always possessed what seemed like a supernatural power to settle my nerves, no matter what crisis was eating away at me. But this time, it wasn't entirely working. I'd walked into her cottage determined to take on the world, but a nagging doubt was beginning to creep in even as the grim reality of my task draped itself around my neck like an iron chain.

"How can anything possibly work out?" I asked, succumbing to the fear of failure that had haunted me all my life. "I left the Academy, which is totally against the rules. Even if I don't get brutally murdered by angry wolves in the next twenty-four hours —which, by the way, is *extremely* likely—I'll probably never be allowed to go back there. I certainly won't be allowed to compete in the Seekers' Trials after what I'm about to do."

With a dismissive wave of her hand, Nana made a *tsk* sound that told me that I was being just a little *too* melodramatic. "Come now. Have you already forgotten what I told you about your bloodline?"

I ground my jaw. It was true, after all. A few minutes earlier, she'd revealed to me that the Headmaster of the Academy for the Blood-Born, a highly skilled wizard called Merriwether, was my biological grandfather.

Not to mention that Nana herself had been selected as the Academy's Chosen Seeker many years ago, and by all accounts, she'd kicked major butt. So as it turned out, I was the descendant of two amazing people from two different worlds.

It was why I'd developed into what was called a *Multi*—a magic user with multiple skills.

It was also why I seemed to have more enemies than anyone else at the Academy.

"I don't really see Merriwether playing favorites, even with his own granddaughter," I protested.

"It's not a question of favorites. It's what's best for the Academy and both our worlds. He knows how special you are, Vega. He knows he'd be a fool to let you go. The Otherwhere needs you, and this world needs you, too, more than you could possibly know. You're special, and it's time you faced up to that fact."

*Special.*

That cursed word kept coming up lately. Yet I'd proven worse than useless in combat situations at the Academy. I was clumsy and slow when it came to using weapons, to the point where I was as much a danger to myself as others. I could do exactly two things:

*1. Summon magical doors.*

*2. Disappear.*

"The only thing special about me is my special ability to run away," I half-mumbled.

"It's time you banished the word 'only' from your vocabulary, Granddaughter of mine. You've just recently come into your powers, and you haven't even begun to scratch their surface. So stop making excuses, and go save the world from the woman who's hell-bent on destroying it."

With that, she circled around the table, hobbling a little with age. After giving me a surprisingly strong hug, she twisted around to open a drawer under the counter.

When she turned back to me, she handed me a small glass vial, pressing it into my left palm.

I closed my fingers around the object. "What's this?"

"A potion. A drop of it will make you—or anyone else—forget the Otherwhere ever existed. Tuck it into your pocket and keep it with you always, just in case you need it sometime."

"Wait—forget the Otherwhere? Why would I want to do that?"

"Because that land is beautiful. And it's wonderful in so many ways. But sometimes it hurts to remember what we've had and lost." For a moment it sounded like her voice was going to break, but she composed herself and went on. "I came close to using the potion myself, once. But I decided that I'd rather remember my time in that faraway world, even if the memories sometimes bring pain. Your journey is just beginning, and you might find yourself experiencing things you'd rather forget."

I couldn't imagine a time in my life when I would ever want to forget about the Otherwhere. That would mean forgetting the amazing, beautiful world I'd discovered, a world that few could access, hidden somewhere beyond our own.

It would mean forgetting a certain boy I'd grown to care about so much that the thought of him made me want to open up a door and head straight back to the Academy.

Then again, the potion would also make me forget all the confusion, torture, humiliation and near-death experiences I'd endured since my seventeenth birthday.

With my hand trembling a little, I tucked the small vial into my pocket and nodded thanks before giving Nana one last hug.

Did I make a mistake, coming back here?" I asked. "Niala—a friend at the Academy—told me time passes differently in this world. What if I'm too late to help Will and Liv? What if months have already passed in the Otherwhere by the time I get back there?"

Nana gave me an unreadable half-smile. "A deep magic binds our worlds together, and yes—it affects time." She took me by the shoulders and looked me in the eye. "Hours and days don't matter, not where the Old Magic is concerned. Finding Will and Liv won't be easy, Vega. With the way time works, you're right— it might already be too late. The only thing to do is get there as fast as you can."

Offering her a seriously pathetic attempt at a grin, I turned and stepped out of her small cottage on the coast of Cornwall, only to be greeted by the salty smell of sea spray lingering on the air. It was the scent of sailors and fishermen, of explorers setting out for adventures on the high seas. Of ancient, long-forgotten stories laced with magic and danger.

Unfortunately, my sense of adventure was quickly being over-shadowed by a grim sense of foreboding. My hands were shaking, and my legs were two seconds away from buckling under me.

But I reminded myself that there was no time to let doubt cloud my mind. I knew exactly what I needed to do. This wasn't some nagging high school-level worry that I might get a C on a test or some conundrum about what to wear to prom. The mission I was about to undertake was literally a matter of life and death.

"Go, Vega," Nana said from behind me. "Follow your destiny."

*Destiny,* I thought. What a terrifying, fatalistic word that was. As if I had no choice in any of my actions. I was pre-ordained to embark on this new life of mine—a life that terrified me at every turn.

But I had to admit that it also thrilled me more than anything ever had.

I spun around to see Nana leaning against the door frame, her arms crossed. As our eyes met, her face seemed to alter. Her wrinkles disappeared, her eyes brightening, and for the briefest moment I saw Mariah Sloane, the young woman who had served the Academy so many years ago.

But then the illusion faded, and she was Nana once again. Still beautiful, but older, wiser, and full of secrets.

"Remember, I have faith in you," she said with a final smile before closing the door gently.

Taking a deep breath, I closed my eyes and summoned a door to the last place on earth I wanted to go.

# THE DOOR

WHEN I OPENED MY EYES, a sharp gasp lashed at the air, and it took me a second to realize the sound had come from my own throat.

Most of the doors I'd conjured had been elegant, carved with scrolling images of dragons, landscapes, idyllic forests, or majestic fruit trees with their branches intertwined like intricate Celtic knots. The wooden surfaces were usually immaculate and exquisite, delicate, and powerful beyond the wildest dreams of even the most masterful craftsman.

But the door that stood before me now was dark and decaying, the wood riddled with scratches, holes, and twisted iron nails. A thick liquid—molasses dark and as gross-looking as slime from a slug—oozed down in slow, seeping streams. If there had once been an image of some sort carved into its surface it was gone now, rotted away as if by the ravages of time. The door was a horrifying reminder of just how little control I had over this new summoning ability of mine.

Inhaling deeply, I reminded myself that I'd chosen this path. I'd chosen to leave my comfortable, albeit boring, home in

Fairhaven to attend the Academy for the Blood-Born. And though I'd only been there for a brief period, the place had come to feel like a second home.

For the first time in years, I felt as though I belonged somewhere.

But it was because of my choice to attend the Academy that the woman known as the Usurper Queen had seized the opportunity to kidnap my brother Will and my best friend, Liv. The queen hoped their imprisonment would be enough to blackmail me into returning to Fairhaven, to give up any aspirations I had of becoming the Academy's Chosen Seeker.

But there was no way in hell I was going to give in to her demands. Which meant I had no choice but to go through the horrifying door I'd conjured. I needed to find Will and Liv. I needed to bring them home. I had to save their lives, even if it meant losing my own.

With trembling fingers, I pulled the dragon-shaped key off the chain around my neck and reminded myself of the importance of my task. Chewing on the inside of my cheek, I was just about to thrust my shaking hand toward the lock when the vivid image of a young man flashed through my mind, bringing a much-needed smile to my lips.

I froze in place, closing my eyes in an attempt to bring the picture into sharp focus. As I zeroed in on the exquisite face forming in my mind's eye, I found myself breathing deeper, my body and mind calming.

If anyone could give me courage, it was Callum Drake. The boy with the bright eyes, the chiseled jaw, and the deep, soothing voice that melted me each time I heard it.

I'd grown to care for him more than I wanted to admit, even to myself. He was brilliant, amazing. He was the most beautiful person I'd ever known.

He was also incredibly gifted.

Not only could Callum shape-shift into a majestic golden dragon—a feat that was mind-blowing in and of itself—but I'd discovered he was also the rightful heir of the Crimson King, the former ruler of the Otherwhere. It was Callum's throne that the Usurper Queen now occupied.

Many of the Academy's students and instructors were endowed with magical powers, of course, but Callum…well, he seemed to exist on a whole other level. He was powerful in ways that I could barely fathom. Miraculous, even—though that word might have come with just a *little* bias on my part.

I was convinced that the only reason he hadn't taken his throne back from the wretched queen was that he was too kind and gentle to wreak fiery havoc on her followers. Callum was thoughtful, sensitive and patient—everything a great leader should be. I had no doubt that he would find just the right moment and take back what was rightfully his. And, if fate allowed it, I'd be there to help him do it.

"You *will* succeed, Vega. And when you do, I want you to come back to me."

Callum's rich baritone seemed to breathe the words into my mind as I stood frozen in front of the still locked door.

Though I was sure I was only imagining his deep voice, it came to me as clearly as if he'd been standing only a few inches away.

But after a moment, the image in my mind faded away to swirling nothingness.

"Great. Now I'm hearing things," I said out loud. With my chest tightening, I opened my eyes and stared up at the hideous-looking door. Holding my breath, I pushed the key into the lock and gave it a firm twist. The mechanism clanged and crunched in protest, but the last of the lock's tumblers finally fell.

I heaved the huge door open and stepped through, blinking into an oppressive, velvety-thick darkness.

The air was frigid and smothered in the scent of dampness, reminding me of days spent playing hide and seek in our basement back in Fairhaven.

Only this was no basement.

And I definitely wasn't in Fairhaven.

# DARKNESS

THIS PLACE I WAS IN…I wasn't even sure it *was* a place. It felt more like a void, an empty abyss of darkness and despair. Wispy shadows of dense blues and charcoal grays flitted around me. The air moved in a swirl of tangible-looking ribbons and rolling vapors, like undulating ghosts hovering above a graveyard.

*Great,* I thought. *I've managed to open a portal to…absolutely nothing.*

A chill was already beginning to penetrate my clothing, sending my very bones into a hard tremor. I felt like a little girl, alone and lost in a world that was almost too daunting to confront. There were no lights to guide me, no sounds to direct me one way or the other, except for the occasional screech from somewhere overhead that sounded like a soaring hawk. Or was it an eagle?

All I knew for sure was that I was outside, which meant this definitely wasn't the location where Liv and Will were being held hostage. I'd seen their dark prison projected like an ominous hologram in the Orb of Kilarin, the magical sphere currently in Merriwether's possession.

In the orb's glimmering surface, I'd stared at two helpless

forms trapped in large glass cylinders filled with green liquid, surrounded by the impenetrable moss and mold-covered walls of what looked like a dank underground dungeon.

Wherever I was at the moment—this empty vacuum of a void —I definitely didn't seem to be near any prison. In the engulfing darkness it was impossible, in fact, to tell if I was near anything at all.

What felt like a series of icy fingertips made their way over the surface of my skin as I realized I'd never felt so vulnerable or alone in my life. But I wasn't leaving this desolate place until I either succeeded in my mission or else failed horribly.

Unfortunately, the second of the two was beginning to look like the much more probable outcome.

After what felt like several minutes of silent, petrified panic, I watched the moon emerge from behind a thick blanket of clouds, revealing wispy images of the world around me in bits and pieces. The dark ribbons began to settle into tangible forms and objects. Beneath my feet, a pattern of uneven cobblestones materialized from the nebulous haze. To my right and left, buildings of heavy gray stone were beginning to take shape, their surfaces stained with lichen and moss, punctuated with leaded windows of warped, soot-stained glass.

The surrounding façades might once have been welcoming and beautiful, but in the dark of night, sullied as they were from neglect, they'd turned grim and foreboding. The squat, craggy buildings looked like massive tombstones, warning me to steer clear of whatever lingered behind their walls.

As I took a few tentative steps forward, signs advertising one business or another began to appear in the grimy windows of a series of long-neglected shops. Most of the signs had been faded by time and were all but unreadable. The small establishments, packed together in lopsided rows, looked like they hadn't been open in years. Or possibly even centuries.

I walked silently along the bumpy cobblestone road as more

details began to emerge and solidify. To my right, I could see what looked like an old bookshop, with a few decaying, leather-bound tomes sitting in a messy pile just inside the window. A sign half-hanging overhead read "Montague's Reading Nook." A cheerful name for such a desolate place.

To my left was an ancient candy store. The lollipop on its sign, which was probably once colorful and welcoming, looked like it had half melted into a pathetic, gray mass.

"What *is* this place?" I whispered to the engulfing emptiness. "Nothing about it feels...right."

Overtaken by a shudder, I wanted to kick myself. Why hadn't I asked Callum to join me on this ill-advised adventure? He should have been here with me, holding my hand, reassuring me with his strength and his unwavering ability to stay calm in awful situations.

And it didn't exactly hurt that he could morph into a dragon and barbecue anyone who threatened us.

*But he's not here,* I reminded myself. *And I'm terrified.*

Then again, fear was probably my best defense. If it wasn't for a moment of abject terror during a combat lesson at the Academy, I may never have discovered that I possessed the extraordinary ability to disappear, to enter what was called the Shadow Realm.

Right now, though, there was no need to hide from anything or anyone. This old town, which was piecing itself together before my eyes, seemed to be completely deserted. Death hung over the place like a grim veil, and I was pretty sure that even ghosts would find these streets too inhospitable to haunt.

"Okay. I need to get the hell out of here," I said into the stillness, trying my best to sound strong. "Sooner, rather than later."

Eager to find my way to somewhere a little more welcoming, I picked up my pace, putting one foot in front of the other in the beginnings of a determined stride. After a few minutes spent navigating the irregular terrain under my feet, I finally emerged from the narrow street of uneven stones onto another, wider road, which led up a steep hill between a series of gabled buildings toward an imposing structure towering up in the distance.

At first, I could only make out a large silhouette of something massive and portentous. But when the clouds parted, making way for the almost full moon, the structure's outline came into sharp, terrible focus.

With a jolt of horror, I realized I'd seen this place once before, with its jagged turrets and grim contour. I was staring up at the one place I needed and dreaded to go.

The castle of the Usurper Queen.

## INTO THE FIRE

I'D NEVER SEEN the queen. I didn't even know her real name.

Only that she was a thief, a liar, and a murderer.

What she'd done to Callum by stealing his rightful place on the throne was reason enough for me to despise her.

But I hated her even more for what she'd stolen from my brother and me. The queen may have robbed the Otherwhere of its rightful heir, but she robbed Will and me of our parents when her Waergs took their lives.

It was her fault that I'd watched Will struggle for years balancing jobs and school, all so he could look after me when he should have been enjoying his life like any other teenage boy.

A potent combination of hatred and rage swirled inside me as I started the long climb up the steep, twisted road to the castle's entrance, wondering how on earth I was going to find my way inside.

As I drew nearer, I spotted something, or someone, moving around by a set of large open doors. At first, I could only make out the silhouettes of two broad-shouldered men. But as I narrowed my eyes into the dark, a four-legged outline came into focus, padding along to their right. I recognized the distinct shape of one of the queen's Waergs, the shape-shifting creatures that could change between human and wolf in the blink of an eye.

I'd met my first Waergs in Fairhaven and would have been only too happy to live the rest of my life without ever encountering another one. In their animal form, they looked like normal wolves, except for the fact that they were enormous, their paws as thick and broad as a lion's. They were terrifying, malicious, and endlessly obedient to the woman they called the *Mistress*.

Their eyes were more intelligent than most animals' and shone with a hatred I'd never seen on any wild creature's face. It was more than mere viciousness. This was a feral vindictiveness —the look of an animal who wants to torture and maim, not out of a survival instinct or because of its master's orders, but for the pure pleasure of it.

And their human sides, from my limited experience, were just as awful. Each time I dared look into the eyes of a Waerg I felt like it was stripping my soul bare, reading my mind, and reveling in my fear, all at once.

So I wasn't about to take any chances with the one that was currently patrolling in front of the castle gate.

With my heart pounding, I pressed my back to the nearest wall and called on my Shadow form to hide me from the creature's keen eyes.

At first, nothing happened.

*Concentrate, Vega.*

Slowing my breathing down and doing my best to keep myself from trembling to pieces, I tried again. This time, I succeeded.

The transition was excruciatingly painful. Like every cell in my body was collapsing on itself and every bone disintegrating, all in the space of a split-second. *Suck it up,* I told myself as I suppressed a scream. *A little momentary pain is easier to tolerate than a Waerg's fangs tearing out my throat.*

I felt myself go weightless as I morphed from flesh and bone to a swirl of mist, relieved to know that no weapon could hurt me now. No hands could grab me.

I was invincible.

Well, *sort of.*

As I moved toward the castle gate, I wondered if there was even the smallest chance that the queen's guardians would be able to detect me. I may have transformed into little more than vapor, but I knew from experience that I wasn't entirely invisible to the naked eye. There was a reason I was called a *Shadow* and not an *Unseeable.*

Fortunately, it turned out I didn't have to worry too much about detection. As I drew near, the two guards began to argue.

"But I was supposed to be done at three hours past mid-dark!" one of them was yelling at the other, shooting a spray of saliva into the air after every other word.

"Nah. Shift ends at sun-up," the other protested. "You ain't leavin' 'til then."

"Oh yes, I am!"

"Over my dead body, lazy-arse!"

One man leapt at the other, grabbed him by the front of his leather tunic, and threw him against the stone wall. The wall and the man's body shuddered as if trying to decide which one was going to break first.

The first guard pressed his attack, charging with his shoulder lowered. He slammed into his partner, and the two of them crumpled in a heap to the ground, cursing, rolling around, and throwing thudding punches into each other's sides.

Seizing the opportunity, I slipped toward them undetected, only to spot the large gray wolf again, pressing its chest to the ground and growling at the two tussling guards. I could only hope it would leap into the fray and keep the two guards distracted long enough to let me pass by.

Of course, it would have been even more convenient if they'd all had the decency to kill each other and put my mind at ease.

But that was probably a little too much to ask.

As I made my way past them, the wolf raised its muzzle and sniffed the air. I was relieved when it quickly turned back to the task at hand, which consisted of nipping at the heels of both guards, seemingly agitated by their juvenile bickering and chaotic wrestling.

With a sigh of relief and one final push forward, I went gliding through the entranceway and into a large, open courtyard with thick stone walls rising up on all sides. There had to be six or more doors embedded along the various walls, each of which probably led to a different destination.

*Well...crap.*

It was impossible to tell which door might lead me to Will and Liv. All I knew for sure was that the prison chamber where they were being held was windowless, which meant that it was probably in the castle's basement—which was no doubt vast, dark, and labyrinthine.

Taking a wild guess, I headed left and made a beeline for the first door I saw. When I reached it, I tried to grab its handle.

That was when I realized my plan had one fatal flaw.

"Well, that's not great," I muttered, watching my misty fingers swirl uselessly through the air as they tried to take hold of the handle. It seemed I'd forgotten about one little complication: a girl entirely made of mist couldn't actually take hold of solid objects.

With a shudder of frustration, I realized that if I wanted to find my way into the castle, I'd have to revert to my solid form. That meant becoming visible, which meant becoming vulnerable.

Taking a deep breath and scanning the courtyard to make sure no one was around, I called on my body to change back to its normal state.

The transformation into flesh and bone was agony. Brought back into the relentless pull of gravity, my entire body filled with a brutal ache all at once, like I'd been hit by a truck then backed over for good measure. Once again, I tried to ignore the pain, reminding myself that I had far more important matters to contend with.

Once my feet were planted firmly on the ground, I pushed the door open and slipped through, delighted to find the castle so easy to penetrate. I didn't exhale again until I'd pushed the door closed behind me and turned to glance at my surroundings.

I found myself inside a long, broad corridor of stone, lit here and there with torches in iron holders angled away from the walls. Unlike the Academy, which teemed with magical and strangely modern touches like floating digital projections and gravity-defying lamps, this place felt utterly devoid of modernity, stripped of the twinkling loveliness that I'd grown used to in the Otherwhere.

It was cold and ghastly, an ominous, cavernous tunnel leading to some unseen destination. The few windows that flanked the corridor were cracked, filthy, or boarded over entirely.

Still, part of me wanted to burst into a triumphant dance. After all, I'd managed to find my way inside the evil queen's castle unseen. I was so close to completing my mission that I could taste victory. I'd have Liv and Will out of this awful place in no time. Then, I'd go back to the Academy and throw my arms around Callum, and we'd live happily ever after.

I would even have been satisfied with happily *for now.*

Unfortunately, the optimism of my fantasy was about to crash up against one of those cold, stone walls.

# CAUGHT

"Oı!" a loud voice bellowed from the shadows at the far end of the hallway. "Just where do you think yer goin', Missy?"

*Crap. Crap. Crap. Crap.*

From out of the darkness a large man, with shoulders nearly broad enough to touch the walls on either side of the corridor, was stomping his way toward me.

With muscles bulging out from under his thick, steel-studded leather armor, he brandished a very long, very sharp weapon in the air as the soles of his boots thundered on the stone floor.

The silver blades of a three-pronged spear glinted in the firelight. It was a huge weapon with a handle as big around as my arm, but the man carried it as easily as I could hold a number-two pencil.

I wasn't sure if he was a guard or someone higher up in the castle's hierarchy. But whatever he was, he definitely didn't look like the chairman of the welcoming committee.

Panicked, I called on the Shadow to overtake me once again.

*It'll be fine. I'll disappear then slip by him, just like I did to the others.*

I closed my eyes and poured every ounce of energy into the change.

But the Shadow didn't come.

And the guard was getting closer with every passing second.

*Please*, I whispered into the chilly air. *I need you. Don't desert me now.*

I slammed my eyes shut and tried again, focusing so hard I felt like my head might split down the middle.

*Nothing.*

Desperate, I tried to call up a door to bring me to Fairhaven, to the Grove at the Academy, to Nana's cottage. Anywhere but here.

But no door appeared.

"Answer me, girl!" the man bellowed. He was close now, and the rage ripping through his face reflected the vicious wolf lingering inside him. If the weapon didn't kill me, the wolf certainly would. "What are you doing here?"

I stammered, searching for any answer that wouldn't result in my dead body lying on the cold floor. *Why the hell didn't I bring a weapon? What kind of idiot infiltrates her greatest enemy's castle without so much as a butter knife for protection?*

Unable to come up with anything clever to tell the man, I spun around, hoping to leap out the door I'd come through.

But there was no sign that an entrance had ever existed.

The castle had let me in, but it had no intention of letting me leave.

"Are you serious right now?" I blurted out as I stared at a vast surface of thick, gray stone.

Panicked, I spun around again to face the guard. He was as big and thick as one of the castle's turrets, but he moved with a speed of a sprinting cheetah. I cried out in pain as he leapt at me, slinging his weapon onto his back and locking both of my wrists in one of his meaty hands.

With a lightning shot of pain searing through my forearms, a hit of the man's foul breath swirled through the air next to my face.

"You're Vega, aintcha? The Mistress has been waiting for you. Welcome to castle Uldrach, your own personal Hell."

The words were followed by a round of chuckling so tainted with malice I could practically taste the bitterness on the air.

Dismayed by my own stupidity, I cursed under my breath. I should have known this had all been too easy. Merriwether had warned of a spy at the Academy—one who had reported to the Usurper Queen about my powers, and I couldn't even guess what else.

So of *course* the queen knew I was coming.

Of course she'd set a trap for me.

And I'd walked straight into it.

As I kicked myself for being so cocky, my rancid-smelling captor threw an even more awful-smelling sack over my head. I didn't really want to think too hard about what might have been inside it before it found a new life as a makeshift blindfold.

I half-held my breath as the man dragged me down a series of hallways that grew progressively colder and damper the deeper we ventured into the bowels of the castle.

I tried to tell myself not to worry about what might happen.

*Somehow, this will all work out.*

*Just like Nana said.*

*It'll be fine.*

The only problem was, I couldn't see how. I was now a prisoner of a murderous monster. I'd lost the ability to escape or to hide. The castle was probably crawling with Waerg guards who would gladly shift into their wolf forms and bite my face off with one word from their beloved Mistress.

And, to add to my misery, I had no idea where we were going —though I was pretty sure that wherever it was, it wouldn't get me any closer to finding Liv and Will.

In fact, my chances of finding and saving them had just taken a radical nose-dive.

After being dragged down several winding hallways with the man's hand gripping my arms hard enough to cut off the circulation to my fingers, I heard a voice in the distance calling out, "What have you got there, then?"

"A present for the Mistress," grunted the guard who'd caught me. "Pretty little thing. Shame I had to put a bag over her head, really. Give me a hand bringing her down to the dungeons, would ya?"

"Are we putting her in the—"

"Shh! Idiot! She may not be able to see, but she can *hear*!"

"I only meant," the other man whisper-hissed, "are we putting her in the *special* cell?"

*Special cell?*

That didn't sound great.

"Shut it. It's none of your damned business where we're bringing her."

A second pair of rough hands grabbed me under my legs and started to lift me.

Seeing my chance, I lashed out with a storm of crazy kicks as I twisted and flailed as hard as I could. For a moment I thought I was making progress.

But what I suspected were the man's groans of pain turned out to be amused chortles of laughter.

"You'll have to do better than that," the guard grumbled through a thick belly-laugh. "Teenage girls don't tend to do well in matches with Waergs. Or did the old geezer at the Academy tell ya you were invincible?"

Mentally and physically defeated, I collapsed into a panting heap. The huge guard slung me over his shoulder and stomped down the stairs with me bouncing, wheezing, and writhing in pain the entire way.

At the bottom of what felt like a mile-long stairwell, he set me down and dragged me by my wrists along another frigid corridor. My soles bumped and scraped on the pitted concrete floor until we came to another stop.

With the screech of what sounded like old hinges and the creak of a door, I was shoved forward. I stumbled, slamming my shoulder and the side of my head against a rock-solid wall. I winced against the painful ringing in my ears.

When I heard the door slam shut behind me, I ripped the damp sack off my head, grateful that at least the bastards hadn't bound my hands.

"Thank heavens for small mercies," I muttered. It was something my mother used to say whenever she managed to find a silver lining in an awful situation.

But as it turned out, being able to see my surroundings wasn't exactly a blessing.

The only light in the small cell came from a tiny window crisscrossed by thick iron bars, twenty or so feet above me. Way too high to climb.

Miserable, cold, and hopeless, I slumped down onto the cell's cold floor, knees pulled up under my chin, my arms wrapped tight around my legs. I was shaking, but I didn't know if it was from fear, from the cold, or from the throbbing in my head that I was sure was the first symptom of a serious concussion.

Drifting in and out of bleary-eyed consciousness, I had no idea how long I stayed curled up, shivering, and in pain like that. Hours, at least. All I knew for sure was that it felt like an eternity of wondering if Merriwether had noted my absence.

Was Callum worried yet?

Or had he already given up on me?

If he had, I probably deserved it. I'd done this to myself. I was alone now, with only the darting shadows of long-legged bugs scurrying around to keep me company. I told myself to shut down my heart, to push away thoughts of him. It was a survival mechanism, more than a desire to be rid of him. A need to preserve my last vestiges of strength for whatever atrocities were yet to come.

To make matters worse, the sun had begun to work its way into the sky, only to vanish again beyond a heavy layer of dark clouds, leaving the grim night behind to make room for an even grimmer day. I'd already begun to miss the sun like I'd rarely missed anything in my life. I wondered with a wave of self-pity if I'd ever see it again.

Funny how things begin to matter deeply in the moment you think they may be gone forever.

Pushing the thought of my ghastly situation from my mind, I closed my eyes, hoping to find myself drifting to sleep and waking to discover that this had all been a horrible dream. My whole body was sore from getting dragged such a long distance, and my mind had kicked into serious overdrive, concocting an assortment of possible tortures I might have to endure in the very near future.

"Way to go, Vega," I whispered. "You've ruined your own life. And it was all for nothing."

# HOPELESS

I WASN'T sure if I fell asleep or merely drifted into a state of mindless oblivion. But after a time, the same beefy guard who had lugged me down the stairs and thrown me into the cell pushed the door open and ordered me to my feet. Several other guards stood behind him, staring at me as if I was some exotic zoo animal they'd come to gawk at.

When I'd pushed myself up onto my very tired and very sore feet, the man told me to step toward him.

I hesitated for a second. "Why?" I asked.

"I want something that you've got," he said, lurching toward me.

"I don't think so," I replied, taking a giant step backwards with an angry glare, horrified to think what he could possibly be talking about.

Apparently, that was the wrong answer.

He reached out, grabbed the front of my shirt in his hairy-knuckled fist, and lifted me clean off the ground, pulling me toward him. With his free hand he reached out for the dragon key that still hung from its chain around my neck.

But when he wrapped his meaty, dirt-crusted fingers around

the key, he let out a loud yelp like a dog that just got its tail stepped on. Despite being tired, in pain, and, frankly, scared out of my mind, I still had to fight back a cheeky smile at the giant man's high-pitched squeal.

He dropped me and staggered back a full step, sucking on his fingertips.

"I guess you don't know," I said, narrowing my eyes at my greedy assailant. "The key belongs to *me*. Even if I die in this place, I have faith in its loyalty. It's mine until I offer it freely. That's the rule."

Growling and holding his injured hand in a cramped ball under his chin, he took a half step toward me before freezing in place.

"Unless you want to try that again?" I mocked, standing tall and looking as brave as possible despite the shiver of pure terror pulsing through my bones.

The other guards laughed as the wounded man scowled, shoved me against the wall with his uninjured hand, and retreated back into the hallway. As the door closed, I could hear them assuring him it didn't matter anyhow and to let me keep my precious trinket.

"It won't do her any good in here," one of the guards grumbled. "Not as long as the queen's keeping her from usin' her tricks."

They were right, of course. Since I'd been locked up, I'd tried more than once to summon a door, but to no avail. Nothing worked. No amount of concentration, need, or desperation helped me break through whatever force was keeping me from casting my limited repertoire of spells.

I was weak. Useless. Broken. And I was being forced to face a cold, hard truth:

I was probably going to die in this place.

I DIDN'T KNOW how much time passed after that, but I could only guess it was a *lot*.

I must have paced the cramped, gloomy room a couple of hundred times. The small window sitting so high up on the wall teased me with the thin streaks of hazy light it let in—like it was reminding me there was an outside world I couldn't get to and a freedom I'd never have again.

I tried over and over again to use my spells. I strained to summon a door. I clamped my eyes shut and tried to will myself to transition into my Shadow form.

But all I got for my efforts was a massive headache and the gloomy realization that I'd been completely caught off-guard, outsmarted, and out-muscled. The tiny spark of hope inside of me, the one that flickered with the weakening light of my grandmother's voice, was starting to fade.

*But it's not gone yet*, I reminded myself. *They might beat me, but I'll never just give up.*

After what I guessed were at least another two or three hours spent shivering in isolation, the door clanked and creaked open to reveal the guard who'd hurt his hand on my dragon key. From the look on his contorted face, he remembered that moment *very* well.

Without taking his eyes off of me, he took one step into the cell and knelt down to place a bowl full of something that looked like cold, gloppy porridge on the floor. I refused to touch it. There was no way I was about to trust any of the queen's subordinates. I could just imagine them trying to poison me for fun and placing bets on how long it would take for me to die.

"Suit yourself, my beauty," the guard said, his eyes narrowing as he began backing out of the cell. "Starve, for all I care. But you should know the queen wants you alive for now. She'd be devastated if she missed the chance to meet the great Vega Sloane." He slammed the door shut, and once again, I heard the sound of muted laughter through the tiny cracks between thick wooden beams and rusted iron braces.

I slipped over and pressed my ear to the door to hear the muffled conversation.

"Thinks she's so high and mighty, the little brat," one of the guards said. "Just because she's one of 'em Seekers."

"Yeah, well, I heard she's got skills, that one. She's not just a Seeker. They say she's a Multi. A Summoner *and* a Shadow. She's dangerous. That is, she *would* be if she could use her powers."

*If*, I thought. *The most loathsome and unfortunate word in the English language.*

"I don't understand why we can't just kill her," another guard grumbled back. "Why keep her and them two *Worlders* alive? Best be rid of all three of them."

*Worlders?*

If only for a moment, my heart leapt with something like joy. I'd never heard that word before, but there was no doubt in my mind that he was talking about Will and Liv. Hearing confirmation they were still alive was enough to bring a brief smile to my lips and a shot of energy to my very tired body. The flicker of light that had nearly snuffed itself out was finally getting its second wind.

Now, if the stupid guards would just say where my brother and Liv *were*…

One of the men cleared his throat, snorted, and made a loud spitting noise. "I heard the Mistress say she needs the girl for something. But don't ask me what."

"Oh, so she'll use her, *then* kill her. Sounds like my kind of plan. Well, I'll tell you what. As long as we get to watch, I'm happy."

A series of cackles rumbled from the other men's throats.

I clenched my fists, a grimace undoing my all too brief moment of optimism. Use me? What could the queen possibly have in mind?

Then again, maybe I didn't want to know.

IT WASN'T LONG after the guards' voices and footsteps faded into the distance that a fist pounded heavily on my cell door.

"Hey, Girl!" a voice belted out. "Word is the Mistress is making room in her schedule for you, a few days from now! You'd better practice your curtsies!"

"Exactly when will I see her?" I called back.

"That's none of your damned business, is it, Missy?" he replied with another thudding fist to the door. "Now shut your face and behave yourself!"

I wanted to swear at him, but from the sound of things, he was already clomping away. Besides, letting out the string of expletives that were barreling through my mind would probably have resulted in the door flying open and a hard fist to my jaw.

*A few days,* he'd said. Who knew if that meant two or ten? I wanted to weep to think I was going to be in this god-awful cell for days before the Usurper Queen decided once and for all what to do with me.

Days before I'd find out if I'd ever see the Academy again. By the time I got out of here, my fellow Seekers would probably already have competed in the Trials. Someone else would be declared the winner, and I'd be sent home.

*If* I ever got out of here.

Broken by the thought, I resigned myself to the idea of spending the remaining daylight hours thinking about my dashed hopes and dreams.

My regrets, which were too many to count, marched through my mind in a parade of misery. I pondered the fact that I would never see Fairhaven again—never finish high school, never go to university, start a career, get married, have a family, or do anything else that people were supposed to do if they actually made it to adulthood.

Part of me wanted to curl up into a pathetic ball and let myself drown in the sea of fear and anxiety that was surging its way through me. Instead, I forced myself to remain upright, huddling against the cold of my dank prison of foul air and impenetrable stone. I had to stay strong. I had to come up with a plan.

But every time I tried to point my mind in that direction, it filled instead with thoughts of my greatest regret: the fact that I might never see Callum again.

I hated to admit it, even to myself, but I wished more than anything that he would find a way to come for me. I wanted desperately for him to be my saving grace, my lifeline, my light at the end of a terrifying tunnel, as he had been more than once before. As much as I liked the idea of being a strong, independent young woman, I wouldn't have objected in the least if my knight in shining dragon scales had shown up one more time to save me from certain death.

More than once over the course of several hours, I closed my eyes and repeated his name over and over again, so softly that I could barely hear it.

But it was pointless. I knew he wasn't going to come for me. No one was. I was alone, with no heroic prince racing to save me, no merciful lord to offer me a stay of execution, and only myself to rely on.

I could only hope that this time, I would be enough.

I reached for the key around my neck, my fingertips slipping over its sharp ridges, gliding over the sleek silver chain my Nana had given me for my birthday.

In the note that had accompanied the gift, Nana had mentioned that the chain once saved her life. I only wished I'd thought to ask her how. What could a simple length of silver links do, aside from hold the precious key in place? Did the chain possess some other special property I didn't know about?

I pulled the key off and examined it under the pale light. The red, glinting stone embedded in the dragon's body. The smaller stones that surrounded it. It really was the most beautiful thing I'd ever owned. And it had led to the greatest series of adventures I'd ever had.

Too bad it would probably also lead to my death.

# THE BOY NEXT DOOR

As the hours ticked by, the thickly overcast sky ruined any chance I had of keeping track of the time of day.

For all I knew, it was late evening by the time I finally mustered the courage to drink a little of the water the guards had pushed through the door toward me. I'd even taken a few bites of a piece of questionable-looking dried meat. I figured if the queen really wanted to talk to me, it would hardly make sense to poison me first.

Restless and anxious, I distracted myself by pondering what I'd do if I ever got out of this place.

*Kiss Callum. Tell Merriwether I'm sorry for leaving without his blessing. Kiss Callum again. Eat a giant cheeseburger. Kiss Callum a thousand or so more times. Accept the fact that I'll never become the Chosen Seeker after what I've done.*

Of course, none of it mattered. I'd never get out of here, at least not until Will and Liv were free. And with every passing minute, that outcome was becoming less and less likely. If I couldn't use my magic, there was no way to free them. And if I couldn't free them…

*I'm sorry, Will. Sorry, Liv. You didn't deserve any of this. It's all my fault.*

I pictured the scene that I'd witnessed in the Orb of Kilarin. Two people floating helpless in tall tubes filled with mysterious green liquid, their eyes staring absently into space. They were in suspended animation, frozen in time, ripped away from their lives in another world.

I was just beginning to surrender to the fresh tears that were welling in my eyes when the faint sound of scratching drew my attention to the far wall.

At first, I thought maybe some rodent or a giant insect was digging among the loose stones somewhere across from me. Crouching down, I crept toward the sound, expecting to frighten the creature into silence. But as I advanced, the scratching only grew louder.

"You'd better not be what I think you are," I said out loud, disgusted by the possibility of a large, fearless rat darting into the cell with me.

Tensely expecting to be met by a pair of horrifying red eyes, I was greeted instead by a meek, hollow-sounding voice that sounded like it was speaking through a paper towel tube. "Hello? Is someone there?"

*Oh my God.*

Someone—an actual human being—was in the cell next to mine. And from the sounds of it, he was another teenager.

I wasn't sure whether to be happy or devastated to know that someone else my age was being held against their will. Still, I couldn't help feeling a little grateful to have company.

I pressed myself to the floor, searching for a hole, an indentation, any small tunnel that the voice may have come through. I finally found it between two chunks of stone midway down the wall. A small opening, barely as big around as a quarter, between my cell and whatever lay on the other side.

I squinted my left eye shut and looked through with my right, only to be greeted by an eye staring back at me. Shocked, I lurched backwards, falling onto my hands.

A second later I was on my feet again, crouching in front of the hole.

"Who are you?" I asked.

"Name's Raff. I'm a prisoner," the voice replied in a surprisingly jaunty tone. "You're new here, aren't you?"

"Yes. But wait—how long have *you* been in here?"

"About ten years. But I only know that because they tell me I recently had a birthday."

*Ten years?*

The thought horrified me. I thought *I* had it bad, and I'd only been in there for a day, tops. To be imprisoned in a cell like mine for so long, never to see the outside world. Never to walk down a street with a friend, to go shopping, to enjoy a simple pleasure like a milkshake…

Did they even have milkshakes in the Otherwhere?

"Why are you in here?" I asked. I could only assume that he'd killed someone, or possibly many someones, and I braced myself for a terrifying answer.

After a few seconds of silence, the voice stuttered out, "This will sound insane, but the truth is, I'm not really sure. All I know is that my mother was one of the queen's servants. They arrested her when they took me. That is to say, they took me *because* they arrested her."

"Wait," I interrupted. "You're in prison in the queen's castle because of something your mother did? That seems pretty unreasonable, to put it politely."

I supposed it shouldn't have come as a surprise that the queen might decide someone—even a child—was guilty by association. Liv and Will were imprisoned because of me, after all. But to incarcerate someone for a decade?

That seemed cruel by any measure.

"Reasonable behavior isn't exactly the queen's strong suit," Raff replied. I could all but hear a shrug in the words, like he'd resigned himself to the notion that the queen was horrible, but what could he do? "She lets me out sometimes, so that's something."

"What do you mean, *out?*"

"You know. Out of my cell. She invites me to come see her now and then. She says she likes my company. But mostly, the guards let me out so they can take me to a room at the other end of the castle. It's where they test me."

"*Test* you?" The conversation had already gone from disturbing to horrifying. "Test you how?"

"They ask me to cast spells. You know, magic stuff."

"What sorts of spells, exactly?"

"Any and all. They try to get me to move things or set things on fire, all with my mind. I'm not so great at some of it, but I'll admit, I do enjoy the puzzles they give me."

"Puzzles?" I asked, shooting a nervous look toward the door in case a nosy guard was on the verge of barging in.

"Mostly," Raff explained, "they give me riddles. They'll read me one and ask me to solve it. It always leads me to something— a goal—like I'll have to find a hidden object in a room, that sort of thing. I'm pretty good at it, too. Especially the one they made me do on my birthday. I turned seventeen a few weeks ago. Or maybe it was months—I can never tell how much time I've spent in here. All the days and nights kind of blend into each other, you know?"

I tightened when I heard how old he was. It was on my seventeenth birthday that I'd first learned I was a Seeker, and my world had begun to alter around me.

Was Raff one of us?

"Happy belated birthday," I replied, trying not to sound utterly freaked out. "Tell me something—what was different about the test they gave you that day?"

"Usually they ask me to look at a picture and tell me to find something specific in its details. Or they'll hide an object in the room I'm in. But the riddle that day was about some location far away, deep in the Otherwhere. It was a place I'd never been. The queen's Waergs said I had to find a treasure for them...they told me it was a matter of life or death. It was pretty weird, to be honest."

"Wait—you said a 'treasure?'" I asked, my palms sweating.

"Yep. And I found it!" Raff added with pride. "I'll admit I was pretty pleased with myself."

"How, exactly?" I asked, trying to hide the quiver in my voice. "I mean, how did you find the treasure?"

"I'm not even sure. When they read me the riddle, I just closed my eyes and listened. I didn't *solve* it. Not exactly, anyway. It was more like my mind figured it out for me without any effort. Like I just...knew."

"What was the riddle, Raff? Can you remember?"

"Remember it? I don't think I'll ever *forget* it. I guess it was more like a poem than a riddle, really."

"Can I hear it?"

"Sure," he said. "It goes like this:

*On an ancient hill stands the oldest house*
*Where glass and stone conceal a prize.*
*Ancient as the world itself,*
*On a king's chest it lies."*

As he spoke, I swallowed up every word, thrusting the verse into my memory like my life depended on it. Though I wasn't sure why I was bothering. If he'd already found the object, the words probably weren't all that important anymore.

Yet something told me I needed to hold onto them.

"When I heard the verse," he continued, "I closed my eyes, and this image just…came to me…of some old ruins on top of a hill. Very distinct-looking, like it was once an important place. One of the queen's men asked me to find the precise location on a map of the Otherwhere. He said there was an object hidden there, something of vital importance. A *trophy of strength* or something…now, what did he call it? I can't quite recall…a…what *was* it?"

"Relic of Power," I said, all but choking on the words.

On the other side of the stone wall, Raff's voice was pure jubilance. "Yes! That was it!"

I felt sick.

Merriwether had mentioned a rumor during one of the Academy's assemblies that the queen had acquired one of the four Relics of Power.

And it turned out it was all thanks to Raff.

If he helped them find any more of them, the queen's power would increase. Merriwether had told me that the Relics gave their possessor the power to open portals between our worlds, to move their armies through and wage war. The queen would be able to send her Waergs anywhere she desired. The Academy, too, would be in grave danger.

I couldn't entirely picture an army of wolf shifters in Fairhaven. Yet I'd seen their kind there with my own eyes. Threatening, malicious, thirsting for blood.

Those few had been hunting me.

I could only imagine what would happen if they were sent to terrorize the entire town.

"But how did you know what they were called?" Raff asked when I didn't reply.

"Let's just say I've seen a Relic of Power. I know how important they are. Listen—the one you found—do you know where it is now?"

"Yeah, it's in the Throne Room, here in the castle. The queen keeps it on display. She's very proud of it. To be honest, I'm a bit annoyed that she acts like *she* was the one who found it. It's not like she lifted a bloody finger or anything."

"What does it look like?"

"The Throne Room or the Relic?"

"The Relic."

"Well…it's a sword—a long one. Silver and quite beautiful. They say it used to belong to someone very powerful, though I have no idea who."

*A sword,* I thought. *A sword could come in very handy if I could get my hands on it…*

Pfft. What was I thinking? Even if I walked right up to the Relic and grabbed it by the hilt, I wouldn't suddenly turn into some skillful warrior. I'd probably drop the thing on my foot and sever a toe or something. And then the Waerg guards would laugh at me as I bled slowly to death.

I definitely needed a more realistic plan.

Not to mention that I needed to get Raff out of this place. If not for his sake, then for the Academy's. He should be working for our side, not for a queen who'd cruelly kept him imprisoned for most of his life.

"So why are *you* in here, anyhow?" he asked. "What did you do to get on the queen's bad side?"

"Does she have a *good* side?"

"Yes. But it's evil."

That made me laugh and, for a second, I took what felt like the first normal breath I'd inhaled in days.

"Okay," I said after composing myself. "Let's just say I walked into the castle uninvited. Apparently, that's against the rules."

A laugh vibrated its way through the wall. "Yeah, that was a bad idea," he said. "I could have told you as much."

"If only I'd met you before I decided to try something so stupid." I gave a little chuckle of embarrassment at my own misplaced confidence and the unqualified failure that followed.

"Anyhow, there's a lot more to it, but I'm not sure I should tell you."

"That's too bad. I'd love to hear a good story. Things are pretty boring around here lately. They haven't taken me for tests in a few days because of the queen's no-magic rule."

"Yeah. What's the deal with that?" I tried to sound casual, like I wasn't desperately digging for information. Last thing I wanted to do was scare off my new friend-slash-informant.

"I probably shouldn't tell you this—she'd kill me if she knew I was talking behind her back."

"I won't tell. I promise."

Raff waited a few seconds, apparently weighing the pros and cons of what he was about to say before replying. "Let's just say the queen's not very skilled with magic."

"You could've fooled me," I said. "When I was at the Academy, a fleet of drones attacked an instructor and me. I was told the queen had cast a spell on them."

"Yeah? Well, I can tell you that's not bloody likely," Raff said. "The queen struts around like she's in charge, but the truth is, she's not really."

I found myself intrigued yet horrified at the idea that there might be someone out there even more cruel and powerful than the Usurper Queen. "Who is?"

"A man," Raff said. "One who scares me half to death. If you ever see him, you'd do well to stay out of his way. He's incredible."

"Terrifying and incredible," I chuckled. "That's quite a combination. So you're saying he's the one around here who's casting the spells?"

"Sort of. I mean, the queen knows some spells, but she's not powerful like he is. The truth is, she's *terrified* of magic users. So she sometimes wears an amulet that keeps anyone who comes to the castle from casting. She has it on all the time these days."

"An amulet, you said? What does it look like?"

"It's yellow. Might be stone. Could be glass. I don't know. Very shiny, though. It reminds me of a wolf's eye. I always feel like it's looking at me, staring at me like it's debating whether or not to kill me. Something inside it keeps other people's magic from working. No one in the entire castle can cast spells while she has it on—not even her closest allies."

So, a small, slightly evil-looking pendant dangling from the queen's neck was wreaking havoc and keeping me from using my powers. Was that really the only thing between me and freedom?

If so, my mission was becoming clearer: I had to get my hands on the precious amulet.

Which wouldn't exactly be easy.

"Not everything is disrupted by the amulet," Raff added. "The Waergs can still shift, of course. Shifting doesn't count as magic. Oh, and I heard the guards saying magical *items* can still be used. I don't suppose you have any of those on you?"

"No," I replied. "No magical items. I mean, I have a key that's sort of special, but it seems pretty useless at the moment. I've tried using it, but no luck."

"A key? Sounds like a great item to have when you're locked in a dungeon."

"It would be. If the door of my cell had a keyhole on the inside."

"Good point. Well, it's probably for the best. You don't want to cheese off the queen. She can be pretty terrifying when she wants to be."

"I'm sure she can." Feeling oddly relaxed for the first time since I'd left the Academy, I stretched my arms above my head and let out a yawn.

"I'm boring you," said the disembodied voice.

"Not at all!" I said. "I guess I'm just tired. It's been a long day."

"Hey—may I ask you a deeply personal question?" Raff asked after a momentary silence.

"Sure."

"What's your name?"

A rolling laugh rose up in my chest as I pressed my forehead against the wall, realizing we'd talked this long without discussing my actual identity.

"Vega," I said.

"Vega," he repeated. "It's nice to meet you."

"You too. Though the circumstances could definitely be less weird. I mean, we've talked this long and I don't even know what you look like."

"Very dirty at the moment," he snickered. "Very dirty *usually*, to be honest. I'm pretty tall. Brown hair, blue eyes. What about you?"

"Not so tall. Not short, either. Extremely curly hair—like, out of control. Hazel eyes, though they keep changing color lately." I didn't feel like going into any more detail than that, or explaining that having parents with very different skin tones meant I was a perfect amalgam of both. Anyhow, he had enough information to start forming an image of me in his mind's eye.

"Well," he said, "whatever happens, I hope I get to see you face-to-face someday soon. I'd like to lay eyes on the girl who managed to sneak her way into the queen's castle and lived to tell about it. I have a feeling you're very pretty."

I chuckled again. "Why would you say that?"

"Not sure. I suppose it's because you have a kind voice. Kindness tends to render people more beautiful. At least, that's what I remember from the outside world. I can't say I've seen anyone particularly gorgeous in this place."

*Beautiful. Gorgeous.*

The words made me think of Callum. Of his incredible features, his extraordinary presence. Raff was right—kindness *did* make people more attractive.

"Well, I'd like to see your face, too," I said with a yawn, lying down to press my back to the floor next to the wall, knees bent. "Someday."

"Someday," Raff echoed. "Go to sleep, Vega. We'll talk tomorrow?"

"I'd like that."

"Me too. Well, good night…neighbor."

"Good night."

# TIME SERVED

THE NEXT SEVERAL days were rendered almost bearable by my ability to converse from time to time with the boy next door.

Raff turned out to be a good companion—always cheerful, talkative, and most importantly, always careful not to speak too loudly. His voice, like mine, rarely rose much above a whisper. On the infrequent occasions that he spoke out loud, the sound echoed through the small stone tunnel between our cells, an aural lifeline that reminded me I wasn't entirely alone.

Our conversations were mostly about banal topics: our favorite foods, favorite childhood games, favorite sports, though occasionally we'd talk about things we'd do if we ever managed to escape the queen's prison. One evening when we were sure the guards were some distance away, I asked him, "What do you miss most about the outside world?"

"Fighting," he replied without hesitation.

"Seriously? Fighting?" I asked. "Like fist fights?"

He paused for a few seconds, and I wished I could see his face.

"You know," he said. "I'm a guy. We like punching each other."

"So when you were seven and younger, your favorite thing was punching other boys?" I laughed.

"I guess it was. I mean, it wasn't like I was into astronomy at the age of six or anything. I liked scrapping. I guess it was about the human contact more than anything."

"I guess that makes sense."

Raff went quiet for a few seconds before asking, "What about you? What do you miss most?"

I was about to say *Callum*, but I stopped myself. I didn't feel like explaining the depth of my feelings for the young man who should rightfully occupy the throne. I trusted Raff as much as I could trust anyone I'd never met face to face, but my instincts told me to keep at least *some* cards close to my chest.

"Everything." I let out a frustrated breath and pressed my back against my cell's cold stone wall. "I just wish I could figure out a way get us out of here."

"Me, too. I suppose the best I can ever hope for is to get to wander around Kaer Uther sometime. The queen told me she'll let me...if I help her solve more of her riddles."

"Kaer Uther?" I asked, my interest piqued once again. "What's that?"

"That's the town. You know, the one down the hill from the castle. You probably went through it to get here. It's where I was born. Where I would have grown up, if not for...well, you know. It was such a brilliant place, full of laughter and fun. There were tons of kids my age, running through the streets, playing games. From what I remember, it was beautiful, too. There were shops everywhere, food, drink, you name it. Everyone knew each other. The townspeople were all friends."

"I did see it." I hesitated to say the next part, unsure if he knew what his birthplace had become. "But...it's not what you describe, not at all. It's empty, Raff. Like a shell of whatever its former self was. I hate to say it, but I don't think you really want to go back there."

"I know it's changed," he said, his voice heavy again.

"So what happened to it?"

Raff went silent for a second before replying, "The queen used to collect taxes from the residents. After a while, the townspeople refused to pay—which, if you ask me, was wrong. You can't just go against a queen."

My brow furrowed, though I supposed he had a point. It wasn't like anyone in my world could just decide to stop paying taxes and expect to suffer zero consequences for it.

"So," Raff continued, "the queen sent her Waergs in to clear the place out. Anyone disloyal was banished or killed."

"Holy crap," I said under my breath.

Raff fell silent for a moment before saying, "I hope we can find a way out of here together, Vega."

"I'll get us out," I assured him. "Or else I'll die trying."

I could all but feel Raff's grin through the wall. "So, I heard the guard say you're going to meet her."

"The queen? Yeah. She probably wants to tell me how she plans to kill me."

"I don't know about that. The queen doesn't kill people she can use. She'd rather torture them for a long time first."

"Great. Maybe she'll set me on fire, then jab metal splinters under my fingernails, *then* kill me."

"Or maybe she'll skin you alive!"

"You're not helping at all."

"Sorry."

I turned around and crouched down, peering through the hole in the wall. "Hey, Raff," I said quietly. "Listen to me. Whatever happens when I get taken out of here, it's really important that you don't help the queen anymore."

"What do you mean?"

"That Relic you found—there are three more that she'll soon be hunting. And if she were to get her hands on them, they'd give her massive amounts of power. She'd probably destroy the Otherwhere in the process. This world could go dark forever, just like Kaer Uther did."

Raff was quiet for so long I thought he might have fallen asleep, but at last his scratchy voice filtered through the tiny hole in the wall. "So, what should I do?"

"Nothing," I told him. "If they come and ask you to solve more riddles, tell them you're trying your best. Make them think your skills have stopped working or something. Don't help them, not under any circumstance. In the meantime, I'm going to try to figure out a way to get you out of here, I promise."

"Get me out? How?" he asked. "I told you, the queen's got powerful allies, plus she's always surrounded by her Waergs."

"I'll find a way," I said. "I have to, or…"

"You can't possibly beat her at her own game," Raff interrupted, sounding suddenly angry. "Honestly, I don't understand why you even came here. Most people would stay a million miles away if they could. You don't know how she works. What she's capable of. It's foolish to think you can win this battle. Foolish, and honestly, a little arrogant. The queen is so much stronger than you know…"

"I thought you said she was weak," I replied. "You said she's terrified of magic users. That she's not good with spells."

"She's strong enough to kill you and everyone you've ever cared about," he snapped. "And don't think she won't do it."

"I know that, better than you think," I muttered.

I was taken aback by his hostile tone, but I couldn't exactly blame him for being short with me. Holding onto hope in a place like this had to be exhausting. I probably sounded like an idealistic idiot to him, thinking I could get us both out when he'd been locked up for a decade.

But I didn't have a choice.

Hope was the only thing I had.

"Look, I don't know if I can get myself out, let alone you. But if I can help you, I promise I will. I could bring you to the Academy with me…"

"What exactly *is* the Academy?" Raff interrupted, his tone calmer.

"You've never heard of it?" I asked.

"No…at least, I don't think so. Not until you mentioned it the other day."

"It's a place where teenagers like us train to be warriors, magic users and Seekers…a place that helps develop our talents. They don't lock you up and treat you badly there. You're looked after, fed well, clothed, and protected by some very kind people."

"Well, I'll admit that sounds a lot better than hanging onto life in a dark, incredibly boring cell."

"Trust me, it is." Much as I had mixed feelings about the Academy and its combination of friendly and hostile students, I couldn't deny that Merriwether, Callum, and Niala were some of the best people I'd ever met in my life.

"Hey, Raff," I said. "Speaking of cells, tell me something—what does yours look like?"

"I imagine it's just like yours. Why?"

"Just humor me. I have my reasons for asking."

Not that I was about to delve into them just now.

"Okay," he replied. "It's…not very big. Square, like a box. There are three windows up near the ceiling."

"Three?" I asked. "I only have one!"

"They're pretty small," Raff assured me.

"Describe them for me."

"They're round. Perfect circles, quartered by a cross of iron bars."

I closed my eyes and pictured what he was describing until it was clear in my mind. "Tell me more."

"The floor is stone. There's a chunk out of it in the far corner. Oh—and there's a place on the wall where I carved my name a few days ago."

"Perfect," I breathed. "Thank you. That's all I need."

Raff let out a snicker. "Whatever floats your boat. Well, I'm too tired to think anymore. I'm going to crash. Good night, Vega. Don't let the stone beetles bite your ear lobes."

"Wait—stone beetles?"

"Don't worry. They're probably asleep by now. They only chew on ears when they're feeling energetic."

"I'm going to pretend you didn't say that. Night, Raff."

I didn't sleep a wink that night. And it wasn't because of the fear of beetles, the anguish of being imprisoned, or the haunting images of the decimated town of Kaer Uther.

It was that I couldn't get Will, Liv, or Callum out of my head.

And I didn't see any way that those images—the ones of my brother, my best friend, and my almost-boyfriend—could ever be made real again.

# THE THRONE ROOM

THE FOLLOWING MORNING when I called out a greeting to Raff, no answer came.

At first, I assumed he was still sleeping. I'd discovered over time that he usually slumbered until noon, and I could often hear him snoring in soft, rhythmic waves. The sound was weirdly soothing—as soothing as *anything* could be during an indefinite period of incarceration.

But when I called out a few hours later, I was met once again with stony silence.

I told myself the guards had probably taken him for a bath. Or maybe they'd brought him somewhere to run more of their questionable experiments on him.

Hopefully he was taking my advice and refusing to cooperate, because if he *wasn't*…

As I contemplated the worst-case scenario, the shuffling of feet outside my cell startled me into alertness.

*Guards. Two of them, from the sound of it.*

When I heard a key scraping its way into the lock, I leapt to my feet, my breath coming in short, frantic gasps.

The door to my cell began to creak open, and I spun around

to face it, giving myself a dizzying head-rush in the process. A combination of hunger and fear was rendering me so wobbly I felt like I was going to collapse in a spiraling heap, and it took some effort to focus my eyes on the silhouettes of the two men who were now standing in the doorway, staring at me and snickering sadistically.

Without asking, I knew my time in the cell had finally come to an end.

The first guard had an off-kilter slouch that made him look like a mutated hyena. His bulbous brown eyes stared in two different directions, and I couldn't tell if he was eyeing me or the upper corner of the prison cell.

The second guard was tall but remarkably round, his face glistening in the dim light with either sweat or oily secretions.

I didn't particularly want to know which.

In a moment of weakness, my eyes darted to the small opening between my cell and Raff's.

"Your friend's not there, Missy," the googly-eyed guard grunted.

"Where is he?" I asked, anger surging up as I tried and failed to meet his unpredictable gaze.

"Gettin' punished for talkin' to you, I expect," the oily-faced guard said, striding toward me with creases of feral rage embedded in his forehead. "Oh yeah. I should probably tell you the Mistress knows about all the goings-on in this place. You can't get away with anything. Not even an innocent chat with your next-door neighbor."

My body tightened, my fingers trembling.

"What are they going to do to Raff?" I asked, my mouth dry.

"That's none of your damned business, is it?"

"But it's not his fault! I was the one who—"

But before I could say another word, the men rushed over, grabbed me by the arms, and yanked me toward the door.

"Time to meet the Mistress," one of them said. "They say she's eager to see you, though I'm not sure why she'd waste her time on the likes of a Worlder like you. I can only imagine she wants to size you up a little before she chucks you out the window to plummet to your untimely death."

The other man let out a piercing, high-pitched laugh, which only strengthened my theory that he was an unholy hyena-human hybrid.

"Window, huh?" I retorted with as much of a snarl as I could muster. "That sounds fun. I've always wanted to learn to fly."

The oily-faced guard looked taken aback for a moment, as if his brain had zero sarcasm-detecting capacity. Then he scowled, gripped my arm hard, and led me out of the cell.

"You're to shower first," he snapped as we moved down the hall. "You're filthy, and the queen has a sensitive nose. Can't have her meeting with smelly useless girls, now can we?"

I wasn't about to say it out loud, but the thought of getting clean was a massive relief. I'd never in my life gone so long without a shower or bath. My face felt greasy, and I was sure I smelled like death, though I was too horrified to actually sniff my armpits to verify my theory.

The two guards dragged me along until we came to a locked door that looked as decrepit as all the others. But when they pushed it open, I was pleased to find myself greeted by walls of pristine white tile. There was a small, steel-covered drain in the middle of the floor, and on one wall was an elaborate-looking shower system of twisting, polished silver.

"You have this room to yourself," Oily-face said. "There's a change of clothes waitin' for ya when you're done. Be quick. If you're not out in ten minutes, we're comin' in."

With a wince and a shudder that I hoped he couldn't see, I nodded and stepped into the room, waiting for the door to close behind me.

There was nothing there but a small wooden stool with a set of clothing folded up on top of it, a couple of dingy gray towels that looked like they'd once been white, and a bar of soap. The room was lit by a series of flickering lights dancing high over my head. No windows, which wasn't entirely surprising.

Still, it was a lot more cheerful than my desolate cell.

I tore off my clothes and dropped them to the floor, turned on the shower—which, mercifully, was hot—grabbed the fresh bar of soap that had been left for me, and reveled in the sensation of scrubbing off several days' worth of grime before reluctantly shutting the water off again.

The clothing they'd left me was comfortable-looking enough. After reaching into the pocket of the pants I'd been wearing for days to retrieve the small vial my grandmother had given me, I threw the outfit on: a gray linen tunic and loose-fitting trousers that tied at the waist, as well as undergarments that fit remarkably well. I pulled on the boots I'd been wearing when I left the Academy and knocked on the door, my curly hair soaking the back of the tunic.

Without a word, Googly-eyes pushed the door open, grabbed my left arm and began to lead me down the hall. I trudged along beside him in silence, tripping over my feet occasionally as we moved along a series of damp, dreary corridors stained with lichen, moss, and mold.

The now familiar smell of death and decay met my nose at every turn. Looking at the arching stone ceiling above us, I was beginning to imagine that this castle might once have been majestic and beautiful. In the days when the Crimson King had sat on the throne—the days when the Otherwhere was a happy land where people were treated well—I suspected the castle they called Uldrach had teemed with life and laughter.

Now it was in a state of desolation, nothing more than an above-ground crypt. A place where all living things came to die. And if they weren't fortunate enough to do that, they simply festered in despair.

I couldn't help imagining that the Usurper Queen must

resemble her surroundings. Gray, decaying, coated in a thin layer of lichen. She probably had warts on her face and hair like cobwebs. I pictured an old crone who looked like she might crumble to dust if a soft breeze blew her way. A ghoulish, soulless entity who occasionally walked the streets of the now-abandoned town below the castle, leaving a trail of rot in her wake.

But when the guards led me up a long stone staircase and pulled open a massive set of double-doors leading into the most beautiful room I'd ever seen, my theory began to fall apart.

Unlike the wings of the castle that I'd already been dragged through, the Throne Room was bright, cheerful and airy, lined on either side with high-arching windows that invited sunlight to flow in broad streaks onto the glistening marble floor far below. The walls were covered in gleaming cobalt and silver mosaics arranged into intricate works of art that seemed to tell the story of several great leaders in action.

The ceiling was accented by a dome of stained glass reaching high into the sky. A spectrum of blues and whites drew my eyes upward to joyful images of forests and seascapes displayed under an umbrella of airy clouds that gleamed in the glass.

I felt like I'd stepped into someone's vision of Heaven, in spite of the fact that I knew I was far closer to Hell.

I had to wonder if the cheerful room was a remnant of the Crimson King's reign. Surely the woman they called the Mistress would never come up with a design so uplifting as a sunny sky. She'd probably prefer a scene of carnage, burning towns and cities, and the screaming, bloodied victims of her cruelty.

"Come on, then," Googly-eyes croaked, squeezing my arm hard enough to make me wince with pain.

As he and his partner began to walk me toward a large golden throne at the front of the vast chamber, I glanced around to see that there must have been at least twenty of the queen's other men milling about the room, eyeing me every few seconds like the wary half-animals that they were. Some carried swords while others shifted into their terrifying wolf forms as we passed, as if to remind me they could rip my throat out at a moment's notice if the lady of the manor requested it.

Next to each guard was a rounded silver brazier containing a cool blue flame that danced skyward, as though trying to escape its confines. The fires flickered wildly as I was escorted past, and I could swear I saw eyes staring at me from inside their ever-moving outlines. But each time I'd try to focus on one, the eyes would disappear.

As my angry-looking escorts reminded me to keep moving, the reality of my situation hit me once again. I may have been out of my cell, but I was still very much a prisoner, completely at the mercy of a woman who'd already proven cruel enough to rob me of everything I loved.

*I'd be a fool to assume I'm going to leave this place alive,* I thought wearily as the guards dragged me toward the waiting throne. *It's never going to happen. Not without a miracle.*

As we moved further into the room, two deep alcoves appeared on either side of the cavernous chamber. The open spaces stretched off to the right and left like a cathedral's transepts—a word I'd learned from Nana on one of our family trips to England.

A disturbing, high-pitched series of sounds pierced the air as we advanced, prompting me to pull my arms away from the guards and slam my hands over my ears. The two guards did the same, protecting their own ears from the horrific, gut-churning cries.

Pulling my head up, I saw a series of enormous, iron-barred cages suspended from the impossibly high, arched ceilings of the two alcoves. Inside the cages, crying out from the constraints of what looked like huge leather muzzles, was a heartbreaking sight:

Dragons.

# DRAGONS

My mind flashed back to a conversation I'd overheard one night, when Merriwether had sent me to eavesdrop on two of the queen's underlings. One of them had insisted that the queen had taken dragons captive, though I'd hardly dared believe it at the time.

Yet here they were, imprisoned.

Just as I'd been.

Only their cells were far more cruel and torturous-looking than mine, fashioned out of crisscrossed, thick iron bars on all six sides. The dragons looked unnaturally contorted, as though they'd been forced into boxes three times too small to accommodate their enormous bodies, and I couldn't help wondering who —or what—had managed to force such majestic creatures into those cells.

Three of the cages hung from the high-arching ceiling to the left, two on the right. Each dragon had a different dominant color—red, blue, green, purple, or silver. Their snaking tails curled protectively around their feet, which were accented by a series of enormous, razor-sharp talons.

A feeling of pity filled me as I stared at the beautiful creatures, their wings tucked tight to their sides, presumably to avoid slamming them on the thick black bars of their confining cells. I could tell just by looking at them that they would wither and die if they couldn't find their way to freedom soon.

Caging wild animals like this—especially ones so massive and majestic—was one of the greatest sins I could imagine. It was a crime against nature, a slap in the face to everything good in the world.

Rumor had it that the queen wanted to recruit more of their kind as soldiers to fill out her army of beasts, just as the Crimson King had once done. The Usurper Queen wanted the dragons to fight by her side, to form an alliance that would ensure her victory against anyone in the Otherwhere who dared defy her.

But I could already tell that these noble beasts would sooner die than serve a mistress so cruel and merciless. There was an intelligence in their eyes that told me they would never agree to an alliance with anyone who abused their kind. They were wild, proud, loyal. They weren't the sorts of creatures who would commit atrocities for the sake of the queen's own glory and ambition.

They reminded me of the only other dragon I'd ever seen—a golden beast, flying above the Academy, protective, glistening, extraordinary.

A pang of sorrow shot its way through my chest as I found my mind focusing for the millionth time on Callum.

I hadn't thought it was possible, but I missed him more now than I ever had.

Reluctant to wear my emotions on my face as I braced myself for the meeting to come, I ground my jaw and pulled my chin down to fix my eyes on the large throne that sat on a raised platform beneath the vast dome of glass.

I had to admit, if only to myself, that the throne was impressive. Upholstered in red velvet, its arms and legs were ornately carved out of wood and coated in fine gold leaf. Its feet looked like those of the captive dragons, with large, imposing talons at the ends of shapely legs.

The seat was empty, though two giant wolves stood like statues to either side of it, their bright eyes fixed on me as I came to a stop.

Above the throne, dangling from a long, thin chain that extended all the way up to the center of the dome, was a long, glinting silver sword. Its tip pointed down, threatening to drop and impale anyone who dared step too close. It glowed an eerie metallic blue in a sudden burst of sunlight pouring in through the stained-glass windows.

But as I stared, the sword flickered, seeming to blink itself in and out of existence like the Orb of Kilarin did. Which was...odd.

Merriwether had told me the Orb was soon going to disappear after serving its time at the Academy, to hide itself in a new place and await its discovery by a Seeker. So it made sense that it was gradually fading away like a flitting shadow.

The sword, on the other hand, had only been in the queen's castle for a few weeks. So why did it look as though it, too, was on the verge of disappearing?

Telling myself not to think about it, I pulled my eyes back to the throne and stood as still as I could, holding my breath as I tried to calm my racing heart.

The two guards who had escorted me from my cell joined me as the dragons' cries faded to grim silence in the depths of the alcoves on either side of the cathedral-like room.

"You'd best not try anything, girl," Oily-face said. "Or the queen will feed you to her hungry pets."

"Don't worry," I muttered. "I'll be good. I prefer not being devoured."

It felt like minutes passed before a door finally creaked open off to the left side of the room, and a tall, elegant wolf came striding out so gracefully that his massive paws seemed to float just above the marble floor. He was bigger than any Waerg I'd ever seen. His fur was metallic silver, as were his dark-ringed eyes, which gave him a ghostly, ethereal appearance.

My lungs took my breath captive as I stared at him. Maybe it was his beauty that froze me in place, or simply the overwhelming sense of power he exuded with little more than his presence. All I knew was that he wasn't like the other wolves who milled around this awful place.

He seemed to be *more*, somehow. More intelligent, more noble...and, I had no doubt, more cruel.

As he approached the throne, he shifted into his human form without missing a step, turning into a tall, slender man with a shock of silver-gray hair that swept in a wave away from his face. Dark eyebrows arched over fierce, light eyes. He wore a long silver tunic, its collar embroidered with two symmetrical red wolf heads.

I knew without asking that he was the man Raff had mentioned—the magic user whose powers far exceeded the queen's.

He raised his chin and shot me a look sinister enough to send a shiver through my neck and shoulders, all the way to the tips of my trembling fingers.

But he said nothing.

After several seconds of agonizing silence, a tall, slim woman in a flowing dress of liquid-looking red silk strode into the room and glided toward the throne. She stopped only when she'd reached the lavish chair, turning to look down at me with a tight smile on her dark red lips.

"I'm glad to see our young prisoner has joined us," she said, lowering her chin and scrutinizing me from head to toe. "Welcome, Vega Sloane, to the moment that will decide whatever is left of your life."

# THE USURPER QUEEN

CONTRARY to every gruesome image I'd ever conjured of her in my mind, the Usurper Queen was shockingly beautiful.

Her face was youthful, yet wise beyond what appeared to be a limited number of years. Her lips were full, her cheekbones so sharp they looked like they could cut glass. Her mass of shiny light brown hair was twisted into an intricate set of braids, looped up on her head like a crown.

She was regal, elegant, and, much as I hated to admit it even to myself, impressive beyond words.

Everything about her was a disconcerting surprise. But perhaps the strangest thing was the color of her eyes. When she locked them onto mine, their glittering turquoise shade felt uncomfortably familiar.

Under any other circumstance, I might have instinctively bowed before her out of sheer intimidation. Instead, I reminded myself that in spite of her disarming beauty, she was a horrible creature who didn't deserve to lick the soles of my shoes.

I glared at her, my jaw set in a tight grimace as my mind reeled under a storm of confusion and fury.

Ignoring my expression with a graceful pivot, the queen took a seat on the red and gold throne, the long skirt of her crimson dress flowing to the floor like a river of blood.

The man with the silver hair positioned himself behind her, his hands gripping the back of the throne, his piercing metallic eyes fixed on my face.

"How lovely to meet you at last," the queen said through a condescending grin. "But I should really introduce myself properly. My name is Isla."

*Such a pretty name for such an ugly-hearted person.*

"I'm sure you know by now that my servants refer to me as the Mistress," she continued when I issued her a sullen stare. "Those on your side refer to me as the Usurper Queen, though I'm not so fond of that moniker."

As she shifted in her seat, I noticed something hanging from her neck—a large piece of yellow glass or stone, unevenly shaped and wrapped delicately in silver wire. The object glowed unnaturally against her chest, as though she'd somehow harnessed the sun and imprisoned a small portion of its light.

There was no doubt in my mind that I was staring at the amulet Raff had described.

"It's a pleasure to come face to face with the girl who is supposed to be such a threat to me. Although I must say, you look positively harmless, if I'm to be honest. I expected someone a little less…mousy."

"And I expected someone with fangs, claws, and drool dripping down her chin, but here we are," I snapped, surprised by my sudden surge of confidence. "For the record, it's no pleasure to meet *you*. Or your army of mangy dog-men, for that matter. You're a pack of monsters."

"Monsters? That's a little harsh, particularly given the fact that I've looked after your brother and your friend so carefully. They're quite comfortable and at peace, you know."

I wanted to leap at her and claw at her perfect skin for daring to mention Will and Liv as if she was doing them some sort of favor.

"You separated them from their homes, their lives. How is that *at peace*? How can you justify taking them? They have nothing to do with any of this. It's not their fault I was invited to the Academy. It's not their fault I'm a Seeker."

"Taking them brought you to me," Isla said. "Which was exactly what I wanted. *That* is how I justify it. You should know that when I want something, I obtain it by any means necessary—yourself included."

"Okay, Machiavelli," I muttered as I eyed her, anger roiling inside me.

"Believe me, Vega," she added in a sickly sweet tone that made me want to throw up, "they're fine. They may as well be in a deep sleep, enjoying pleasant dreams. I can't think of a nicer existence. Besides, I fully plan on returning them to their homes when I'm done with them. That is, as long as you comply with my demands."

"So glad you see human lives as bargaining chips," I shot back. "What a noble and kind queen you are." I pressed my left forearm to my ribcage and threw in an exaggerated bow for good measure.

"Shut your mouth, girl!" Isla snapped. "I tried to negotiate when you were still at the Academy. I offered you the option of leaving that wretched place of your own free will. You didn't accept, so perhaps you will listen to reason now. Help me, or believe me, your brother and your friend will suffer, as will you."

"*Help* you?" I asked, using every ounce of self-control I had to keep myself from full-on laughing. "Even if I wanted to, how exactly am I supposed to do that?"

Isla's delicately arched eyebrows met in a temporary expression of rage before relaxing again. "I've heard you're skilled. I know whose blood runs through your veins, so I have no doubt that the rumors are true. The granddaughter of the great Merriwether must be full of secret talents."

Out of the corner of my eye, I noticed a few of the Waergs turning to ogle me as if they were waiting for me to do something impressive.

"My offer is simple," Isla continued. "Tell me you'll help to bring the remaining Relics of Power to me, and I'll let the prisoners go back to your world unharmed. All I ask is an alliance. A truce, if you will."

"I haven't competed in the Trials yet. I'm not the Chosen Seeker. And even if I was, what makes you think I'd ever help the woman responsible for killing my parents?" I asked, barely containing the wrath that was searing me from the inside out. "How could you think I would ever align myself with a woman like you?"

She narrowed her eyes at me for a moment, a palpable hatred bubbling beneath the surface of her flawless skin.

So, it seemed she didn't like being called out for her crimes.

"I'm nothing if not fair-minded," she said after she'd regained her composure. "If you're not willing to help, my original offer still stands. The one I made to you while you were still at the Academy. Surrender your precious dragon key and agree to leave the Otherwhere, never to return. Do those two simple things, and you can have your brother and the girl Liv." She rose to her feet and strode down the steps toward me, stopping only when she stood mere inches away.

I froze as she reached for the key dangling from my neck and held it up in front of my face. "This trinket of yours is of no use to me, of course," she said, staring at the dazzling red gem that glinted in the light of the Throne Room. "Such a key can only be used by a Seeker…but I would like to destroy it, all the same. No mere child should have the power to move between our realms as easily as you can. It's not…*natural*."

I yanked the key away from her and shoved it back under my

linen tunic. "If I leave—if I do as you ask—you'll really release Will and Liv? You'll let them go back to their lives in my world?"

She nodded, an unreadable smile tracing its way over her lips. "Of course. Who knows? I may even reconsider punishing your new friend for his over-active mouth."

"What new friend?" I asked, trying desperately to sound oblivious.

"Don't be foolish, Vega. I know you've spoken to the boy. I know he told you about the sword." With that, she gestured toward the suspended weapon hanging in mid-air above her throne. "A pretty thing, isn't it? I'll bet you'd love to get your hands on it."

"Where is Raff?" I asked, my chest tight. "What have you done to him?"

"Don't worry your silly little mind. He's fine...for now." But her disconcerting smile told me he wouldn't be fine for long. "I simply removed him this morning to ask him a few questions. I believe he's back in his cell as we speak, awaiting his fate. I suspect you just missed one another."

I chewed on my lower lip, relieved that he was alive and safe, at least.

But if she'd hurt him...

He was my friend, and didn't deserve such cruelty. Besides, it was my fault he'd gotten into trouble. If I hadn't talked to him—if I'd just ignored him—the queen would never have punished him for fraternizing with the enemy.

Isla seemed to revel in my discomfort. I could see the unmitigated joy on her face as I squirmed. She thrived on my empathy, which she no doubt saw as a weakness.

"If I agree to leave," I blurted out, "then I want you to let him go, too."

"I'll consider it," she said. "Though he has been *very* helpful."

By now, I wasn't even sure anymore if I was trying to negotiate or merely buying myself a few precious minutes. I shifted my gaze to her amulet once again, eyeing the chain around her neck, trying to work out if there was a way I could possibly grab it.

I wasn't particularly quick, and I definitely wouldn't beat the queen or her Waergs at hand-to-hand combat. But there had to be *something* I could do to separate her from her precious magical token.

"You will have to return to Fairhaven, of course," she said, drawing my eyes back to her own. "One of my people will open a Breach just for you, since you will no longer be able to do it yourself. You'll go on living your life without the likes of Merriwether…or Callum Drake, for that matter."

My chest tightened to hear Callum's name on my enemy's lips. She'd uttered it with an irritatingly knowing look, as though she was privy to my most private thoughts and emotions.

But how could she possibly know about my feelings for Callum? I hadn't said a thing to Raff about him.

*Of course. The spy at the Academy. Someone's been watching us.*

I pulled my eyes to the floor even as my cheeks reddened with a mixture of embarrassment and anger.

Isla let out a mocking giggle. "So, the rumors are true. You're quite taken with Callum, aren't you? Ah, well. It's unfortunate for you that he's such a weakling. If he was on this throne, he would have the power to keep you here in the Otherwhere with him. You wouldn't be confronted with this horrible choice. But then, he's never been the type to go after what he wants." She curled the fingers of her left hand into her palm, eyeing her cuticles with a deliberate casualness. "My brother has always been *such* a fool."

Wait…

Did she just say her *brother?*

# SHADOWS

I FELT like I'd been punched in the stomach.

I finally understood why the Usurper Queen's bright eyes looked so familiar. Why I found her beautiful despite her cruel nature.

And the very thought of it filled my throat, my veins, and my heart with acid.

Though it seemed impossible, the despicable woman who was in the process of ruining my life for the second time was Callum's *sister*.

"You really didn't know?" she asked with a smile.

"It's not true," I said, shaking my head in a desperate attempt to prove her wrong.

"So, he didn't tell you. Well, well. I guess you two aren't that close after all."

A hideous tsunami of nausea surged through my insides. Of all the things she could have done or said in that moment, pointing out the gulf between Callum and me was pretty much the worst. Those words hurt more than any beating I could've endured at the hands of her barbaric guards.

A thousand questions and twice as many doubts flashed

through my mind. How could the honorable young man I'd come to know have such an evil and vindictive woman for a sister? Why hadn't he told me?

"You have to be lying!" I shouted.

"You make an awful lot of assumptions for someone who didn't even know this realm existed until a few days ago," the queen laughed. "Of course I'm not lying. Callum is my flesh and blood. I'm sure he'd tell you himself, if only he thought highly enough of you to let you in on his personal affairs."

"Do you have the same powers he does?" I stammered, ignoring the sting of her words and shooting a look toward the dragons suspended in their high cages. I'd been thrown for a loop, and all I could manage was pointless questions to keep my mind off this mind-churning turn of events. "Can you shift?"

The queen tensed, lowering her chin to stare down at me with a haughty, angry glare.

But she said nothing.

"No one with Callum's powers would ever treat dragons like you do," I growled. "It would be like going after someone in your own family. It would be a betrayal." Narrowing my eyes, I continued. "Then again, you're an expert on betrayal, aren't you?"

She glowered at me. "My brother's so-called powers are an abomination. He is inhuman, like all those with dragon blood in their veins. He is not my *family*—not any kind of family I'd welcome, anyway. Even our parents knew he was an atrocity from the time he was very young. It's why they…"

"Why they what?" I asked into the queen's silence.

Isla sucked in her cheeks. "No matter. Suffice it to say that no dragon shifter will ever occupy the throne again."

She seemed to accentuate the word *shifter*. Looking around, I wondered if the queen considered her Waerg minions abominations, too. But, for whatever reason, they looked utterly unfazed by her ranting.

Maybe they weren't intelligent enough to realize they were being insulted.

"Callum is more human than anyone I've ever met," I said. "And he's the true heir to that throne you've been sitting on. That's what really bothers you, isn't it?"

"The throne belongs to the strongest person in the Other-where, and that is me. Callum is more than welcome to try to take it for himself. But of course, he won't. Above all his other flaws, my dear brother has a fatal weakness known as respect for life. He's unwilling to risk others' lives to gain power, which means he'll never, ever find himself seated in this Throne Room. He'll never be the leader that I am. A true queen—or king—understands that compassion is a weakness, not an asset."

"You think not caring about life is a strength," I scoffed. "But Callum has more strength in his little finger than you have in your entire army of wolf-men."

She pursed her lips tight and shot me a glare that could have melted iron. "Your beloved *boy* is a coward who hides behind the walls of a wizard's fortress, Vega. The sooner you learn that, the better it will be for you."

I could feel her anger growing at the mere mention of Callum's power. It wasn't just him she hated. It was his strength, his goodness.

But there was more than hatred behind her words.

There was fear, as well.

She was terrified of what her brother could do. It was all becoming clear in my mind now: She hated that he shared the Crimson King's ability to change into a dragon. She hated that he was everything she could never be, no matter how many Waergs served her, or how many people's lives she destroyed.

She was an impotent and cruel leader. And she was afraid Callum would reveal the truth about her to the Otherwhere, that he would show its residents just how weak she really was.

If we could keep just her from getting her hands on the remaining Relics…he could regain the throne he so deserved.

For a moment I was tempted to prod the Usurper Queen further. To taunt her, just to watch her grow more and more defensive.

But I thought better of it. After all, I'd ventured to her castle to rescue two prisoners, and I couldn't risk their lives for the sake of a fleeting moment of sadistic pleasure.

"What is your decision?" she asked, her tone dripping with venom.

I closed my eyes and fell silent, contemplating my horrible options.

I had no desire to leave the Academy. And the thought of severing my bond with Callum felt like the cruelest sort of self-inflicted agony.

But what choice did I have? I didn't stand a chance of leaving the castle, not until I knew Will and Liv were safe. And that meant surrendering the dragon key willingly.

If I had to suffer a great loss, at least I'd know I'd done it to save two people I loved.

But it would mean losing someone else I loved, too. Someone so dear to me that the thought of never seeing him again was enough to make me want to double over in pain.

"If I agree to your terms," I said slowly, my jaw tense with a churning combination of anger and sadness, "if I give you the dragon key…I need you to release Liv and Will immediately. I need you to stay true to your word."

The corners of the queen's mouth curled up.

"Of course, Vega."

I could feel my heart breaking as I reached up and took hold of the key, its sharp edges digging ever so slightly into my skin.

The loss I was about to suffer was the worst since the day I'd lost my parents.

*I'm surrendering my chance to become Chosen Seeker.*

*I'm giving up a relationship with a grandfather I barely know.*
*But worst of all...*

I closed my eyes, wincing with the onset of pain.

*Callum, I don't want this for us,* I said internally. *I want you. But I don't have a choice...*

In the darkness of my mind, a sweet, deep voice echoed a reply.

*You'll never lose me, Vega.*

The words were as clear as a cloudless day, gliding through the air around me as if spoken by someone close at hand.

But I knew the voice wasn't real. It was nothing but an illusion, my mind playing tricks on me. Wishing for something that could never be, and trying to will it to life.

With nothing to lose, I answered it anyway.

*You'll never lose me either, Callum.*

Shaking, I pulled the key away from its chain. As always, it slipped off easily.

But something strange happened then—something I would never fully understand.

Normally, when I pulled at the dragon key, it detached itself from the silver chain, leaving the links around my neck intact. The feat had always seemed like a magic trick that I couldn't quite explain.

But this time, the chain also slipped off, falling into my palm alongside the key.

At first, I assumed it was because of the queen's magic-suppressing spell. The chain was behaving like any normal necklace would—one of its links had probably broken, and it had tumbled off my neck to land in a useless silver heap.

But instead of staying in my palm, one end began quietly twisting its way under my sleeve, wrapping itself around my wrist and sliding up my arm like a coiling snake. It moved slowly, concealing itself from the queen's eyes as it lengthened and grew thicker, heavier, and stronger in the space of a few seconds.

Without understanding why, I sensed the chain was trying to help me.

"You want this?" I asked Isla, lifting my fisted hand before letting the dragon key drop to the stone floor with a series of sharp clinks. "It's all yours."

"Very good," the queen said, her eyes flitting toward it for only a moment before looking into mine once again. "Now, are you going to agree to my other demands?"

"Well, that all depends," I said.

"On what, exactly?" she asked with a hard sigh and a roll of her eyes. I could tell she'd had just about enough of me, and I was savoring every second I got to spend annoying her.

"On whether or not this works."

As I spoke the words, I grabbed the loose end of my silver chain with my right hand and pulled, marveling at its length as the other end quickly uncoiled itself from my arm and slunk down to the floor.

The sound of metal scraping on stone met my ears as the chain grew longer and thicker, each link increasing in girth until it began to look like it might become too heavy to lift.

But to my surprise, when I drew my right hand upwards, it flew into the air with all the lightness of fishing wire.

"What is this?" Isla cried, her eyes wide with the sudden onset of fear. "What are you doing?"

"Taking control!" I snarled. With that, I lashed out with my hand and watched the chain whip its way the air, coiling itself around the queen's elegant neck and tightening. She made a hideous choking sound, grabbing at the links with both hands. But to my delight, she was helpless to remove them.

Startled into action, her Waerg guards advanced, surrounding me on all sides. Some shifted into their wolf forms. Others pointed their spears and swords at me. They snarled, but the sounds were more like anguished grunts of confusion than dire warnings.

I pulled on the end of the chain and its grip tightened. The queen shook her head weakly as she gasped for breath.

"Stay back!" I called out to the encroaching Waergs. "Come closer and I'll choke her to death!"

I gave the chain a quick pull. The queen tripped toward me, stumbling clumsily over her own feet. She didn't seem so daunting anymore, nor so beautiful. Her face was red, her knuckles bone-white, and she looked terrified.

We were face to face now, and I held all the power. I smiled, reached out, grabbed the amulet from around her neck and yanked it, breaking the delicate chain that held it in place.

Holding the glowing trinket up in front of her face, I gave her my snarkiest grin.

"This is your greatest weapon," I said evenly. "It's the only thing you have that can save you from people like me. And I'm about to destroy it."

With my breath trapped deep inside my chest, I opened my hand and let the amulet drop.

# SEEKING

A SOUND HALFWAY between a cry of sorrow and a scream of rage erupted from the queen's throat as the pendant crashed to the ground, shattering into a thousand shards that scurried across the stone floor until what remained was nothing more than a trail of yellow dust.

From their cages suspended high in the deep alcoves, the dragons were growing agitated. Perhaps it was the queen's rage that set them off, or maybe they somehow knew her trinket was destroyed. They were screeching again, flailing around their iron prisons, their powerful wings slamming against the bars and blasting peals of metallic vibrations throughout the queen's chamber.

At the same instant, a dozen of Isla's wolves took a threatening step in my direction, ready to pounce at her command. In response, I tightened my grip on the chain that remained around her neck, cutting off her ability to utter so much as a faint whimper.

My chest was heaving now, my heart hammering as I narrowed my eyes at the woman I hated more than anyone I'd ever met.

I had her life in my hands. One more pull on the chain and I could end it.

But my mind flashed to something Merriwether had told me when we'd first met. I wasn't welcome at the Academy, he'd said, if my sole motivation for being there was revenge. I wasn't being trained as a Seeker in order to kill. I was being trained to defend myself, to help others. I was no Zerker thirsting for blood; I was someone who sought light and good in the world.

As I pulled my eyes to the trail of finely shattered glass littering the ground, a rush of renewed strength drove its way through my veins, my muscles, my mind. I'd destroyed the one thing that was keeping me from using my powers. I was free of the queen's shackles now, stronger than I'd ever been.

And the queen knew it.

I lunged down to snatch my dragon key from the floor. Still holding fast to the chain around Isla's throat, I raised my head to stare into the blue eyes that reminded me so much of her brother's.

"In case it's not perfectly clear by now," I said, "I do *not* agree to your demands. I will never, ever agree to them. And I'll spend my entire life making sure Callum takes the throne away from you, if I need to. You are no queen. You're an evil harpy."

As the words tumbled out of my mouth, I silently commanded the chain to return to its rightful place. The length of silver links immediately released its grip on the queen, shrinking rapidly as it slithered its way up my arm and shoulder and fastened itself back around my neck.

Off-balance, the queen stepped back, grabbing at her throat and struggling to regain her voice.

"Cat got your tongue?" I asked, pleased with my handiwork. "Good. I hope he keeps it."

Still smiling, I called on my Shadow form, which overtook me immediately. Before anyone could figure out what had happened, I vanished through the still open door that the queen and the silver-eyed man had come through a few minutes earlier.

Somewhere behind me, I heard Isla's hoarse voice call out, "You know what to do. Quickly, now! We don't have much time."

*Your Waergs can pursue me,* I thought. *But there's no way in hell I'm letting them catch me this time.*

I FOUND myself gliding down a long, bright corridor accented with shining marble columns and walls covered in large, gold-framed mirrors. It reminded me of photos I'd seen of the palace of Versailles in France—a lavish dwelling fit for an opulent, wasteful king—or queen—who enjoyed accumulating mass amounts of wealth on the backs of his or her subjects.

As I swept past one reflecting surface after another, I was pleased to realize just how little I could see my own reflection. Even when I looked closely, I was just barely aware of a vague outline of a ghostly figure about my size and shape making its way down the broad hallway. I'd become little more than a figment of a person. I really *was* a Shadow.

Not that I had the luxury of scrutinizing my non-reflection for long. By now, a small army of Waergs was attempting to pick up my scent somewhere behind me, and I still needed to find my brother and Liv before the queen brought the full wrath of her vengeance down on me by sending them to the guillotine, or whatever other horrible punishment her twisted mind might decide to inflict on them.

Clutching the dragon key to my chest, I could feel it slip silently onto the silver chain that was now back to its normal size around my neck.

And just like that, everything was right with the world again.

*Almost.*

I still needed to find the two people I'd come for, free them from their prison, and somehow get them out of this hellish place before anyone figured out what I was up to.

I'd just darted into a large bedroom when an open door on the far wall drew my gaze. I ran over—or rather, *floated*—hoping that my Shadow form would hold up long enough for me to remain concealed from the enemy's prying eyes. I slipped through the narrow opening, which couldn't have been more than a few inches wide, and tucked myself into what I soon discovered was a large walk-in closet. It was more or less empty, aside from a few silk robes and some old, well-worn boots.

*Okay, Vega. Think for a second.*

*You should be able to summon doors again. You just need to find your way to the room where Will and Liv are being held.*

I closed my eyes, calling up a memory of the ominous prison chamber I'd seen in the Orb of Kilarin. Immediately, my mind conjured a vivid image of Will and Liv, suspended helplessly in those awful tubes filled with some unidentifiable liquid.

*I need more detail. There's no time to play guessing games.*

I opened my mind, exploring the memory of the place I'd seen in the Orb. I recalled stone carvings of dragons looming above the tubes. Frightening, fierce-looking creatures, their eyes fixed on the room's center as though to make sure no prisoner escaped. Cruel sentinels, immovable yet threatening.

I focused on the image, adding more and more detail as my mind freed itself of all other thoughts. I wanted nothing more than to create a link between us, an invisible thread that I could use to pull myself toward them.

*My brother's eyes.*

*The dark sleekness of Liv's hair.*

I felt a rush of cool air as the room grew clearer in my mind's eye. I was so close…

"I'm coming for you," I mouthed. "I'll be there soon. I promise."

To my delight, when I opened my eyes again, a tall, light-colored wooden door stood before me. On its surface was the image of a strange, troll-like creature with angry eyes. A gargoyle-dragon hybrid, staring me down.

Too excited to wait a second longer, I pushed away my Shadow form and allowed my body to turn solid again. Just then, I heard a commotion erupting in the room next door. "Check the vestibule!" someone was yelling. "Quick, now!"

"Here goes nothing," I muttered, shoving the key into the lock and turning it. I leapt through the door, pulling it shut behind me.

# REUNION

A SECOND LATER I was standing in a large, cold room, and the door I'd summoned was fizzling away behind me.

The room was enormous and cavernous, with high vaulted ceilings. It might have once served as a meeting place or a ballroom, except for its grim lack of windows.

At its center were two massive glass tubes. Inside them were Will and Liv, their eyes and mouths open as though they'd been in the midst of speaking when the queen had frozen them in time. I couldn't tell if they were conscious, or even breathing. They didn't look dead. But they didn't look entirely alive, either.

They just…*were*.

A desperate yelp leapt from my throat as I lunged forward, pressing my palms flat against Will's glass prison. I shouted to him and banged on the tube, but he didn't respond.

"How do I open these?" I cried, circling the tubes frantically, looking for some kind of release mechanism. "Where's the latch? There has to be some way!"

When I couldn't find any sort of handle or button, I raced around to examine the prison chamber's walls. But there was no lever, no switch.

Nothing.

The tubes must have been sealed by a spell. Words the queen or her strange silver-eyed companion had used to ensnare the prisoners.

Unfortunately, my knowledge of such spells was exactly zero.

"Damn it!" I shouted, tears welling up in my eyes. My brief moment of glory had passed. As powerful as I'd felt a minute ago when I'd beaten the queen at her own game, I wasn't strong enough to shatter the thick glass with my bare fists.

Maybe if I had a sword or even a bow and some arrows. Or if I had…

*Callum.*

*He* could break through, if only he was here. The chamber was huge; there was plenty of room here for him to shift into his golden dragon form and free the prisoners.

But it was a pointless thought. He was hundreds—maybe even thousands—of miles away.

In the end, I'd lost.

I crumpled to the ground, faint with exhaustion and hunger, and pressed my face into my palms before pulling my eyes up to look at the stone creatures perched near the ceiling. The statues I'd seen projected in the Orb of Kilarin. Carved dragons of different shapes and sizes, staring menacingly down at Will and Liv.

Cold, soulless enemies, witnessing my failure.

Or…maybe they *weren't* enemies.

Maybe they were protectors.

So strange to think that until a few days earlier, I hadn't believed dragons had ever existed. Everything I knew about them came from fairy tales and myths. But now, all those fictions had turned out to be one-hundred percent fact. Not only did they exist, but their relationship with humans was far more complicated than I could ever have imagined.

In the old stories about the Crimson King, he'd called upon

the majestic beasts to fight in his army. Their bond was so strong they even traveled with him between our two worlds and fought in the ancient wars I'd only ever heard of in old legends.

But that all happened centuries ago, in the days when dragons trusted humans. From what I'd heard, their kind had long since gone wild again, turning their backs on people and concealing themselves in the shadows. They saw us as the enemy. And it was no wonder, given what the queen had done to five of their kind.

There was no way dragons would ever be willing help me.

Still, would it really hurt to ask?

I closed my eyes and pictured the beautiful creatures I'd seen imprisoned in the Throne Room—red, blue, green, purple, silver. When their faces were clear in my mind, I sent them a mental message, conveying my thoughts as clearly as I could.

*Forgive me. I'm new to all this. I don't quite know how it works, or if you can hear or understand me. All I know is that I want to free you from your cages.*

*So...be free. Come to me. Help me, and I'll make sure you return to your homes. I'll do everything I can to help you and your kind, to protect you from people like the Usurper Queen.*

*That is my solemn promise.*

I waited a few seconds, then opened my eyes, unsure of what I expected to see.

But nothing had changed. I was still alone in the vast, cold prison chamber.

And Will and Liv were still trapped.

"I'm not strong enough," I moaned. "I'm not the Crimson King. I'm a seventeen-year-old girl who has no idea what she's doing."

I was ready to break down weeping when a strange, low buzzing sound met my ears. A moment later, the air around me began to grow hot, as though I'd just stepped into a sweltering summer's day.

The large forms appeared slowly, carefully, as though

sketching themselves on the air. Huge winged creatures, coming to life, emerging from the shadows around me.

"Holy crap," I said softly, pushing myself to my feet. "It worked!"

I'd transported them from their cages in the Throne Room to this place. I'd actually summoned freaking *dragons* to my side.

But my delight was short-lived. As I stared at the beasts, my head began to spin out of control. The massive forms turned fuzzy before coming into focus again, and I struggled to hold onto the image of their faces.

The spell had taken everything out of me. I reached a hand out and pressed it to Will's glass prison, steadying myself as I slowly regained the ability to see clearly.

The dragon nearest to me let out a puff of air through his nose, accompanied by a shot of dark smoke. Like the others, he still wore a large leather muzzle, but his head was raised as he stared at me with curious eyes.

Focusing my own eyes on his, I sensed an intelligence in him, an understanding of why I'd called him there—and a knowing look that told me he had faith that I would never hurt him.

The trust was mutual.

"I need your help," I said, my voice shaking with emotion. "Please."

He didn't answer. But his eyes softened, and his head lowered toward me.

It was all the reassurance I needed.

# THE DUNGEON

THE DRAGON'S scales were a deep shade of crimson. His pale, cat-like eyes were a cluster of yellows and golds with a vertical black pupil at their center.

And strange as the thought was, I couldn't help thinking he looked sad.

"I'm so sorry," I said. "Sorry that the Usurper Queen imprisoned all of you. Sorry that you were in those cages for who knows how long. I'm going to free all five of you from this place. But first, I need to ask you to do something for me, if you possibly can. It's very important."

The red dragon pressed his muzzle close to my face and let out a sound somewhere between a growl and a purr. The barbecue odor of charcoal and smoke filled the air, and I flashed back to peaceful days of family cookouts. A wave of warmth overtook me as the image of my smiling parents sprang into my mind.

Somehow, this extraordinary creature, who should have been terrifying, was summoning memories of the days when I was at my happiest.

"I'm going to take that as a yes," I told the dragon. Swallowing hard, I looked around at the others again. "My brother and my friend are in these tanks," I announced, gesturing to the tall glass tubes. "I need to get them out without hurting them. Do you think you can help me?"

With a series of low, conversational rumbles, the dragons exchanged a conferring look far more knowing than any expression I've ever seen on most human faces.

And then, nearly in unison, they turned their backs on me.

"Please?" I said, my voice hoarse with confusion. "I'm begging you."

With their backs still facing me, the red dragon let out a sharp, short cry. Then, in a coordinated surge, all five tails swept upwards.

I leapt back in terror as they crashed down.

Only they didn't hit where I was standing. Instead, the five slender but powerful tails sliced through the air and smashed sideways against the two glass tubes.

A spray of glass shards exploded outward, followed by a sea of thick green liquid splashing over the floor and walls.

Faster than my eyes could follow, two of the dragon's tails whipped through the explosion of glass and green goo, curling around Liv and Will and snatching them out of midair before setting them gently on their feet.

Trembling and dazed, the two prisoners stood ankle deep in the green liquid with the dragons looking on.

I sprang forward and waved a hand in front of Will's face, hoping to draw his attention. It didn't take long to realize he still couldn't see me.

"He's still under the spell. They both are," I muttered. "I need to get them back home."

The only question was where exactly should I bring them? In all likelihood, very little time had passed in my world since I'd first come to the Otherwhere. The sensible thing to do was bring

Will and Liv to wherever they were when I'd first come through the Breach on the day I'd met Merriwether.

"Will would have been at the airport," I said, "waiting to get on his flight to California. Liv was most likely packing for her family's planned road trip."

At least I hoped so.

Because if I got this wrong, I was about to seriously screw with two people's lives and minds.

Closing my eyes, I summoned a door to Liv's house first, even as the dragons shifted around until they were standing next to one another, watching with curiosity.

When the Breach appeared, I opened it and took hold of Liv's hand, urging her to take a step forward. To my delight, she seemed to be waking up, even becoming vaguely aware of her surroundings.

The spell was breaking at last.

I reached into my pants pocket and pulled out the small vial my Nana had given me—the liquid that was supposed to make anyone who drank it forget about the Otherwhere.

I took Liv's chin in my hand, lifting it gently, and let one drop fall on her lips.

Confused, she licked it off.

"Come with me," I whispered. "We need to get you home."

She took a single sleepy step, then another, until I guided her through the Breach into her family home in Fairhaven. As she passed from the Otherwhere into our world, her clothing and hair, which had been coated in the strange green liquid, dried up without a trace.

Watching from the doorway, I smiled to see her take a few steps into her living room.

She was finally back where she belonged.

"Liv!" her mother called from the kitchen. "Are you finished packing?"

"Um…I…just about…I think?" Liv called out, looking around as if trying to figure out what she was doing there.

Before she had a chance to see me, I shut the door quietly, watching as it disappeared in front of my eyes.

"Bye, Liv," I said. "I'll see you again soon."

When I'd taken a breath, I did the same for Will, calling up a door that opened into a dark alcove at Fairhaven Regional Airport. After I administered a drop from the vial, I took my brother's hand and led him through the doorway in a trance-like walk.

As with Liv, Will's hair and clothing dried up without so much as a trace of the queen's awful green liquid.

Disoriented, he turned and walked toward a bright, sunny waiting area where other passengers were seated. He plopped down with a groggy groan next to his blue backpack, which was still waiting for him as if he'd never left. His eyes were glazed over, but he didn't look too disoriented or distressed.

If he wasn't on the road to clarity yet, at least he was heading in the right direction.

"Bye, Will," I said, tears stinging my eyes. "I don't know when I'll see you again, but I hope you stay safe."

I jumped back through the door before anyone had a chance to spot the weirdly-dressed girl who had just conjured a portal from another world. Fortunately, it seemed like no one had noticed me—even those who were a few feet away. It was like I was still in the Shadow Realm, and the people in my world were oblivious to my existence.

Which was fine with me.

When I stepped back through into the vast dungeon, the dragons were still crouched in the cold, damp room, their muzzled heads meeting in the middle. A sea of green liquid and glass shards lay all around them, but they didn't seem to care.

They drew their attention to me, expectant and eager.

"There's just one more thing I need to do," I told them. "One more person I need to free. Then we'll get out of here. I'll bring you all somewhere safe, I promise."

A low, approving rumble came at me from all five of the dragons, eliciting a much-needed smile from my lips.

"Give me two minutes," I said. "I'll be right back."

# RESCUE

A MOMENT later I was standing in a cell with three circular windows high on one wall, a set of iron bars crisscrossing each of them. Wincing into the darkness, it took me a second to see that a boy was sitting on the floor in the farthest corner, his face so dirty that all I could make out of it was a pair of shining blue eyes staring up at me. The letters R-A-F-F were scrawled clumsily on the stone wall next to him.

"You're Vega, aren't you?" he stammered, pushing himself to his feet. He was taller than I expected, with long legs and broad shoulders. "How did you…I mean, I can't believe you actually came for me!"

"I'm glad I made it to the right cell," I said with a smile, gesturing to the door I'd summoned. "I need to be able to picture the place I'm going very clearly. It's a good thing you described it to me."

"I…yes," he replied with a stunned grin. "I suppose it is."

I stared at him for a second, trying to work out what he looked like under all the dirt.

"Is everything okay?" he asked.

"It's just so strange seeing you in person. And your voice…you sound a little different when we're standing in the same room. I'm trying to process all this."

"Your voice sounds different, too," he said. "I guess the hole in the wall changes things."

"I suppose so," I replied, still in shock to see just *how* different he was from the boy I'd expected. But there was no time to muse over his appearance. I needed to get him back to the Academy before the guards came storming in.

"Are you hurt?" I asked. "Can you walk?"

He looked confused. "I'm fine. Why?"

"I wasn't sure if the queen's men did something to you when they came for you."

"Oh, that. They…pushed me around a bit. But I'm okay."

"I'm so sorry, Raff," I said miserably. "That was all my fault. They knew we were talking—I should never have put you in danger like that."

He looked taken aback, like my emotional reaction came as a shock. "It's fine, really. Don't worry about it."

"I'll do my best not to. But listen—we need to go."

"Are we going to the Academy?"

I nodded. "Come on. We need to get out of this castle before they figure out what's happening. The guards could be here any second now. Honestly, I'm surprised they haven't found me yet."

Without another word, he followed me through the summoned door, which disappeared as soon as we'd stepped into the dungeon where Liv and Will had been imprisoned.

When Raff saw the dragons, he recoiled in fear, pressing his back against the wall and tucking his chin into his chest. I couldn't say I blamed him—I hadn't exactly warned him there would be five giant, fire-breathing creatures waiting for us.

The dragons, too, seemed to tighten with the appearance of the new human in their midst. The red one blew out a huff of smoke but seemed to calm down when I raised my hand, palm out.

"It's okay," I assured him. "We're friends."

"Right," Raff muttered through tremulous vocal cords, his eyes pointed at the floor. "Friends."

"Okay, there's no way you five will fit through one of my doors," I said, turning to face the huge figures as I eyed the thick stone walls around us. "And I'm assuming you won't be able to break out of here."

The red dragon pressed his head to the ground, his eyes staring up at me like they belonged to a sad puppy.

"I take that as a no."

He let out a groan and shook his head, an oddly human gesture both surprising and adorable.

"Don't worry," I said with a reassuring smile. "I brought you into this room without breaking walls. I can get you out. Just... stay here. I have a plan."

Thirty seconds later, Raff and I were standing in the main courtyard at the Academy for the Blood-Born, the sound of clashing steel coming at us from all sides.

I looked around to see that thirty or so students—mostly Zerkers dressed in red—were paired up for their morning sparring matches. Their swords, daggers, and other weapons were still clenched in their fists when they stopped to turn and gawk at the two people who'd just walked through a magical door.

As I scanned the courtyard, my heart sank with the realization that Callum was nowhere to be seen. Since the moment I'd left the Academy, I'd tried to hold onto some minuscule scrap of hope that I'd somehow find a way to lay my eyes on him again.

But it looked like I'd have to wait a little longer before that particular dream came true.

*Snap out of it,* I told myself. *You have more important things to think about right now. Like how to explain to a bunch of Zerkers what the hell you're doing here.*

Wishing I could ask my Shadow form to hide me from so many prying eyes, I threw the students a sheepish smile. My forehead beaded with perspiration as I tried to summon a reasonable explanation.

"Vega!" someone shouted behind me. I turned around to see Niala, with Rourke in his black Husky form by her side, both sprinting toward me from a far corner. When they reached me, Niala wrapped her arms around my neck and hugged me tight.

"You're back!" she said, pulling away and eyeing my dirty companion curiously. "I thought you'd...actually, I don't know what I thought. But I'm so glad to see you. We've been so worried!"

"I'm glad to be here," I told her with a half-frown. "At least, I think I am. We'll see if that changes when I run into Merriwether."

"Don't worry. He'll just be happy to know you're back safe. He even delayed the Seekers' Trials for you."

"Really?" I asked, my jaw dropping.

She nodded. "I suppose he had faith that you'd be back soon enough. He wants you in the competition, after all."

"I hope you're right." When the boy standing next to me cleared his throat in a not-so-subtle way, I added, "Oh, hey—this is Raff. He's...actually, it's too long a story to tell just now."

"Nice to meet you," Raff said as Niala offered him a cautious grin. Rourke took a tentative step forward to sniff him before drawing back abruptly and pressing against Niala's left leg. I hadn't noticed any foul body odor coming from my new friend but, given that the last time Raff had bathed was probably weeks ago, he must have smelled terrible to any creature with a powerful nose.

"Nice to meet you, too," Niala told him before turning to me.

"You're going to have to explain all this to me at some point," she added under her breath.

"Yeah. I know."

I perused the multitude of students who'd now completely abandoned their class to gawk at me, no doubt trying to figure out exactly where we'd come from.

"Hi, everyone," I said with a wave of my hand as the Zerkers shot me daggers with their eyes. "Listen, I'm really sorry, but I need you all to move back against the walls. It's really important."

"You do not give the orders around here, Miss Sloane!" barked a loud, angry voice as the class's instructor emerged from behind two large male students. He was a short, stocky man, a sword clenched in his right hand. Though we'd never spoken, I recognized him from my first day at the Academy. His name was Strunk.

"Look," I replied in a less than patient tone, "I need some space, and I need it now. You'll see why in a minute, I promise. There's someone coming. A few someones, actually. And I think the Headmaster would be extremely upset if he found out you'd kept them from finding their way to the Academy, given how important they are."

Strunk paused long enough to give me a once-over accompanied by two very evil eyes. Either he could hear the urgency in my voice, or he realized I was about to start crying and felt sorry for me. Either way, he issued a quiet command for everyone to get back.

Scowling at me the entire time, his students obeyed.

*Well, it's nice to know the Zerkers still hate me.*

"Thank you," I said, my voice meeker than I wanted it to be.

I positioned myself at the center of the courtyard, closed my eyes, and focused all my mental strength on my next task. I had no way of knowing if I could summon creatures who were as far away as the queen's captive dragons. But if I could...if I could somehow set them free...

It would be the best thing I'd ever done.

"Come," I said silently, picturing their beautiful faces in my mind as I sent my voice their way. "I'm giving you your freedom. Come to me. Leave that horrible place behind."

When a chorus of shocked gasps met my ears from the edges of the courtyard, my lips ticked up in a smile.

Gasps could only mean one thing.

*Success!*

I opened my eyes to see all five dragons standing in a row in front of me, facing me like eager soldiers awaiting orders.

"So glad you made it," I told them, trying to conceal my utter relief. "And I'm especially glad to be able to do *this*." One by one, I walked up to them, unbuckled their leather muzzles and let them drop to the ground. "You're really free now."

I gestured to the sky, granting them the liberty I'd promised.

But instead of taking off, they just stared at me, lowering their heads to the ground and moaning.

"What is it?" I asked, turning Niala's way. "I don't get it...what are they waiting for?"

She shrugged. "Not sure. I've never dealt with dragons before. To be honest, they're a little...terrifying."

Rourke seemed to agree. He'd shifted into his panther form and was stalking low to the ground, eyeing the creatures cautiously when a deep, familiar voice behind us said, "Maybe I can help."

# HOME

MY HEART THREATENED to explode when I spun around to see Callum walking toward me from the far end of the courtyard. It was all I could do to resist sprinting over, throwing my arms around him, and kissing him full on the lips as I'd fantasized about so many times during my captivity.

But I was in enough trouble with the Headmaster already. There was no sense in getting Callum reprimanded for fraternizing with the rule-breaking enemy.

"There are metal clips on their wings," he said casually as he sidled up next to me, pressing his upper arm against my shoulder for just a second before leaning away.

Although he sounded relaxed, I could sense the tension in his body. He was putting on a show for the others, acting like he wasn't overjoyed to see me. Like it was no big deal that I'd left abruptly and returned with five dragons in tow.

"You see?" he said as he gestured toward the joints of the silver dragon's left wing. For the first time, I noticed a small, jagged piece of metal, clamped onto the wing's joint like a monstrous-looking vice. "It's an inhibitor of some sort, to keep him from flying."

As I stared at the cruel device, rage swelled inside me to think of all the nasty punishments the Usurper Queen had inflicted on these beautiful creatures. "These keep them from spreading their wings fully," Callum explained. "It's like clipping a bird's feathers, only much worse, because it causes constant pain."

I could hear the strain in his voice as he tried to conceal the anger that was building inside him.

"What can we do?" I asked. "We need to set them free..."

"We take the clamps off," Callum said without hesitation.

With one hand held high, he walked up to the silver dragon. "It's all right, Tefyr," he said before adding something in a language I couldn't understand. The creature bowed its head to the ground in a gesture of submission and let out a thankful purr when Callum pulled the first of the clamps off.

"Tefyr?" I asked.

"It's his name," he replied, turning my way as he did the same to the second clamp.

As I watched, he moved around the courtyard and liberated one dragon after the other, speaking each of their names in greeting. When he reached the blue dragon, he paused, pressed a hand to its face, and stroked its scales for a moment.

"I'm sorry for what happened so long ago, Dachmal," he said softly. "I'm sorry the trust was broken between your kind and ours. Please know, you have nothing but allies in this place."

To my shock, the dragon turned my way, narrowed his eyes, and let out a grunt of protest...or at least what *sounded* like protest. He raised his head, curving his neck, and breathed a puff of threatening blue flame, which quickly dissipated in the air.

At first, I was sure he was trying to tell Callum he didn't consider me his ally. But when I twisted around to look behind me, my eyes landed on Raff, who was half-cowering, his chin lowered again.

Callum shot Raff a quick glance before turning back to the dragon. "Don't worry. Vega brought him here, and I'm sure she had her reasons." Dachmal lowered his head, pushing his muzzle against Callum's hand as though in silent agreement before Callum released him from his bonds.

"I'm worried the queen will find a way to capture them again," I said, stepping forward. "Are the dragons going to be safe?"

Callum nodded. "They're free now," he replied. "Those clips held some dark magic…" he added, pointing to the piles of large metal chunks on the ground as they faded into mounds of toxic-looking dust, "but it's gone now. You've released them."

"With your help," I said with a smile.

I took a step toward Dachmal and said, "Thank you so much for your help. Please tell your friends that not all humans are awful."

The creature let out a shrill cry, spread his wings like he was stretching after a long sleep, then shot toward the clouds with the other four following close behind.

I backed away, watching the silhouettes of the magnificent beasts fill the sky, and let out a long breath. Today, I'd rescued three humans and five dragons from captivity. For once in my life, I really did feel like I had a purpose.

"You should be proud, you know," Callum said as the others stared at the unbelievable sight high above us. "You've done a great thing."

"You know what? I *am* proud of myself." Smiling, I turned toward him. "But tell me something—how did you know their names?"

"They told me."

"They *what?*"

Callum chuckled. "There's a lot you have yet to learn about dragons, Vega Sloane. Maybe when we have a little time, I can teach you a thing or two."

"I'd like that."

Behind us, someone coughed.

We turned around to see Niala and Raff stepping forward. I

introduced Raff to Callum, who nodded a greeting, eyeing him with the same kind of careful scrutiny I'd seen on Niala's and Rourke's faces.

"Hello," Raff said, his voice shifting to a timid, almost mousy tone. It was no surprise that he seemed intimidated, really. Callum was an impressive figure, with his piercing eyes and regal air. Not to mention the fact that he'd just spoken to dragons in a language none of us understood.

"You were in the queen's castle?" Callum asked.

Raff nodded then pulled his chin down again as if deliberately avoiding eye contact.

"Yes. For years," he muttered.

"I can't believe what the queen did to him," I added, sensing Raff's reticence. "Cruel as she is, I never thought she'd be the type to lock up kids. Those cells of hers aren't exactly the Ritz Carlton."

"No," said Callum. "I'm sure they aren't. Well, I'm sorry for what you've been through, Raff. Welcome to the Academy."

"Thanks. I'm...looking forward to exploring the place." Staring up at the walls around us, Raff smiled, his lips stretching into a strange, almost mischievous grin. For the first time, I noticed that his teeth were gleaming white.

As I eyed him, trying again to discern what he might look like under the layers of dirt, a deep voice cut through the air like a cannon blast. Three syllables echoed through the courtyard, sending a tremor through my entire body.

"Vega Sloane!"

I braced myself as I peered upward only to see Merriwether's face staring down at me from an open window high above us.

"My office, this minute!" he bellowed before disappearing again.

"Who's that?" Raff asked.

"Who that is...is a long story," I sighed. "Let's just say he's the man who's probably about to kick my butt out of this place."

AFTER SENDING Raff off with Niala to get cleaned up and fed, I turned around to look for Callum, who'd been standing by my side only a minute earlier. But he was nowhere to be seen.

I tried to tell myself that he had somewhere to be. A meeting, or a class to instruct.

But my instincts told me otherwise.

*He's angry with me. Disappointed, upset, hurt.*

I could hardly blame him. I'd left the Academy abruptly, without so much as an explanation. I so desperately wanted to tell him everything now, to help him understand. But how was I supposed to do that if he was intent on running away the moment we finally had a chance to talk in private?

With the students from the class I'd just interrupted still buzzing and gawking up at the dragons fading into the distance, I made my way inside to begin the dread-filled hike up to the Headmaster's office. I would have much preferred to take a shower, change my clothes, and go track down Callum. Right now, all I wanted was to feel his arms around me. I needed to know he'd forgiven me. Or merely that he still cared.

But Merriwether had issued an order, and there was no sense in postponing the inevitable.

Too bad the inevitable totally sucked.

# CONSEQUENCES

WHEN I OPENED the door to the Headmaster's office, he was sitting behind his sprawling wooden desk, staring down at a pile of papers with an enigmatic expression on his face.

"You certainly took your time getting here, Miss Sloane," he said, pulling his chin up to shoot me an appraising look. "Tell me, exactly what part of 'this minute' evaded your comprehension?"

"I…," I replied. "I was just…" *No. Do NOT tell him you trudged up here like an anesthetized turtle because you were preoccupied with thoughts of Callum.* "I'm sorry, Sir."

Merriwether rose to his feet and swept a hand through his mass of gray hair before combing his fingers over the layer of white stubble on his cheeks and chin. His finely carved features looked harsh under the hovering overhead lantern. His bushy brows cast shadows over his eyes that made them daunting and unreadable.

I'd all but forgotten what a textbook example of a wizard he was.

Well, minus the long white beard or flowing robes.

"Come in, then," he snapped, gesturing impatiently toward a

chair on the other side of his desk. "Close the door behind you. Quickly, now."

When I'd seated myself, he said, "Well, it seems you've finally figured it out."

"Figured it out?" I asked, furrowing my brow. Did he somehow know I'd talked to my grandmother about him?

Was *that* what this meeting was about?

"That you possess great skills. You've proven you have the power to take on a foe as dangerous as the Usurper Queen. In your own rather unique way, you've shown yourself to be a skilled warrior, Vega. Well done."

His tone, which had been so chilly a few seconds earlier, had altered to one of profound warmth, even admiration.

Which only served to further confuse me.

"I'm not sure I'd go that far," I replied. "What I did was stupid. I thought I was going to die in that castle. The queen…"

"Found a way to keep you from using your magic. Yes, yes. She does have a healthy fear of those who are more powerful than she is. As I'm sure you discovered, she'd rather shut down every magic user—even her closest allies—than risk being beaten by one." Merriwether's lips twisted into a crafty smile. "I suspected she would try such a thing when confronted with the possibility of your presence."

"You *suspected*?" I blurted out before I could stop myself. "If you knew what might happen, why didn't you warn me how much danger I was in?"

The Headmaster's smile faded, and once again, his eyebrows met. "*Warn* you?" He seemed to grow several inches as he spat out the words.

Or maybe I was shrinking.

"Need I remind you," he continued, "that you left here against my wishes? I *did* warn you that the queen's castle was impenetrable." His voice calmed as he continued. "Yet you not only penetrated it, you freed quite a few prisoners in the process. All of that, despite the fact that your magical skills were hindered." With that, he let out a quiet snicker. "I must confess, what you pulled off was nothing short of a miracle."

He opened a desk drawer and extracted the Orb of Kilarin, which he placed on the desk in front of him. The Orb lifted for a moment, hovering, flickering, and fading in and out of visibility before coming to rest on the desk's surface.

In its shadowy depths I could see a dull projection of the room where Liv and Will had been prisoners. Its floor still shone with green liquid and shattered glass, but there was no longer any sign of life.

"You saw everything that happened," I said. "You saw us…you saw me…"

"The Orb's time with me is coming to an end, and its power is weakening with each hour that passes. But I did manage to watch your adventure in the Throne Room as it unfolded, and all that happened to you afterwards."

"But I…" I began before stopping myself. I was on the verge of telling him I hadn't really accomplished anything. But the truth was, I'd done something amazing.

Albeit incredibly stupid.

And the craziest part was, despite the fear, mayhem, and madness involved, I would do it all over again. "I'm sorry I left without telling you," I said. "But I didn't have a choice. I couldn't let my brother and best friend die, and I knew you'd never let me go if I asked."

"Ah yes. *It's easier to ask forgiveness than to ask permission*," Merriwether said softly. "Well, I can't say I approve of your methods, but you did what you felt was right, and that's admirable. Your friend Liv needed you, and I understand your need to help her."

"And Will," I said, irked that Merriwether had left his name out of the equation.

"Will, yes. Your older brother."

His voice filled with an affection that seemed tainted by profound sadness. For the first time, it hit me that I wasn't Merriwether's only grandchild.

I wondered if I'd ever bring myself to tell my brother the truth about our bloodline. He didn't know about any of this—the Academy, my powers, the Otherwhere. I could only imagine how he'd react if I tried to explain my strange new life to him.

*"Hey, Will…I need to tell you something, so please, just hear me out: I can summon doors out of thin air and turn invisible, and my sort-of-boyfriend can turn into a dragon, and there's a magical world beyond our own, and also, we have a grandfather who's a wizard. Crazy, huh?"*

And then he'd tell me to lay off the drugs and probably send me to get my head examined.

"I…think I need to tell you something," I stammered after a pause.

"Mmm?"

"Before I went to the queen's castle, I spoke to my grandmother. I went to see her in Cornwall."

Merriwether raised an eyebrow. For once, he actually looked surprised. Perhaps even a little excited.

"Oh?" he asked, his voice higher than usual.

"Why didn't you tell me that you…that we're…?" My eyes moved from his to the floor and I found myself intertwining my fingers into a nervous knot.

"You want to know why I didn't tell you I'm your grandfather."

"Well…yeah."

Rising to his feet, Merriwether strode over to a bookshelf at the far end of the office to finger the spine of a leather-bound tome, his back facing me. "I suppose it was because you would have expected all sorts of unfair treatment. Or perhaps more accurately, because the other students would have assumed I'd treat you with special care. I wanted you to sort out for yourself how special you are, regardless of bloodlines or genetics. I had no intention of spelling it out for you. A true magic-user learns for herself exactly what she's capable of. You are not invincible, Vega —no Seeker ever is. But you *are* strong. I needed you to find that out for yourself."

I shook my head. "You're wrong, though. I'm not really that strong or special. I wouldn't have accomplished anything without five dragons helping me."

Merriwether turned my way with a twinkle in his eye. "Five dragons that you managed to move from one place to another with nothing more than your mind. And yes, they helped you, but only because you made allies of them. You have created five lifelong, powerful friends, all because you did the right thing in a difficult situation. A situation where you were far braver than anyone had a right to be."

My lips twitched into an involuntary grin. "Okay, that *was* pretty cool, I'll admit."

After a brief shared chuckle, Merriwether frowned. It seemed his mind had shifted back to the business at hand.

"Now, what do you propose we do with you?"

"What do you mean?" I asked, swallowing nervously.

"Students are not to leave the Academy's grounds without an instructor. Yet you did so without my authorization. You went to the Usurper Queen's castle—a very dangerous, even stupid, venture. Again, without my permission. There need to be consequences for those actions, don't you think?"

I stared at him, expecting him to tell me what those consequences would be. But when he stayed silent, I knew I had no choice but to defend myself.

"I…I rescued three people who should never have been there and managed to transport them to safety. I freed five dragons who are now our sworn allies. You said so yourself. I'd say that almost makes up for any, um…insubordination."

"You risked a great deal, and you set a very bad example for the other students." His bushy brows met once again above his expressive eyes, a grave look overtaking his lined face. "However noble your deeds, you've broken the rules, Vega. Actions like yours have consequences."

"Punish me, then!" I blurted out. This slow reveal was more like unbearable torture. I just wanted to know my fate so I could get on with it. Was he going to send me back home to Fairhaven? Or was the punishment somehow even worse? "I can't stand not knowing what you're going to do, so please, just do it."

But Merriwether didn't reply. Instead, he stared at me, waiting for something more.

I got the distinct impression that he was enjoying himself.

"Look, I get that you need to make an example of me. I want to participate in the Trials, I really do. I want to become the Chosen Seeker. But more than that, I just want to help. What we're up against here—the queen—we both know she's pure evil. I've looked into her eyes. I've seen the inside of that castle of hers —Uldrach, they said it was called. I've seen Kaer Uther. It's… dark, decaying. There's a feeling of death in the place that I'll never forget. Like a disease that's waiting to spread. Nothing good will come of any of this if we don't act soon."

Merriwether was still staring, silent.

And it was freaking me out.

"If you want to punish me," I stammered, "then fine. All I know is that Isla—the queen, I mean—is the cruelest person I've ever met. And trust me, I go to high school with teenage girls, so I know malicious when I see it."

"I don't *want* to punish you. But I must." Merriwether flicked a hand toward the far wall, and a weightless screen sprung up between him and the old bookshelf. A map of the Academy shimmered to life on its surface.

"I know you've suffered," he said. "You were in a cell for days. From the looks of it, they didn't feed you very well. Under other circumstances, I might say that was punishment enough."

With another quick gesture from my grandfather, the map zoomed into the southwest corner of the Academy's grounds.

"But these circumstances are unique. For too many reasons to name, I cannot let you off with a mere warning. If I do, what's to stop other students from following your example?"

"I understand."

"With that in mind, you are to muck out the stables each morning before your training session begins. This will continue until you leave the Academy."

I looked at the map, only to see a long row of horse stalls. I'd always liked horses, so the punishment didn't seem bad, if you didn't count the intolerably inhuman hour at which I'd have to get out of bed each morning.

"Seems fair," I said with as much enthusiasm as I could muster.

"Good. Now that we've sorted your penance, we need to talk business. As you know, the queen is already in possession of the Sword of Viviane. A very special weapon. Legendary, even."

"Yes. It's hanging in the—wait a minute. *What* did you call it?" On my birthday, a stranger in Fairhaven had referred to me as a Daughter of Viviane. I'd since learned that was the name of the Lady of the Lake—the woman who'd allegedly handed a sword to a young man who would eventually become known as King Arthur.

I still remembered the stories my parents had read me when I was little. There were various versions of the legend. Some said Viviane had emerged from the watery depths and held out the sword, but others said Arthur had proven himself by pulling the blade from a stone.

To be honest, both versions had always seemed pretty out there to me.

"You know it by another name, of course," Merriwether told me.

"Wait...you mean the sword I was staring at...the sword

hanging over the throne…that's King Arthur's sword? That's *Excalibur?*"

"Yes, I'm saying exactly that."

"Well, Excalibur, or whatever it's called, is suspended above the throne in the queen's castle," I said, my voice thin with wonder as I realized how close I'd come to getting my hands on such an incredible legend of a weapon.

"And do you know how the queen got hold of the sword?" Merriwether asked.

"Raff," I said. "He—he was her prisoner. She made him find it for her."

"The boy you brought with you to the Academy," Merriwether said.

"Yes. He seems to be a Seeker."

"Ah. Interesting."

I eyed Merriwether curiously. What did he mean by that, exactly?

But before I had a chance to ask, he spoke again.

"Given this new information, I'm beginning to rethink my strategy with regards to the Seekers' Trials. I will need a few moments to ponder it." He pressed his palms onto the desk, pulling his eyes to mine. "In the meantime, there's something else you and I need to discuss."

# MERRIWETHER

EVERY INCH of me tightened as I stared into my grandfather's unreadable eyes.

Merriwether may have been my flesh and blood, but it was entirely possible that he'd changed his mind and decided to make Raff the Chosen Seeker and kick me to the curb.

And judging from the extremely serious look on his face, that was *exactly* what was on his mind.

For all I knew, I might find myself back home in Fairhaven within the hour.

I held my breath as the daunting Headmaster began to pace the room, seemingly searching for the right words as I did everything I could to resist biting my nails. The longer he remained silent, the more I became convinced I was about to be expelled.

*He's having a hard time figuring out how to break the bad news*, I thought. *Trying to work out how he can let me down easy.*

I ground my teeth as I watched him, trying my best to keep my chin high and to stop my eyes from welling with tears. But my stomach was doing backflips, and my legs had gone tingly and numb.

I was glad to be sitting down.

Finally, after a brutally long silence, Merriwether laid a hand on the edge of a shelf, his back turned toward me. His voice was even and measured.

"I need you to know, Vega, that I wanted to remain in your world all those years ago. I desired nothing more than to stay with your grandmother, and I would have gladly spent my life, however short it might have been, by her side. I didn't want to leave her, not ever."

As I listened, my eyes began to go wide with shock. This was *not* the subject I'd expected to discuss right now.

"But she asked me to go," he added, "and I obeyed."

"I know," I replied, resisting the sudden desire to leap to my feet, stride over, and lay a reassuring hand on his shoulder. "I know it must have been hard for both of you to say goodbye. I mean, I've never exactly been in that situation, but I think I can at least *imagine* how you felt."

"It was difficult. Of course it was. More difficult than I can say. I want you to understand…." Merriwether drew his gaze toward the door that I'd walked through a few minutes earlier. "I know you and Mr. Drake care for one another—probably more deeply than either of you wants to admit. But do yourselves a favor and be sure you don't find yourselves in the same position your grandmother and I were in. Don't give yourselves the brief gift of great joy, only to find you'll pay for it later with great pain. It's an agony you'll have to live with for the rest of your lives."

I felt my skin heat up as the full impact of what he was saying smacked me square in the chest. Wait a minute—did he think I was going to end up pregnant with Callum's child? Was that *seriously* his primary concern?

"We haven't done anything!" I blurted out. "I mean, we've kissed. But I'm not in any danger of ending up like my grandmother did, if that's what you're afraid of."

For a moment Merriwether looked surprised, then he broke out in a full-on smile. "That's not what I'm worried about," he said, the smile fading. "I'm worried about your heart. There is danger in love, always. And you find yourself in a particularly perilous situation. Callum Drake is no ordinary young man."

"I know. That's why I—" My cheeks were scorching by now. "I mean, that's why he's...*interesting* to me."

I wanted a hole to open up in the floor and suck me in.

But no such luck.

"It's one thing for him to be interesting. But be mindful of him. He is kind and good, yes. But there is a side to every person that remains hidden. Like the rest of us, Mr. Drake has his secrets."

For the first time in years, I felt like I was being lectured by a concerned parent. It was a strange yet familiar sensation, and I hadn't quite realized how deeply I'd been craving it.

Will had always acted as a sort of surrogate father to me since our parents' death, of course, but this...felt different. Merriwether was the mentor I'd lost when my mother and father died. I felt safe, all of a sudden, like there was a new person in my life who would always look out for me, no matter what.

It was a bittersweet feeling, to say the least.

"I'm not issuing you a command or trying to interfere in what, let's face it, is your personal business," Merriwether added. "I'm only telling you this to protect your heart. Callum is a fine young man. I see how you look at him, and I must admit that in those moments, you remind me of your grandmother. I see love in your eyes, just as I saw it in hers. I just don't want to see you crushed beneath the weight of the truth."

I was about to issue a weak denial. But I stopped myself. The truth was, I already knew I loved him. If I hadn't been sure of it when I set off to liberate Will and Liv, I was sure of it now. There was nothing quite like incarceration to make you realize where your priorities—and deepest affections—lie.

Whatever Callum's flaws, they were of no significance to me.

If anything, it would probably be a relief to discover that he *had* actual flaws.

All I'd ever seen of him was perfection.

"I'll be okay," I told Merriwether. "I'm being careful. Besides, I've barely talked to Callum since I got back. I don't even know what he's feeling."

"I can guess," he replied, his eyes sad. "Look—I just don't want you to be crushed when the time comes to say goodbye to him forever, which may be sooner rather than later."

"I understand. I'll take that all under consideration. I promise."

I thanked him, stood up, and headed toward the door. But he called out my name just as I reached it.

"There is one more thing I want to ask you," he said. "About something of a rather delicate nature."

"Yes?" I asked, turning around and wondering what could possibly be more delicate than talk of his secret relationship with my grandmother, or my not-so-secret relationship with Callum.

"The boy you brought back with you...the boy you say found the sword..."

"Raff?"

He nodded. "How well do you know him?"

"Fairly well," I shrugged. "But at the same time, not at all. He told me the queen held him prisoner for years because of something his mother did." I cocked my head to the side. "Wait—you must have heard it all. Didn't you use the Orb to eavesdrop on us?"

Merriwether shook his head. "No. For a time after you left here, I couldn't get a clear image of your whereabouts. The Orb's powers are unpredictable, at best. I saw that boy for the first time just a few minutes ago, when you appeared in the courtyard. Yet...something about him feels familiar."

The look that passed over the Headmaster's face just then sent a tremor of unease through me, though I wasn't sure why.

"Is there something about Raff you're worried about? Something I should know?"

"No. All is as it's meant to be." The words should have been reassuring, but for some reason they had the opposite effect.

"Why does that make me nervous?" I asked.

"Hmm?" replied Merriwether, who seemed to have grown deeply preoccupied with some very distant thought. He waved his hand in a way that reminded me of Nana. "Oh, don't be nervous. Everything will work out. And if it doesn't..."

"If it doesn't?"

"If it doesn't, then I suppose we'll learn a valuable lesson. But listen—I will be calling for an Assembly in an hour or so. I'd like you there, in the front row with the other Seeker Candidates."

"Okay," I replied. "Then I'll see you in a bit."

"Yes, yes. In a bit."

I left the room, closing the door behind me, grateful to have escaped the Headmaster's office with little more than a metaphorical slap on the wrist.

# ASSEMBLY

AFTER SCARFING down a quick snack stolen from the Academy's kitchen, showering, and changing into clean clothes, I found myself seated in the front row of the Great Hall, awaiting Merriwether's arrival. I was dressed in a training tunic and a pair of gray cargo pants, my small silver dagger tucked into a sheath at my side.

From now on, I wasn't going anywhere without a weapon. Even if I had no real idea how to use it.

As the Academy's student population made its way into the Great Hall and seated themselves behind me in rows of green, blue and red uniforms, the other Seeker Candidates filed into the front row to tuck themselves into seats on either side of me, leaning in eagerly to ask questions about every topic imaginable.

*Hey, Vega, how did you get the dragons to listen to you?*

*Was the queen's castle beautiful or terrifying?*

*Can you tell us about how you rescued Will and Liv?*

I did my best to answer all their questions, though the task wasn't exactly pleasant. I had no desire to suffer through flashbacks of Will and Liv suspended in vats of green ooze, or of crying out in horror and frustration as I pounded on the glass, helpless to get to them.

Each time I thought about the queen's malice, I wanted to scream all over again.

At one point, Oleana leaned forward to ask me a question, though she looked hesitant.

The Candidate the other Seekers had nicknamed Olly was one of the prettiest girls I'd ever set eyes on. I almost hated to admit it now, but when I'd first met her, I'd disliked her immediately. At first glance, she reminded me of the three Charmers at Plymouth High: the matching-lipstick-wearing torture machines whose sole reason for living was to make other girls feel small and insecure.

Over time, I'd come to realize Oleana didn't really have much in common with those malicious creatures. Yes, she was competitive, proud, and occasionally confrontational. But she could also be surprisingly down-to-earth, even humble. More than once she'd even sung my praises, which came as a shock to a girl like me who was so used to being torn down by the "popular" crowd.

"Is the Usurper Queen as beautiful as they say?" Olly asked, her voice uncharacteristically meek, almost like she was afraid of what my answer might be.

"The queen *is* beautiful," I replied through gritted teeth. "Physically, anyway. But inside, she's the ugliest person I've ever met in my life. I can't imagine hating anything more than I hate her."

"Not even onions?" asked Desmond, the rosy-cheeked, dark-haired Seeker from England who was staring at me from the seat to Olly's right. We didn't know each other well, but he'd always reminded me of a choir boy, innocent-looking to the point of charming naiveté. He looked more like someone's kid brother than a potentially powerful Seeker—even though I knew perfectly well he was a Digger, a mind controller who could manipulate the intentions and actions of his opponents. "Surely you don't hate the queen more than you hate onions!" he added, sounding like a frightened mouse.

Though the question was absurd, he looked utterly earnest.

"I take it you don't like onions," I replied with a chuckle.

He shook his head. "God, no. They make me gag. Like, retching, dry-heaving, bloody awful gagging. There's nothing on earth more vile than those hell-vegetables."

"Well, multiply that loathing by a million and maybe you'll start to scratch the surface of my hatred for the queen."

His face went white then slightly green. "That must be horrid. Just horrid. The way they feel in your mouth…the texture of them…"

"Don't worry, Des," laughed Olly, "It's unlikely that anyone will be forcing you to eat a slice of the queen."

"Still…Now I'm thinking about onions, and it's making me want to up-end my lunch."

"Hey—what's the difference between the Usurper Queen and an onion?" asked Meg, who was sitting to my left. Of all the Seekers, she was probably my favorite. She was quiet and a little shy, and she wore her self-doubt on her sleeve. But I'd seen flashes of courage in her, and an admirable streak of determination. She had the potential to rise to the level of Chosen Seeker, if only she could find the confidence.

"I'm not sure I want to know," Desmond answered, cupping a hand over his mouth.

"Tell us!" laughed Olly.

"Nobody cries when you chop up the queen," Meg replied with a smirk.

The others laughed, but I found myself pressing my back into my seat. With a shudder, I remembered the feeling that had flooded me when I'd had my hand on the chain wrapped around Isla's neck. For a few seconds the desire to take her life had overwhelmed me, even excited me. As much as I despised the woman, the thought of murdering people was too raw, too real.

Stealing lives was something the *other* side did.

I did my best to push thoughts of bloodlust from my mind. I wanted to forget the feeling. Or better still, never experience it again.

While we awaited Merriwether's arrival, the other Candidates assaulted me with more questions. What was it like being in prison? Did I use a chamber pot? Did I ever think I'd get away? Did I use a tiny spoon to try and dig a tunnel? And what was the story with the boy…Raff? Did he help me escape? Or did I help him?

To my relief, after a few minutes Merriwether, dressed as usual in a long, tailored purple jacket of rich velvet, walked onto the stage and saved me from having to reply further to the never-ending interrogation.

The Headmaster was alone, which was unusual. I pulled forward in my seat and turned around, only to see that the majority of the faculty members were standing at the sides of the massive room, surrounding the students. They were looking to the Headmaster as though they, too, were eager to hear whatever it was he had to say.

It took me a few seconds to locate Callum, who was standing alone in a far corner of the room, his face unreadable. I was contemplating raising a hand to try and get his attention when Merriwether began to speak.

"You're no doubt wondering why I've called you all here today," he bellowed as if in response to the puzzled looks, inspiring a chorus of speculative murmurs. He held up his hand to silence them. "I have my reasons, as you can imagine. Many reasons. But first…" He drew his eyes down and issued me a quick smile. "Vega Sloane, would you come up here and join me, please?"

*Come up there? Really?*

*The. Horror.*

My fight or flight instinct kicked in, minus the fight part. A violent urge overtook me to summon my Shadow form and vanish without a trace.

But instead, I rose slowly to my feet and headed to the side of the stage to scale the steps, not entirely sure what I was doing. I shot Merriwether a "Do I really have to?" look before turning to face the sea of students in their multicolored tunics. At the back of the Hall, a few of the Zerkers were firing their usual dart-like glares of irritation in my direction. And once again, I found myself languishing in a state of self-conscious terror as I tried to will the ground to open up and swallow me whole.

As I struggled to calm my shaking knees, I almost wanted to laugh. After all, I'd taken on the Usurper Queen. I'd freed her captive dragons, summoned doors out of nothing, turned invisible…and yet, standing there on a stage in front of a room full of teenagers still terrified me more than anything.

When I positioned myself beside Merriwether, he gestured elegantly to the back of the Great Hall. I watched as the large double-doors flew open, seemingly of their own volition. A tall, brown-haired figure, dressed in the silver tunic of a Seeker Candidate, began to make his way toward us.

As he drew near the stage, I realized with a shock that I was staring at the boy I'd personally rescued from his prison cell.

# THE RECRUIT

RAFF HAD BATHED since I'd last seen him. His hair was tidy, his face clean of the layers of dirt that had coated it. He actually looked…good.

No.

Better than good.

He looked *handsome.*

Oddly enough, his face in its clean state even reminded me a little of Callum's, which was no small feat. His jaw was broad and square, his cheekbones elegantly pronounced. They even had similar piercing blue eyes, though Raff's seemed to lack the charm and warmth of Callum's.

He didn't look underfed, considering that he'd spent much of his life in prison. And despite his wretched upbringing, he walked with a surprisingly confident air. He bore no resemblance to the image I'd conjured of the boy who'd whispered stories about his youth from the cell next door to mine, or even to the boy who'd cowered fearfully in the presence of dragons.

A murmur rose up in the Great Hall as Raff leapt onto the stage and joined me in front of the large crowd. Guessing it had to freak him out to see so many eyes focused his way, I turned to him to say something reassuring.

But to my surprise, he looked perfectly at ease.

"I would have thought being up here would make you super-nervous," I whispered.

"Nah. I was born for this," he replied, thrusting his shoulders back confidently.

My brow furrowed with confusion. *Born* for this? He was a former prisoner. The son of a woman who'd been killed by the queen. He'd spent most of his life in a cold, damp dungeon.

Meanwhile, I was literally the Headmaster's granddaughter, and even *I* was just barely convinced that I deserved to be here.

"Well, I'm glad you're feeling good about being put on display," I chuckled. "Because that makes exactly one of us."

Raff shot me a quick glance, his chin raised high, and for a moment I felt extra-small, as if he was looking down on me both literally and figuratively. I had no idea where this weirdly haughty attitude came from.

Nor could I say I liked it.

I drew my eyes away, my cheeks flushing hot.

"As many of you know," Merriwether called out, addressing the crowd and calming the din of puzzled voices still crescendo-ing in the audience, "Vega Sloane recently found her way into the Usurper Queen's castle—the castle known as Uldrach. There, she made a few discoveries, most of which were worrisome. But she did make one fortuitous one. Raff here," he said, gesturing toward the boy standing to my left, "was a prisoner of the queen, and Miss Sloane managed to free him and bring him to us. But before we get to his part of the tale, I think we should hear from the Seeker Candidate who defied my orders and went on a one-person rescue mission. For the record, I have issued her what I feel is a suitable punishment."

As he added the last sentence, he turned my way and threw me a quick, almost imperceptible wink.

My heart began running laps inside my chest as Merriwether focused his gaze on me. "Vega, would you please tell your fellow students what you witnessed in the castle? I believe it would be best if the details came from you."

I stared, panicked, at the wizened Headmaster before swallowing hard. He issued me a warm smile that calmed me down, if only temporarily.

Turning away from him, I fixed my eyes on the doors at the far end of the Great Hall and began to speak. "I, um...well, the thing is, the queen..." My eyes landed on Callum, whose lips twitched into a smile encouraging enough to send me a quick shot of confidence. "The queen has Waerg guards—a lot of them. They keep watch over the castle's main gates and the prison cells. They're strong and loyal. They'll do anything for her."

Merriwether's face was expressionless, but he shot me a quick look before gesturing to me to continue. "Go on. Tell our students what you saw in the Throne Room."

"The queen recently trapped five dragons, hoping to use them for her own purposes, but I...I managed to set them free, as some of you know. But I have no doubt she'll try to catch more of them and hold them captive until she figures out how to control them and use them as weapons. She'll figure out a way to bend them to her will, even if it means torturing them. We can't let that happen. If she manages to tame dragons, we can't possibly beat her."

I was surprised at the tone of authority that was beginning to lace my words, and I was pleased to see a series of approving nods and murmurs make their way through the crowd.

When the hum of surprise and approval died down, I continued.

"There's something else. Something even more important. The queen has a Relic in her possession—the one called the Sword of Viviane."

In an instant, the murmurs turned into full-volume, panicked voices. In the back of the Great Hall I saw looks of abject rage on the faces of Zerkers.

It seemed some of the students knew how powerful the sword was.

Merriwether took a step forward, holding a hand up to silence the students. "As you know, the Relics of Power bestow upon their possessors the power to open portals between this land and the other world—the one where some of you were born. But they also grant their possessors other sorts of benefits. Spells cast by Casters become more potent. Armies, too, gain strength. There is an old magic in the Relics that is immeasurable. So let it be known that the Sword of Viviane, in the queen's hands, is a danger to us all."

With that, Merriwether gestured toward me to continue.

"She has the sword on display," I added in a voice loud enough to draw the students' attention back to me, "in her Throne Room. I'm sure she hopes to find more of the Relics before the Chosen Seeker is named, though we've slowed her down somewhat by stealing her secret weapon." Gesturing to Raff, I paused for a moment, enjoying the blissful calm inside my mind.

Confident, I pulled my eyes down to my peers, only to see that even the Zerkers had begun to look at me in a sort of stunned silence. They were hanging on every word, waiting to see what I'd say next. I was sure their admiration was only fleeting, but I had to admit it felt good.

"The Usurper Queen lives in a place of darkness," I said. "A place that used to be beautiful and joyful—a castle that once belonged to the Crimson King. But she's destroyed the town that surrounds the castle, and broken the souls of those who once lived there. She thrives on keeping her servants miserable and making sure they depend on her for their own survival. But we must remember that she's not all-powerful, not yet—she relies too much on her trinkets and her minions to keep her strong. As with any tyrant, her only true strength lies in keeping others down. That's the only reason I was able to escape—I figured out how to take away her power, if only temporarily. We have to find a way to take it *permanently* away from her."

Once again, I found myself picturing the look on Isla's face when I'd wrapped my chain around her neck and tightened it. It was the look of a woman who was helpless, frightened, vulnerable.

"Make no mistake," I said, "we are all in danger as long as she's on the throne. And if she manages to get her hands on the other Relics of Power, her strength will only grow. She will become unstoppable. We…"

I shot Merriwether a look, suddenly hesitant to offer another unsolicited opinion. When he nodded solemnly, I continued.

"We have no choice but to act fast. We need to stop her by any means necessary—whatever that may mean."

The expressions on the other Seeker Candidates' faces turned grim. I wanted to lean down and tell them I knew how they felt, that I shared their fear and anxiety. Stopping the queen meant fighting. It meant leaving the safety of the Academy and confronting an actual threat.

It meant risking our lives.

"Thank you, Vega," Merriwether said, patting my shoulder. "I wanted you and your fellow ex-prisoner up here with me—the girl who broke into the queen's castle, and the boy who *knows* the queen's castle…" Merriwether stepped over and clamped his other hand hard onto Raff's shoulder. The young man stood firm, his feet planted, and grinned at the crowd. "Remind me, Raff. What is your surname?"

It was a strange question, and I wasn't sure why Merriwether was asking it in front of the entire room full of students. Then again, it was a relatively innocent thing to ask.

To my surprise, Raff shuffled his feet for a moment, suddenly hesitant to speak.

"Miller," he finally said.

"Ah. Well, Raff...*Miller*," Merriwether continued, "Since you are allegedly the only person present who's found a Relic—the only Seeker who has actually *sought*—I have a rather important announcement to make."

I watched the other Candidates shoot each other looks of horror. I knew exactly what they were thinking: that Raff would be named the Chosen Seeker, right there and then.

But I knew better.

At least, I hoped I did.

"As you may have surmised, I have decided..." Merriwether continued, pausing dramatically, "...to include Raff in our training. For the next several days, he will attend classes with the other Candidates, and when the time comes for the Trials, he will compete, just like everyone else."

I'd just begun once again to search the Great Hall for Callum when Raff, who'd been standing tensely still, twisted his head around sharply, his eyes laser-focused on Merriwether's face.

"But I found the first Relic!" he snarled. "The Trials should be canceled! I should be the Chosen Seeker!"

"Do you see the Relic here?" Merriwether asked, gesturing to the room in front of us. "Because if not, you cannot possibly expect me to give you credit for finding it."

A sneer slipped over Raff's lips that sent a shiver down my spine. Suddenly I was happy every conversation we'd had had taken place through a thick stone wall.

"There are no shortcuts to Chosen Seeker, Mr. Miller. I will not be sending the other Candidates home, despite your apparent wish that I do so. You will be participating in the training and Trial, just as the other Candidates must." He turned back to the students in the front row. "The Seekers' Trial—yes, that is *Trial*, singular—will take place one week from today, though I cannot yet tell you what will be expected of you. I can only say that this will be unlike any Trial that's come before now. Our world is changing rapidly, and so, therefore, must we."

"But..." Raff choked out.

Merriwether raised a hand that silenced him at last, even as Raff shot me a dark look that felt like a dagger piercing my stomach.

"There is one other thing," Merriwether bellowed, addressing the entire crowd this time, his fierce eyes moving over each face like a terrifying scanner. "Some time ago, I discovered that there is a spy among us, here at the Academy. This spy has provided secret information to the Usurper Queen. Information that gravely endangered at least one of our students."

Grateful that he hadn't pointed out that I was the endangered student, I watched my peers squirm in their seats, shooting accusing looks at one another or whispering speculative guesses.

"I have some idea of the spy's identity," Merriwether continued. "But I have no intention of acting on my theory, at least not yet. In the meantime, I ask that you all be vigilant. Trust no one. And always be prepared to fight for what is right. Let him—or her—be aware, however, that his or her time at the Academy is limited."

I turned toward my grandfather, wanting to ask why he didn't name the culprit right then and there. The spy was the reason I slept in my own private quarters, away from the other Seeker Candidates. The spy had provided secret information about me to the queen and might even have been the reason Isla had anticipated my arrival at her castle.

Which meant the spy very nearly cost me my *life*.

There was no way I wanted to spend another week in this place, knowing someone was out to get me.

But Merriwether shot me a quick smile laden with meaning. *Trust me. I have a plan. I won't do anything to endanger you.*

"You may all go now," the Headmaster finally said, turning back to the crowd. "Get some rest, have some food, look after yourselves. Tomorrow morning, your training resumes."

He turned to look at the back of the room and flicked his

hands in the air. The large wooden doors at the chamber's far end opened up again. Students began filing out, excitedly muttering to one another about what the next days might entail.

As for me, I figured I already knew.

And the thought of what was to come filled me with dread.

# RESPITE

As I FOLLOWED the other students through the doors of the Great Hall, I called upon my Shadow form. The last thing I wanted was to run into my colleagues and have to answer more questions about what happened in the queen's castle, or to speculate out loud about what might occur over the next several days.

Eager to find Callum, I began to make my way unnoticed around the large group of students who were now milling around in the corridor, chatting about what they'd just seen and heard.

"The new Seeker is pretty amazing, isn't he?" one of them said.

"I don't know about that," another replied. "He seems sort of arrogant."

"Well, he should be. He's definitely going to win the Trial. He found a Relic of Power. He's already proven himself."

"He doesn't seem that impressive to me," a third interjected with a shrug.

"Doesn't matter," one of the female Zerkers replied with a smile. "Whether he wins or not, he's super hot. That's all *I* care about. I was craving fresh male blood in this place."

"Shallow much?" one of her fellow Zerkers sneered.

Ashamed of myself for eavesdropping, I'd just begun to distance myself from the group when I spotted Raff concealing himself behind a suit of armor on one side of the corridor, his arms crossed over his chest. As he listened in on the conversation, he grinned from ear to ear.

For a second I contemplated leaving my Shadow form behind to ask him why he was acting so strange. But all I could think of was the rude and off-putting way that he'd snapped at Merriwether. Somehow, over the last several hours, he'd changed from the sweet, somewhat innocent boy I'd met in the queen's prison into someone brimming with confidence, bordering on outright hostility.

But I decided against confronting him. All I wanted—all I'd wanted for days—was to spend time with Callum. Raff was nothing more than a distraction now. A confusing one, at that.

Grateful to leave him and the others behind, I raced to the end of the hall, turned the corner, and sprang at full speed until I came to a dark, secluded alcove where I tucked myself in and summoned a door to the Grove.

With a pang of agony, I shifted into my solid form, slipped the dragon key into the lock, and stepped through into the idyllic, top-secret tree-filled courtyard where Callum and I sometimes met for private talks. Aside from our isolated bedrooms in a tower at the far end of the Academy, the Grove was the only place where we could truly be alone together, away from the watchful eyes and judgmental glares of students or faculty.

I could only hope Callum would have the same idea and find his way there after the strangeness of the Assembly. I was dying to know what was on his mind, to hear his impressions. But I had to admit that most of all, I was dying to feel his arms around me. I craved some tangible evidence that nothing had changed between us. That we were still close, even after everything that had happened over the last several days.

But the second I stepped into the Grove, my heart sank.

There was no sign of him.

I paced among the rows of short, delicate fruit trees for a few minutes, biting my nails as I waited for a boy who might never show up.

*Why aren't you here? I need to see you so badly that it hurts.*

I'd just begun to give up hope when I spotted a tall, broad-shouldered figure, silhouetted against a row of apple trees, walking toward me in the distance.

Relieved beyond words, I raced toward him and threw my arms around his neck, pressing my face into his broad, solid chest. In turn, he wrapped his arms around me so hard that I could feel every bit of his body's substantial heat penetrating my skin through my clothing.

In those few seconds, all my worries melted away.

I was home. I was whole. I wasn't afraid. It felt so good to finally find myself alone with him, to feel engulfed and protected. I'd craved this sensation so deeply when I was in the queen's prison. More than food, water, even air. He was all the sustenance I needed.

After what seemed like several minutes of silence, he pulled back to look at me, slipping a hand over my cheek before pushing an errant handful of dark ringlets behind my right ear.

"Your eyes are so bright right now," he said. "I can tell you've been using your powers."

"Of course I have. I had to get to you. I had to see you."

I spoke the words without inhibition. It was the truth, after all. I'd nearly lost him once. I needed to remind him that he meant something to me, before it happened again.

"Well, I'm glad we both had the same urge." With that, a shallow smile drew its way over his lips. "That Assembly was…strange."

"So, you stayed the whole time? I lost track of you after a while."

"I suppose I didn't want to be seen, but yes, I was there."

"So you heard what Merriwether said about the Trial."

"That it will take place soon," he nodded. "Then we'll know your fate."

I could tell that he was trying to sound calm and confident, but his tone was closer to that of someone announcing a coming death.

"We're back to training in the meantime. I don't see what good it'll do, though, at least for me. Every training session has been a disaster. I may as well just sit in my room and read a book called *The Art of War for Idiots,* for all the good the actual sparring will do me."

Faced with his charming smile, I could hardly resist pushing myself up onto my toes to kiss him.

Callum shook his head. "Sorry, Sloane, but you know that's not true."

"Oh, do I?" I asked with a grin, glad to know he was finally relaxing a little.

"Come on. It's obvious what you are by now. You're not a weapon wielder, at least not in the swords-and-daggers sense. Your greatest asset is your mind. You proved it by taking on the queen. You shouldn't focus on physical weapons—blades and bows aren't for you. For one thing, you've proven you don't need them."

"Good," I replied with a roll of my eyes. "Because if someone hands me another bow and quiver, I'll scream."

"So will any friendly who ends up with an arrow in the eye when you accidentally shoot them," Callum chuckled.

I smacked his arm. "Hey! I know I suck, but I don't suck *that* much."

"I'm sorry," he laughed.

"Okay. I admit it. Weapons and I don't get along phenome-nally well. But still…that was harsh." I let out a sigh. "So what should I do? I'm not sure I can survive another week in here. You saw how the Zerkers were looking at me. They go from admiring me one minute to wanting to kill me the next. They'll be out for my blood."

"It's not the Zerkers I'd worry about if I were you." His jaw tensed, and I could have sworn I detected a millisecond-long flash of anger in his eyes.

"What do you mean? Who are you talking about?"

He ground his jaw before replying. "I shouldn't have said that." For a second he looked away and winced, before turning back to me with a grin. "Ignore me. I guess I'm just feeling protective of you. So tell me, how was your meeting with the Headmaster earlier?"

"Oh, I was sure he was going to murder me—or even worse, expel me—but I'm still alive and still enrolled, so I guess it turned out okay, all things considered."

"He'd never kill you. At worst he'd maim you verbally a little bit."

"I was stupid to leave without telling him what I was planning on doing," I admitted. "I suppose I deserved a little chastising."

"He's not the only one who was left in the dark, Vega." For the first time, I heard a note of deep sadness in Callum's voice.

"I told you I was leaving," I protested. "I said goodbye to you."

"You didn't tell me *where* you were going. You shouldn't have left like that. You could've asked me to come with you, but you just…took off. And when you didn't come back…"

"You thought I was dead."

He shook his head. "No. Never. I knew you were alive." With that, he took hold of my left hand, drew it to his lips and kissed it. "I could feel you—on the air. In my mind. I knew you were out there somewhere. It was the only thing that kept me from leaving this place and searching for you."

"I could feel you, too. Sometimes it was like you were speaking to me. I thought I was losing it. I kept telling myself it wasn't possible, but your voice was so clear in my mind sometimes…Still, I was sure I was only imagining it."

"I did speak to you," he said. "Though I wasn't sure you could hear me. I've never…spoken to anyone like that before. It's a gift granted by the dragon who lives inside me—one that risks awakening him in dangerous ways. But I was desperate. The thought of losing you, Vega…"

I stroked my fingertips over his stubbled cheek. "I'm sorry, Callum," I said. "I know it's hard for you to understand, but I did what felt I had to. I had no choice but to set Will and Liv free. I couldn't have lived with myself if I hadn't done it. And *they* wouldn't be alive at all."

"I get it. I just wish you'd trusted me enough to tell me what your plan was."

"I trust you completely. But it wasn't about that. I just…I don't know how to explain it. I felt like it was something I had to do alone. But if you knew how much I wanted you with me…If you knew the things I wanted to say, in the moments when I thought I might not survive…" I bit my lip, trying to hold back a flood of emotion. "I wanted more than anything in the world to see you, even just once. I had so many regrets, I can't even begin to tell you."

He smiled, his tension seemingly disappearing. For the time being, at least. "Well, you're here now. I'm just glad Merriwether didn't kick you out of the Academy. He's a lot of things, but tolerant isn't always one of them."

"He *is* a lot of things," I replied, reaching for Callum's hand and squeezing hard as I lowered my chin to stare at the ground. "I have so much to tell you, I don't really even know where to begin. There are so many things to say…"

"What do you mean?"

"Merriwether is more to me than you know," I said softly. "He's more to me than I could ever have imagined before I left here a few days ago."

A slew of questions colored Callum's expression.

I stared up at him again—at those stark, blue, strangely deep eyes that seemed at times to convey every emotion imaginable. "He's my grandfather."

"Wait…" Callum sputtered. Clearly, the news threw him as much as it had thrown me when I'd first heard it. "Are you serious?"

"Completely."

"But…how—?"

"Before I went to the queen's castle, I paid my grandmother a visit in Cornwall. She told me everything about their past. About their…bond."

I filled him in quickly on her scandalous pregnancy, Merriwether's onset of rapid aging when he'd gone to live in my world, and why she'd sent him away to return alone to the Otherwhere. I told him how much they'd loved each other, how it must have crushed them both to say goodbye.

"So, that was the so-called *scandal* that everyone whispers about when they talk about your grandmother," Callum said, scratching his chin absently. "Only everyone's got it wrong. She didn't betray anyone—all those stupid rumors were never anything more than lies." He clenched his hand into a fist and grimaced. "I knew it. I knew there was no way a relative of yours could ever turn their back on the Otherwhere."

"It's true. She only left to save his reputation and make sure he'd have a future. It's all very romantic, when I think about it. But it makes me so sad, to think they're both alive and alone, and can never be together."

"Maybe they'll find a way someday…" Callum replied absently before seeming to focus again. "Well, your genes certainly explain a lot about your growing powers. I mean, I haven't seen anyone summon dragons to their side since…"

"Since the Crimson King," I said. "I know. It's a little weird to realize I share a gift with the man who used to rule over this whole land."

"They say a Summoner as powerful as him comes along once in fifty generations," Callum said. "Well, I can't say I'm surprised to learn Merriwether's granddaughter is so extraordinary. I knew the moment I first laid eyes on you in Fairhaven that you were something special. You're the One, Vega."

My cheeks flushed, and I let out a little laugh. "The One?"

"The One who can stop the rise of the queen. The One who can save this world. And possibly even your own."

I swallowed hard, shaking my head. "That's a lot of pressure, not to mention a major exaggeration. There are people in this world who are much more gifted than I am. Niala's a Healer. You can change into a dragon. And there are others…"

I thought of the man in silver in the Throne Room of the queen's castle. The one who'd stood so still, a sentinel guarding the queen with nothing more than his strange, metallic eyes. He'd held a silent power inside him that I could all but taste, and it terrified me.

"Then again," I said, "I'm discovering that some of those very gifted people aren't very nice."

"Don't I know it," Callum said, stroking his fingers over my neck. His touch was wildfire in my blood, a dose of pleasure in an uncertain world. Seeing the quiet, unmistakable hunger behind those incredible blue eyes of his, I was confident for the first time that nothing had changed between us.

He still cared for me, even if he didn't convey it in so many words.

"Speaking of people who aren't so nice," I said, daring to venture further into sensitive territory, "it seems I'm not the only one with family secrets, Mr. Drake."

"Oh?" said Callum, tightening as he pulled his hand away abruptly and averted his eyes.

"I know you have a sister."

He stared into the distance, a grimace settling on his hand-some features. It wasn't exactly surprising to see that he didn't like being reminded Isla was his flesh and blood. But he looked more than just a *little* upset to hear the words from my lips.

"So," he said, "now you know what kind of stock I come from. You know a little about my past, about my estrangement from my family. But you don't yet know all the reasons why. I guess we have a lot of catching up to do, don't we?"

"We do," I replied. "But I understand if you don't want to talk about it just now." I sighed.

"You're right," he said with the lightest kiss to my lips. "It's not that I want to keep secrets from you. It's only…there is pain, Vega. For so many reasons."

"I get it," I said. "I do. I understand pain better than you might think."

He stroked my cheek and gave me a sad smile. "Of course you do."

"You know, it's so strange," I said after staring into his eyes for a few seconds.

"What is?"

"You have a family—one that you'd rather not be part of. I've lost half my family and would give anything to get them back."

"It's not fair, is it?"

"No. It's not, for either of us."

We both fell silent for a moment before a sly smile spread over Callum's perfect lips. "Listen, on another topic entirely—I have an idea of something that might help you get through the next week."

"Uh-oh. Something tells me I'm not going to like this."

"I think you need to spend some time with a tutor. Someone who will push you. Make you work. Someone who can see your potential."

"I was right. I don't like this."

Callum chuckled. "Come on, you have to admit that you could

use someone who can guide you, help you along outside class time. Someone who's intimately familiar with your…unique skill set."

"Oh? Do you have someone in mind?" I asked, raising an eyebrow.

"I might just," he replied with a mischievous grin, which quickly faded as if he'd mentally checked himself. "Except for one small complication."

I stared at him, expectant but on edge. "Something tells me I definitely won't like *this*."

He reached for my hands, and when he'd taken hold of them he inhaled a deep breath. "The trouble is, every minute I spend with you is another minute we get closer. And the closer we get, the harder it will be when all this comes crashing down in the end."

# FORGETTING

"CRASHING DOWN," I repeated, a swarm of insects angrily buzzing around in my stomach.

Callum and Merriwether, it seemed, were cut from the same cloth. Both were constantly forecasting doomsday scenarios.

At least, where my love life was concerned.

Callum ground his jaw again, his eyes focused on my own. "You and me. This..." he said. "This relationship of ours. I hate to say it, but it's doomed to failure, and we both know it."

*Insects in stomach growing angrier.*

"Why? Why would you say that?" I asked in the calmest tone I could muster, despite the fact that my insides now felt like they were lurching over a series of violent, white-capped ocean waves.

Had something changed in the last several days? Had he decided he didn't care about me as much as he'd claimed? Was this his not-so-subtle way of dumping me?

He turned away, all but confirming my worst fear. I braced myself, hardening my insides in preparation for the inevitable blow to come.

"Because even if you could stay here in the Otherwhere, or

even if I could go live in your world...the truth is, you don't know everything about me yet, Vega."

A shot of relief hit me like an injection flowing directly into my bloodstream. "Of course I don't," I replied with a laugh. "You don't know everything about me, either. Like, you probably don't know my lucky number. My favorite color."

"That's not what I mean."

"So what are you saying, exactly?"

"I'm saying when you see the worst of me, you may not like me very much."

"There's nothing you can possibly tell me or show me that I'd dislike. I know what a good person you are. I've seen it in you a thousand times already, Callum."

He shook his head. "You've only ever seen me when I'm in control of myself. Not when…"

He looked like he was about to say something, but instead he pushed out a hard breath and changed course. "It doesn't matter," he added. "No matter what happens in the next few days, we lose, Vega. You know it as well as I do. At some point, your time here will end, and you'll go home to Fairhaven. Even if you're the Chosen Seeker, you won't be staying in the Otherwhere. The ugly truth is, this romance of ours is doomed to be short-lived, and we'd be foolish to pretend otherwise."

I knew he was right. Whatever happened, I was going to lose him soon.

And when I did, it was going to hurt like hell.

I reached into my pocket to feel the outline of the small vial my Nana had handed me before I'd left her cottage. The potion that I'd slipped to Will and Liv, the elixir that made people forget the Otherwhere.

For a split second I wondered if I would find myself using it in a few days, when someone else beat me out for the title of Chosen Seeker. To numb the pain that would set in if and when I had to say a final goodbye to Callum.

*No,* I thought, pulling my hand out and taking hold of his once again. *I'll never use it on myself. Not for anything. I never want to forget what I'm feeling right now.*

*Not even the pain of it.*

Callum ran his free hand along the branch of a nearby peach tree. "It's always going to be there, Vega, this feeling that the end is coming. It hurts. And to tell you the truth, I feel a little helpless right now." He turned back to me and fixed me with the blue eyes that never failed to steal my breath from my chest. "You're the most gifted Seeker I've met. The most gifted student at the Academy. But there's no telling what task Merriwether plans to assign you and the others when the time comes. The fact is that you and I have to accept that. We need to be prepared, in case..."

I shook my head. "I don't want to accept anything, not yet. I'm still here, and I'm not going anywhere, not as long as I have a chance to be with you." I spoke the words with certainty, though a nagging thought had just begun to infiltrate my mind. "You don't suppose this test—whatever it may be—is going to be Merriwether's way of protecting you and me, do you?"

"Protecting? How do you mean?"

"I mean, it could be that he'll make it deliberately difficult for me, so I fail where someone else succeeds. It could be his way to justify sending me back home. Separating me from you, protecting us from what happened to him and my grandmother. It crushed them to be split apart after they'd fallen in love. Maybe he's trying to save us from that same fate, before..."

"Before...?" Callum repeated.

But I couldn't finish the thought without blurting out a lie. The truth was, it was too late for me already. I had feelings for him that ran deeper than anything I'd ever known, and no Forgetting Potion in the world could ever change that.

"I don't know," I muttered, defeated.

Cupping his hand around my neck, he pressed a kiss to my forehead. "There's no such thing as *before,* not anymore. I've fallen hard for you, Sloane. So hard that it's shattered me and glued me back together, all at the same time. That's why it hurts to think of the end."

My breath caught in my throat. It was the closest he'd come to telling me he loved me, and the rush of pleasure felt *too* good, practically addictive.

I could feel the danger in allowing myself to feel so deeply. It was like standing on the edge of a cliff, staring at jagged rocks far below and wondering how much it would hurt to fall.

"As for the Trial," Callum added when I failed to reply, "I do think Merriwether would protect you at almost any cost. If that means separating you from me, he'll consider it. But he's also a reasonable and responsible leader, one who has to consider the big picture. The important thing here isn't our relationship. It's protecting the whole world from destruction at the hands of a psychotic queen who just *happens* to be my sister. You and I are just collateral damage in a war that's been quietly raging for a very long time."

"I know," I said softly. "I know all of that."

Seeing me deflated, Callum led me to the base of a nearby apple tree, where he sat down on the grass. I dropped down and pressed back against him, pulling his arms around me as he pushed his back against the tree's narrow trunk. I closed my eyes, never wanting this feeling of comfort and warmth to end.

"Why can't someone invent a potion to prolong what we have right now?" I asked. "Or conjure a spell? Anything?"

"Because the way we feel right now—the perfection of this moment—it's something we feel so deeply because we *know* the moment is finite. We know it's a fleeting sensation, based on a fantasy that we both wish could become reality. It's all the more valuable for being such a rarity."

I let out a long, deep breath. "You're pretty wise for a guy who looks so much like a teenage boy, Mr. Drake."

"And you're pretty clever for a teenage girl, Miss Sloane."

For a few minutes we sat in silence, my head leaning back against his shoulder.

"You know," I finally said, "when I first met you in the Novel Hovel in Fairhaven, I thought Liv was crazy for thinking she could set us up together. You were way too handsome for me. I've never trusted good-looking people, and you...well, you felt dangerous."

Callum gave my forearm a playful squeeze. "You rejected me based purely on my looks? How shallow!"

"I didn't reject you completely," I laughed. "I figured maybe, just maybe, I'd consider going out on a date with you. You know, if not for the fact that you were totally out of my league."

"I'm honored you even contemplated me for a second," Callum said with a chuckle.

"To be fair, at the time I figured it was just a fantasy. I never thought anything would come of it. I'm not exactly the kind of girl who goes out with the handsome boy everyone wants to date. So you can stop laughing at me."

"I'm not laughing at you. I'm laughing *near* you."

I smacked his arm gently. "Point is, I never thought I'd actually end up in your arms. You were too...confident. Too mysterious. Too *everything*. You were the kind of person who intimidates me to my core."

He held me tighter. "I never thought you'd end up in my arms, either. I only *hoped* you would—at least for a little while. I told myself I'd be satisfied if I could just have five minutes alone with you, looking into those mysterious eyes of yours and possibly, maybe, if I was really lucky, kissing your lips just once."

I shuddered with pleasure. I never could have guessed that being wanted felt so good.

And being wanted by someone like Callum Drake—someone magical, miraculous and altogether perfect—that was a whole new dimension of pleasure.

I pulled away and twisted around to look at him. Even now, I marveled at how impossibly beautiful he was and felt almost guilty for enjoying such a superficial aspect of him so much. *"Five minutes alone.* That sounds like a metaphor for our entire relationship."

"What do you mean?" he asked.

"I mean, has this little dalliance of ours just been the world's most insane summer fling? A pair of star-crossed, hopeless idiots? A Seeker and a dragon shifter—who, by the way, is rightful heir to the throne of a kingdom that's invisible to the people in my world?"

"I prefer to think of it as a torrid romance," Callum said with a laugh. "And yes, it's probably insane. But I see nothing wrong with a little madness now and then."

I wasn't sure if it was the word *madness* or another trigger that set me off. But in that moment, something overtook me, something inexplicable—a craving, a need so great that I forgot myself. Fire raged through my blood, clouding my mind and robbing me of rational thought.

I grabbed Callum's collar and yanked him toward me, pressing my lips to his. Before I knew how it had even happened, his back was pressed to the ground, and I was on top of him, my fingers raking his forearms so hard that I left angry red scratches along his skin. Blood raged in my veins, my breath coming in shallow, rapid waves.

I was no longer myself. I was a girl possessed, my mind consumed by a desire I'd never known. I kissed him, my head spinning with what I could only imagine was how it felt to be drunk.

Sensing my frenzy, Callum grabbed my wrists and pushed me away gently. His skin was like fire, his blue eyes flashing menacingly with red and orange flame.

I gasped at the sight, which terrified and excited me at the same time.

Loosening his grip, he shook his head and took a long, deep

breath as his irises settled once more to their usual shade of Mediterranean blue.

"Vega," he said, looking up at me with a smile. "You might want to slow down."

I pulled back, my chest heaving. Slipping away from him, I sat down on the grass, pressing the back of my hand to my forehead. "Sorry," I said. "That was…really aggressive. I don't know what came over me."

"I didn't mind, believe me. It's just that…"

"It's just that if we get too close, it'll hurt us both all the more," I said. "I know. You already said it in about ten different ways."

"Yeah." The corners of his mouth sank into a frown. "Something like that."

I gritted my teeth, embarrassed and frustrated. "I understand. This *is* just a short-lived torrid romance, after all." I clammed up, my body turning rigid as I pulled my eyes away, determined not to let him see my pain.

"No, I don't think you *do* understand," Callum said, easing toward me. "I'm not rejecting you. I just don't think either of us realizes what we stand to lose, if…"

"If?"

"If we get so close that we no longer have the strength to pull apart." He took a deep breath before adding, "Like I said, there are things you don't know about me that you may not like very much. I don't want you to have regrets. I worry that my presence in your life could do more harm than good."

"I don't want you to have regrets, either," I said, the initial pain of rejection fading, if only a little. "I just…I want to be with you until my time here ends. If that's all I can have, I'll take it."

He drew his eyes back to mine, and they seemed to soften almost instantly. "Then let's try our best to be together, at least for now." He reached out and took my hand, intertwining his fingers with mine. "Why don't we go find a bite to eat?"

"Together?" I asked.

He nodded. "I promise you, I will stay as close to you as I possibly can. Within limits."

"Within limits," I nodded in reluctant agreement. I didn't dare ask where the limit actually was.

Anyhow, rules were meant to be broken.

Weren't they?

# A DATE

AFTER A QUICK MEAL of leftover stew and bread that Callum and I managed to cobble together in the Faculty Kitchen, we headed out to one of the less traveled hallways in the Academy's northern wing.

Projected along its light gray walls were animated, tapestry-like scenes from the Otherwhere's past: Battles fought on open fields. Casters using powerful, deadly spells against their enemies. A flock of flying, cat-like creatures attacking a massive army of wolves.

I tried not to focus on the sound of clashing weapons, shrieking birds, and growling canines that met my ears while we strolled. It all felt too real, as if the hallway was trying to remind me of a bloody past that was about to rear its ugly head again.

Callum stopped when we got to a scene of the Crimson King in his dragon form, soaring through the sky. From his mouth a rush of flame was shooting toward a sea of enemies on the ground far below. I could hear the cries of the opposing army, though I was starting to think the sound existed solely in my imagination.

"My great uncle," Callum said. "He ruled for a long time."

"And then you were supposed to take over."

"Supposed to, yes," he said, his eyes distant. "That was decades ago."

"Decades?" I asked with a slight smile. "You know, you still haven't told me how old you are."

The truth was, I'd begun to enjoy not knowing Callum's age. It didn't particularly matter to me, anyhow. I liked him just the way he was—a wise young man who sometimes seemed like any other 18-year-old boy, but at other times seemed ageless. From a military standpoint, Callum seemed as seasoned as an admiral who'd fought in many wars.

But for all his experience, there were certain emotional battlefields he'd never yet navigated—including the mine-filled one we'd begun exploring together.

"My parents and sister grew to hate the king," he added as he watched the scene unfold.

"Because the king was a dragon shifter," I replied. It wasn't a question. The Usurper Queen had made it abundantly clear how she felt about his kind.

"Yes. But there were other reasons, too." I watched Callum wince as the Crimson King destroyed an entire battalion in front of our eyes, then flew off into the distance, disappearing over the horizon. "Dragons are volatile creatures," he said. "And unpredictable. People see them and their first thought is that they're beautiful, graceful, elegant, powerful. All the *good* adjectives. What they don't realize at first is how destructive a force a dragon shifter can really be."

He turned my way, and I was sure I detected a flash of fire in his eyes once again. The restless golden dragon alerting me to his presence like a silent warning.

But after a few seconds, Callum took my hand and smiled, seeming to shake off whatever dire thoughts were running through his mind. "What would you like to do for the rest of the day? Other than get some well-deserved sleep, that is?"

"I don't actually need to sleep," I replied, shifting my eyes toward an ornate silver clock hovering in midair at the far end of the corridor. It was five o'clock. Most of the Academy's students would soon be making their way to the Great Hall for dinner. "By my calculations, I should still have a few hours of energy left. Maybe we could, I don't know, go on a date?"

I looked up into his eyes to gauge his reaction to the proposal.

"A date?" Callum asked, his eyebrows rising into matching arches.

"Please don't say no. I've never actually asked a guy on a date before, and if you reject me, I'll wish I could get sucked into a vortex of shame, never to be seen again."

"I don't think I've ever been asked on one, so I wouldn't *dare* say no. It would set a terrible precedent."

"Phew," I breathed. "Well then, I think it's about time we tried one on for size. After all, we *have* slept together already, if you'll recall."

*Best few hours of my entire life.*

"*Slept*," Callum reminded me. "Only slept. I am a gentleman, remember."

"*Mostly* slept. I seem to remember that there was some kissing."

"Fine. You win, little Miss Semantics. So tell me, before I get us both in trouble—what do you have in mind for the next few hours?"

I tucked my chin down and threw him a mischievous expression.

"The extremely respectful, well-behaved gentleman inside me is hesitant to ask what that look means, for fear that I might think it's a good idea."

I laughed again. "I wasn't suggesting anything untoward. I just thought maybe we could…"

"Yes?"

I leaned in even closer and whispered. "Maybe we could leave the Academy's grounds and go somewhere…forbidden."

"Vega Sloane, I'm surprised at you!" Callum snickered. "You do realize the woods and fields around here are crawling with Waergs and other hostiles, right? We can't exactly head out for a stroll. Not to mention that your grandfather might not be entirely pleased if he found out you'd gone AWOL again."

"You just offered to be my private tutor," I protested. "Merriwether told me a student can only leave the grounds with an instructor, and well, you're an instructor."

"Fine."

"You also—very conveniently, might I add—happen to be a dragon shifter. Which means Waergs hiding in the forest aren't exactly a big problem for us. I mean, given that we can just barbecue them if they decide we look like a tasty meal."

"Ah, so you're counting on *me* to extricate us both from any potentially perilous situations?"

"Yes. That's exactly what I'm counting on."

"Fine," Callum said. "There are some beautiful spots in the Otherwhere that I haven't seen in some time. I wouldn't mind a romp through a field of daisies, or maybe a prairie filled with killer wolves who thirst for fresh blood. As long as we're back in a few hours."

"That's the spirit!" I laughed.

"There's only one small problem."

"Which is…?"

"We can't just walk out of this place without being seen. And even if we are abiding by the official rules, I'd *really* not have to explain to your grandfather that I'm stealing you away when you should probably be resting."

"Don't worry. I've got this all planned out."

"Right, of course you do. I keep forgetting you're a walking teleportation device. Okay, then. But I'm very curious to know where you're taking us."

I bit my lip and tapped my chin with my index finger. "Okay, I'll admit I haven't *quite* figured that part out yet."

"What? So how...?"

"Just come on!"

We bolted down the hall, tearing past students and faculty members until we'd made our way to the narrow spiral staircase that wound its way up to our bedrooms at the top of one of the Academy's more secluded towers.

When we'd climbed up to the first small landing, I stopped, huffing with the exertion of sprinting such a long distance. A series of torches floated along the curved stone wall, illuminating the space around us, the reflections of the flames dancing in Callum's eyes.

"This is where our date begins, is it?" he asked. "Well, I suppose it's romantic, if a little cramped."

I frowned. "Let me focus," I said, "or I'll end up summoning a door to the middle of a malaria-ridden swamp by accident. That's not exactly the scenic setting I was hoping for."

"Fine," he said, crossing his arms and leaping down two steps. "But for the record, I'd be perfectly happy in a malaria-ridden swamp, as long as I was with you."

"Aww, that's so sweet. Someone should put it on a greeting card."

Grinning, I closed my eyes and tried to picture an idyllic place, though I wasn't sure at first what I was hoping for.

I didn't know how or why, but the image that immediately took up residence in my mind was that of a vast field of long, swaying grass sprinkled with pretty blue flowers. In the far distance was a range of snow-capped mountain peaks, extending as far as the eye could see.

I wasn't sure what I was looking at. But for some reason, I was absolutely certain the scene unfolding before me existed in the Otherwhere. I could *feel* its presence. I could smell the freshness of the air.

Though how that was possible, I had no idea.

"I think I've found our destination," I said.

"Yes. I think you have."

On hearing Callum's words, I dared to open my eyes, only to see that a door had appeared on the landing, with an outline of carved mountains etched in its surface. Callum edged forward silently, running his fingers along the embossed peaks.

"Amazing," he said softly.

"What is it?"

"A place I haven't been in a very long time. You've summoned a door to the Valley of the Five Sisters."

"Sisters?" I asked, confused.

"They're part of a range of mountains that surround a deep, inaccessible valley. The tallest peaks in the Otherwhere." He spun around to face me. "Wait—you really didn't know about them when you called this door up?"

I shook my head. "To be honest, I didn't even know the Otherwhere *had* mountains. I just asked my mind to envision somewhere nice. It's hard to explain—it's like I wanted to come up with the most beautiful place I could find. To be honest, I wasn't completely sure if what I was seeing in my head was real or not. But I *felt* it was…if that makes any sense."

"Your powers are growing stronger. And I should tell you, you've chosen well. The Sisters are not easily accessible. They're one of the few places in the Otherwhere where the Usurper Queen—my sister, I mean—doesn't dare venture. The valley is too difficult to get to, even for her. These mountains are one of the reasons she wanted dragons."

"You mean for transportation?"

Callum nodded. "If she could fly her fighters in, she'd gain access to every square mile of the Otherwhere. Which would make her all but unstoppable. As it is, there are creatures in the mountains who have the advantage over my dear sibling—a fact that she hates, of course." His tone had turned serious, but he seemed to shake it off as he flashed me a grin and swept an arm reverently toward the door. "Well? What are we waiting for? Let our official first date begin."

With a smile, I pulled my dragon key off its chain, opened the door, and stepped through, with Callum just behind me.

# THE VALLEY

WHEN WE'D PASSED through the Breach, we found ourselves standing in the middle of a broad, deep valley, surrounded on all sides by tall mountain peaks exactly like the ones carved into the door's wooden surface.

The actual mountains were massive, majestic, and definitely more impressive than any carving could ever be. Daunting, even. I felt like I was standing in the middle of the Himalayas with no proper climbing gear and no oxygen. But instead of apprehension or fear, the wild remoteness of this place filled me with excitement.

The air was fresh, cool, and smelled vaguely of wildflowers. It was no wonder this location was inaccessible to anyone without the gift of powerful magic or dragons.

"This is so beautiful," I said, turning around slowly to take in the entire view of snow-capped peaks that framed us in a broad circle. "It's...perfect."

"I only see one perfect thing at the moment."

Curious, I turned to face Callum, who was staring at me, his intense eyes narrowed in an expression of such profound admiration that the surface of my skin heated.

It was still so strange to hear him compliment me without a trace of self-consciousness or hesitation. The boys at my high school back in Fairhaven were childish in many ways, flinging food at each other in the cafeteria, insulting one another, mocking their own girlfriends for sport. It was no wonder I'd never had any interest in getting to know any of them intimately.

But Callum was different. He wasn't the awkward, uncertain adolescent most teenage boys tended to be. He was confident enough to tell a girl how he was feeling without worrying that it would somehow diminish him in her eyes, yet he managed to remain mysterious enough to be relentlessly enticing.

"I'm not so sure that the word *perfect* and I really go together," I said with a timid laugh.

"Sorry, Vega. But you're so very wrong about that."

With that, he slipped a finger under my chin and kissed me. This time, under his control, it was gentle—the opposite of our aggressive kiss from the Grove—yet it consumed me, body and mind. As the world dropped away under my feet, I felt myself tumbling, weightless, through space. Untethered, yet completely grounded.

A tingle of pure magic brought on by the briefest contact.

When Callum pulled away, he pressed his forehead to mine, cupping my cheeks in his hands. "Too good," he said, his breath coming in fast, shallow pulses. "It feels way too good to kiss you like that."

"You're telling me," I replied through a gushing exhalation.

I couldn't decide whether to laugh or cry. All I knew was for that moment, at least, he was wholly mine. The world around us was beautiful, the air fresh, and I couldn't have been happier.

Still, I couldn't help but remind myself that our time was limited, our current bliss tainted by the cruelty of fate.

Reluctant to look at Callum for fear that my eyes might well up, I spun around to stare at the mountains once again.

"I wish I could see them up close," I said, my eyes tracing the lines of the Five Sisters' jagged peaks. "But I'm not exactly dressed for climbing. Plus, it would take days to make our way up even the smallest of them."

"I think you're forgetting something. We can get up very easily, in fact."

"What? You think I should open another door at one of their summits?"

When Callum cleared his throat, I turned to read his amused expression.

"I'll tell you what," he said. "I'll take you up to the top of Aurnia—she's the tallest of them. And I promise you won't freeze to death. But first, I have a little challenge for you. As your tutor, I mean."

"Oh? And here I thought we were on a date, not a study session."

"Hey, you're the one who told me you were only allowed to leave the Academy with an instructor. To make this an honest outing, I am therefore obligated to instruct."

"Ugh," I moaned with an exaggerated eye-roll. "You're *so* responsible."

With a laugh, Callum turned and eyed the edge of a vast, thick forest in the distance, at the base of one of the mountains. A row of skyscraping trees stood in a stark outline against the rocky landscape above.

"I want you to try something for me," he said.

"O-*kay*," I replied, my tone laced with skepticism. "What, exactly?"

"Try summoning an inanimate object. Not a door, but something that could help, say, if someone were to attack you."

"Aw, you're worried that I'll get horribly maimed. How sweet of you to think of me."

"I'm serious, Vega," he said, his brow wrinkled, his voice laced with impatience. He'd gone into full-on business mode. "I want you to be safe when you're put to the test."

I let out a sigh. "All right. I'll try," I said. "But I don't see how this could possibly work. I've only ever summoned doors. Well, and a few dragons. But mostly doors."

"Just try. You might surprise yourself."

I closed my eyes and contemplated what I'd do if someone was running at me.

"What's my enemy?" I asked.

"A pack of wolves. Acting not out of animal instinct, but out of anger, revenge, and a savage and deliberate cruelty."

I flashed back to the queen's Waergs in the Throne Room, watching me silently, ready to spring into action on her command. Gray, silver, black, white, their flashing eyes intent on their prey, teeth bared, ready to rip me apart.

The image was very rapidly growing all too real. I could feel the creatures' presence, smell them on the air. Their low growls met my ears and shuddered their way through my bones. Then, in one fluid movement, they leapt toward me, running at full speed.

Before I realized what I was doing, I thrust both hands into the air protectively, as if to stop them in their tracks.

My eyes were still closed, but I felt something spring up between us, attaching itself securely to my left arm. Something powerful, impenetrable. I knew then that the wolves would never touch me.

Though I didn't understand how I'd managed to stop them.

"Well done," Callum's gentle voice said as his hand landed on my shoulder.

"But I didn't...do...anything..." I began to reply, my eyes still firmly shut. "I was only imagining the scenario..."

"Are you sure you only imagined it? Maybe you should take a look."

I opened my eyes and saw it then: a tall, broad shield, strapped to my left arm. It curved protectively, wrapping itself around my body. It was tall enough to reach from the ground to the top of my head, and broad enough to protect every inch of me.

I could see through it as if it was made of glass, though something told me it was far stronger. Tentatively, I made a fist with my right hand and knocked against the strange material, which felt hard as steel.

"You're saying I did this?" I asked, turning to Callum. "I made this...thing...appear?"

"You did."

"I had no idea I could..."

"No idea?" he asked. "Really?"

"Really. It's like I invented it. I don't even know what it's made of."

"It's made of anything you want it to be made of. Light, heavy, strong, weak. It's your call. It seems you can conjure something from nothing, Vega."

I smiled. "I have to admit, I'm impressed with myself."

"Everything you need is already in your mind, waiting to find its way out. You just have to trust your gifts and to set them loose. Trust that amazing brain of yours."

"Trust my brain?" I snickered. "Have you *met* my brain? It's like a bunch of neurotic squirrels having a cage match in there."

"Liar. Your brain is brilliant."

I shook my head. "You might think I know what I'm doing, that I'm in control. Calm. Confident. But I'm a mess."

"No, you're not. But even if you were, it wouldn't matter to me. You're a very beautiful, very powerful Seeker—one who excites me more than I can say. I only wish I had half your control." With that, Callum drew his eyes to the mountain range in the distance. "Now, I promised you I'd get you up there, and it's a promise I intend to keep."

# THE MOUNTAINTOP

WITH A MYSTERIOUS SMILE, Callum told me to stay exactly where I was.

"What's going on?" I asked as he backed away. "Where are you going?"

But he shook his head and brought a finger to his lips.

When I moved to join him, he held up a hand, stopping me in my tracks.

"You're not going to…" I began.

"Oh yes, I am."

My heart hammered with excitement.

I'd wanted to see Callum's golden dragon up close since the first time I'd laid eyes on him. But to request such a thing seemed a little too personal. I may as well have asked him to bare his soul to me and then let me poke and prod at it.

Magical powers were the private domain of those who possessed them, not to be used or abused for someone else's amusement. It was the same reason I didn't give Niala's Familiar, Rourke, belly rubs as I might to a dog or cat in Fairhaven. He wasn't a pet. He was a *part* of her. He was a walking manifestation of her thoughts, her fears, her needs.

Still, Callum *had* offered freely. And there was no way I was going to ask him to stop or hold back. The prospect of seeing his dragon form in the flesh was way too exciting.

Even if it was also a little terrifying.

When he was about fifty feet away, he shot me one final look before a flash of blinding light filled the air around us. I flung my arm over my eyes protectively.

A second later, when the world had seemingly gone back to normal, I looked again.

An exquisite creature covered in gleaming scales was standing in the field of long grass, wildflowers surrounding the impossibly large claws on his enormous scaled feet.

His head was shaped like those of the dragons I'd met in the queen's castle: a long, almost equine muzzle, tapering a little at the tip. Smoke billowed from elegant nostrils—not in a threatening way, but just enough to remind me what he was capable of. He was a beast of power and flame.

He was incredible.

I froze in place. Was I supposed to approach? Was it even safe? Did Callum in his dragon form even know or care who I was, or was he now a wild animal with no attachment to me whatsoever?

As if in response, the dragon shoved his head toward the ground, his snake-like, shining eyes looking at me like he was trying to encourage me to approach. My body tightening, I took one step, then another, and another, before I finally found myself standing right next to his muzzle.

Without thinking, I laid a hand on his surprisingly smooth cheek, caressing the scales, then slid my palm along his long neck, which was lined at its crest with a mane of threatening-looking spikes. Each was long and jagged, made of something that was neither bone nor scale, but translucent, like gold-stained glass. The beautiful skewers glittered with dancing light like perfectly formed icicles on a mid-winter day.

The dragon's wings were tucked in at his sides, and as I

moved along his torso, I wondered if he was silently encouraging me to get onto his back.

"We probably should have talked this through before you shifted," I said. "I really have no idea what I'm supposed to do."

"That's all right. We can talk it through now," a voice replied, startling me.

I leapt backwards, shocked to have heard what I was sure was Callum's deep baritone. But the dragon was still next to me, and there was no way the sound had come from his mouth of ivory-white daggers.

I stared at his face, eyeing his sealed lips. "You didn't just say something, right? Tell me you don't actually talk. That would be super-weird."

"The dragon didn't, no," Callum's voice said again. "*I* did."

"Wait—you're telling me you're speaking inside my head?" I replied.

"Yes. Just as I did when you were in Isla's prison."

I let out a laugh. "Fair enough. Okay, since you can talk to my mind and I'm definitely not imagining it, tell me, what do you want me to do?"

"Climb onto my back," he replied. "It would be dull to fly up into the mountains without you."

"Really? You're okay with me hopping on, like you're some kind of Shetland pony?"

"Well, you won't exactly have a saddle or bridle at your disposal, so I'll be calling the shots, but yes, I'm perfectly happy to be a pony for now. As long as you don't tell anyone. It's a little embarrassing to be compared to a tiny horse when you're using all your strength to control a big, threatening monster who could decide to scorch the mountainside at any moment."

"Fine, be my fire-breathing pony, then," I replied with a laugh. Abiding by his wishes, I somehow managed to hoist myself up onto the base of his neck, only to find myself sitting just above what I imagined must be his shoulder blades. I grabbed hold of the glassy spike protruding vertically in front of me to help me find my seat, though I wasn't exactly confident that I'd be able to stay on.

"I could use some stirrups," I said. "Or a seatbelt. Even a staple gun would be helpful."

"My apologies," Callum replied. "I've been keeping the whole shifting-into-a-dragon thing quiet, as you know, so I've been a little negligent when it comes to buying safety equipment."

"I suppose I'll forgive you, just this once."

"Good. Now, are you ready?" Callum asked when I'd finally stopped moving around. "I don't want to stay in this form longer than I have to. The dragon, as I've said, can be unpredictable, and the last thing I want is to risk hurting you."

"I'm ready. At least I think so. Although I can't guarantee I won't fall off and die."

"I'll try my best to keep you safe. Now, off we go."

Without any further warning, the dragon surged skyward. For a second my stomach felt like it had stayed on the ground below. I pressed my chest down close to his body and hung on for dear life, terrified that I'd lose my grip and slide off sideways. But Callum's dragon seemed to read the moments when I felt off balance, shifting his weight in one direction or the other until I felt secure again.

His wings beat against the air in slow, heavy pulses, which made the ride remarkably smooth. I realized after a time that I didn't feel what should have been a burst of bitterly cold air as we climbed toward the mountain peaks. It was more like the feeling of slipping along the surface of a lake on a warm day.

I wasn't sure if the unnatural warmth came from the dragon himself or from some protective shell around us, but the sensation made me feel closer to Callum than I ever had. Like his arms were invisibly wrapped around me, protective and powerful.

After a time, I began to feel confident enough to pull up to a sitting position and scan the lands far below. Long white glaciers, punctuated here and there by the topmost peaks of jagged black mountains, stretched out toward the horizon.

"Are you having fun yet?" Callum's disembodied voice asked.

"Actually, yes, I am," I said, letting my hands move in rhythm with the motion of the dragon's neck. "This is amazing."

"I'm glad. Hang on tight."

With a sudden burst of speed, he pulled his head up and surged higher, shooting toward the tallest of the snow-covered peaks. We soared over the mountain range, my eyes fixed on everything below—vast fields of pure white snow, craggy stone formations, a scattering of oddly-shaped trees…and even some kind of horned, hybrid animals leaping along the precarious edges of cliffs.

"What are those?" I asked. "They looked a little like mountain goats, only…different."

"It's a little hard to explain. There's a lot up here that you sort of have to see for yourself. Why don't we go in for a closer look?"

"Closer than this?"

A laugh rang through my mind—a wonderful, warm laugh that made me forget every worry I had in the world—and the dragon shot down toward a large glacier near the summit of one of the Sisters.

He landed with solid confidence, a blizzard of loose snow shooting out from under his huge talons as we came to a stop. By some miracle, I managed not to lose my seat.

When I was confident we'd stopped moving, I slipped down onto the white surface, turning away from the gold dragon only to see that the glacier was lined with a series of dangerous-looking cracks that glowed bluish-white under the sun. Each deep fissure was wide enough for me to fall through sideways with room to spare.

The chasms were beautiful, enticing, and deadly, much like Callum's dragon.

"Crevasses," Callum's voice said. "Don't slip into one, or I may never see you again."

"Sounds like a smart plan." I twisted around, assessing the uneven surface around me for safety. "Looks fairly flat over here…"

Taking a tentative step forward to examine the edge of one of the crevasses, I found my right foot slipping almost immediately. By a trick of the light, the frozen surface looked horizontal. In reality, it curved downward at a precipitous angle, and I shrieked as I realized I had nothing to grab hold of to stop myself from sliding all the way into the bottomless void.

I'd almost disappeared into the narrow opening when a hand grabbed hold of my right arm and stopped me, yanking me backward.

"I told you not to do that, silly," Callum said as he pulled me to him, his warm breath on my neck as his other arm came around to hold me from behind.

"You shifted," I murmured, adrenaline surging through my insides. "That was quick of you."

"I thought it might be a good idea. I know you by now, Vega. You can be a little impulsive, to say the least."

"Not to mention that I'm a clumsy oaf," I replied, breathing hard with the combination of relief and excitement at being in his arms again and safely away from the edge of the abyss.

"Not clumsy—just…"

"*Super*-clumsy?"

He laughed as he wrapped his arms around my shoulders from behind and rested his chin on top of my head. I smiled to feel so engulfed in the feeling of safety that came with being close to him.

"When I was first able to shift, I used to fly around up here," he said. "It was one of the few places I could be alone in those confusing days."

"Confusing?" I asked, pulling away to take his hand and pivot around so we could be face to face.

His eyes smiled, but his voice sounded sad. "I'm not sure you want to hear about those days."

"I do know you've lived quite a...*special*...life. I mean, what with the whole turning into a dragon thing. Not to mention the fact that you have royal blood in your veins. I know there has to be a story there."

"Royalty isn't as exciting as most people think. My life wasn't that different from a prisoner's."

"A prisoner? Really?"

He nodded. "I'm serious. I was kept indoors for most of my youth, though I didn't learn why until years later."

"What do you mean?"

Callum pulled his gaze into the distance and let out a long breath. "My mother suspected that she knew what I was, but she wasn't entirely sure. She was afraid of what lurked inside me. She didn't want a resurgence of the Crimson King."

"Why not? He sounded amazing."

"He was, in many ways. But in others he was...complicated. My mother never let me forget that I took after him. She did everything she could to try to suppress the creature inside me—to turn me into something I'm not. She may as well have tried to stop my heart from beating, but instead, she..." He stopped speaking and ground his jaw, wincing away the pain I knew was eating away at him.

"I'm so sorry," I said. As curious as I was to know what had happened to him, the last thing I wanted was to hurt him further.

"It's ancient history by now. My sister was always the more ambitious sibling, constantly asking how she could find her way onto the throne. My parents would laugh, but I knew all along that Isla's intention was to make sure I never found my own way to power, despite the fact that I'm older than she is. And, as you know, she succeeded. The throne is hers."

"I'm almost afraid to ask how she did it," I murmured.

Callum's jaw tightened. "My sister has a habit of robbing everything and everyone of their souls."

With a pang of heartbreak, I began to wonder what Isla had done to him—what his entire family had done, to make him feel so utterly rejected.

But before I could ask, a flurry of movement caught my eye. I turned to look, only to see a creature sprinting along the edge of the glacier toward a gnarled tree that seemed to have no business growing at such a high altitude.

"What is that?" I asked, grabbing Callum's arm. I could tell the animal was some sort of feline, its enormous canines protruding from its mouth. It looked almost prehistoric, like the saber-toothed tigers I'd read about in my youth.

"*That* is an aegis cat," he snarled in response. "Looks like it's going for a razorbeak nest. Come on, we can't let him reach it."

"Just to get this straight—you want to run *towards* a large feral cat with massive, pointy teeth, so we can protect a bird's nest?"

"That's exactly what I want."

"Someday," I said with an exaggerated sigh, "we really should go on a date that doesn't involve quite so many potentially fatal experiences."

## THE CAT AND THE GRELL

CALLUM WAS ALREADY SPRINTING, his left hand reaching back protectively for mine as I struggled to keep up. I did my best to follow in his footsteps, looking down occasionally to make sure I didn't have any more close calls with deadly crevasses.

When we were clear of the dangerous chasms, we sprinted full-out across a combination of ice and stone, only to stop about twenty feet from the tree.

The massive cat was standing on its hind legs, a set of large paws pressed against the rough ashen tree trunk. Its muzzle was high in the air, sniffing at something in the branches overhead.

A large nest crafted out of twigs and leaves was wedged into a crisscrossed section of branches. Tufts of feathers and loose animal fur splayed out in every direction and gave it the look of a fur coat with mange.

"Is the cat looking for eggs or something?" I panted.

"Yes. And we can't let him get them. Razorbeaks are rare and incredibly intelligent. Not to mention that they're loyal allies. We need to protect them."

"Bird allies? Really?"

"Does it seem so unrealistic? You did recently befriend five dragons, Vega."

"True."

I shut my mouth and watched. After a few seconds the cat started stalking his way up the tree, and in the same moment, a series of screeches erupted from somewhere in the sky above us. I looked up to see two birds flapping their wings frantically, making a beeline through the chilly air.

The cat turned his head toward them, snarled, then froze in place, pressing his body against the tree trunk even as the surface of his fur began to alter.

The cat's coat began to reflect the sun's light, its fur shining oddly bright as it took on the icy-blue shades of the glacier that surrounded us. At first, he looked like he was camouflaging himself by mirroring his surroundings. But after a moment, I began to see that its soft coat was slowly being replaced by a layer of armor, altering to something that looked like gleaming silver chainmail.

"What…what just happened?" I asked. "How did he *do* that?"

"It's what aegis cats do," Callum said. "They have a natural coat of armor that forms when they're threatened. It makes them very hard to beat in a fight. Even if I shifted into my dragon form, I'd have a hard time beating him without cooking him alive. By the time my fire hurt him, I'd have burned the whole tree, nest and all, to the ground."

By now, the birds were dive-bombing the feline in a frenzy, pecking at its back with pointed beaks that sounded as though they too were made of metal.

"The birds are incredibly strong," Callum explained. "Their beaks can cut through almost anything—but not an aegis cat's shield. It's like the two species evolved to survive one another."

As he finished speaking, a dart of pain shot its way into my head. I pulled a hand to my temple, wincing. It felt like a hammer was smashing a nail into my skull.

"What is it?" asked Callum, reaching a hand out to steady me.

"I'm not sure. I…"

*Help…us…*

The voice rang through my mind like the chiming of bells.

It wasn't human.

And at first, I wasn't entirely sure where it came from.

*Help.*

*Please.*

*Help.*

I scanned the sky, where a solitary razorbeak was circling overhead. As I watched, it began a slow descent and finally came to a landing on a rocky outcropping a few feet from Callum and me. It stared at me through bright yellow eyes.

Without understanding how, I somehow knew the voice had moved from its mind to my own.

The bird jerked its head toward the tree, where the cat was stuck in a stalemate with the two other razorbeaks.

"What do I need to do?" I asked. "How can I help you?"

*Pro…tect,* it replied.

I turned to Callum. "It wants me to prevent the cat from getting to the nest," I said. "I don't think they can fight it off on their own. But what can I do? That cat looks like it could tear me apart in about three seconds."

Instead of looking concerned—either about me hearing bird voices in my head or about the possibility of my being shredded by the cat—Callum smiled.

"You're laughing at me," I said. "You think I'm loopy because I'm claiming I can talk to animals, like Dr. Dolittle."

"No, I'm smiling because your powers are turning out to be even more impressive than we'd thought," he replied. "The razorbeaks know what you are. They understand that you can provide them with some sort of defense. So, Miss Sloane, what are you going to do?"

I bit my lip and focused my eyes on the tree. It wasn't large, but it looked strong as titanium. If the cat made it to the branch that held the nest, the tree would support his weight without a problem, and the nest would be toast.

"I could try something," I said. "But it's a long shot."

Callum nodded, his expression turning deadly serious, and stepped back to give me room.

The aegis cat had begun climbing again, despite the fact that the two razorbeaks were assaulting his armor with every bit of their strength. The cat was now only a few feet from the nest.

Desperate to help, I sealed my eyes shut and drew a picture in my mind—a mere sketch—of something that didn't yet exist.

My head began to pound again. My fingertips curled into my palms, and my legs began to weaken beneath me. But I kept my eyes closed until I'd finished my rendering of what I hoped would be the solution to the razorbeaks' problems.

"Vega," Callum whispered. "Look!"

Letting out a sharp breath, I opened my eyes. The cat had stopped climbing and was now staring, puzzled, at the strange sight in front of him. A broad, round sheet of what looked like steel, with a hole at its center to accommodate the branch. As I watched, the steel expanded and morphed around the tree's other branches, blocking any possible route the aegis cat could have taken to get to the nest.

With its ears flat against its head, the cat struck the strange object with a paw, letting out a growl of rage when it realized the attack was futile. The shield wasn't going to move.

Finally, the creature turned and scurried down the tree, leaping and sprinting until it was out of sight.

"Clever girl," Callum said.

"It's a bit rough," I replied, grateful that he was now standing close enough that I could lean on him. "But it did the trick." I was sweating and breathing heavily, like I'd just sprinted up the side of the mountain. These skills of mine were proving exhausting. "Hopefully there won't be any more surprises for a little while."

"I'm afraid you're out of luck on that front. Though the next surprise is a good one."

"What are you talking about?"

"It looks like we have another visitor," Callum said, nodding into the distance.

I swung around, terrified that another predator was making its way toward us. Sure enough, something was scrambling over a series of rocks, head held high as though he was picking up our scent on the air.

At first, I thought he resembled the mountain goats I'd spotted from my vantage point on Callum's dragon's back.

The thing was, he didn't entirely look like a goat anymore. His hind legs were too long, and his front hooves weren't hooves at all.

"What *is* he?" I asked as I watched the figure make his way slowly toward us.

"He," Callum said as the creature in the distance raised himself onto two legs and stared at us, "is Kohrin."

"I'm sorry if this sounds like a horrible thing to say, but is he...human?"

"No—at least he wouldn't say so. He's what some call a mongrel—a hybrid of human and animal—though his kind call themselves *Grells*. Like a centaur, or a satyr."

"Mongrels? Isn't that a derogatory word?"

Callum smiled. "Not to them. It's a point of pride, really. The Grells are the best of both human and animal. Some of them live in the wild, some in cities—at least, the cities that'll have them. They're incredibly hardy and strong."

He pursed his lips and let out a long, low whistle. The figure in the distance froze and sniffed at the air again. After a second he began to run toward us, lowering himself onto four limbs and charging forward at a full sprint, leaping deftly over any crevasses he encountered. He was fast, his movements unpredictable but confident as he bounded from one icy surface to the next.

I reached for Callum's arm, tucking myself halfway behind him. All I could seem to focus on was the set of curling, pointed horns on top of the Grell's head, and I could only imagine what they could do to human flesh.

"It's all right," Callum said. "He won't hurt us."

When the figure was close, he drew himself up once again onto two legs. For the first time, I realized he was fully clothed. His legs were oddly bent, like those of a springing antelope, but his impressively tailored pants fit him perfectly. A pair of what appeared to be long leather boots tapered to a pair of small, delicate feet.

He stopped about ten feet away, watching us intently, his head cocked to the side. His eyes were larger than a human's, bright amber-colored and alert, but difficult to read. His cheeks were covered in a fine dusting of hair, though his forehead was bare.

Kohrin stepped closer and, tucking one arm elegantly into his ribcage, bowed low.

"Lord Callum," he said reverently, his voice surprisingly deep and powerful. "I did not expect to see you in these mountains. It's been a long time since any dragon shifter or human has ventured here. Welcome to you and your companion."

"No need for formalities," Callum said. "I'm no lord, as you know well. Kohrin, this is Vega Sloane. Vega, Kohrin Icewalker."

"Nice to meet you," I said, extending a hand. In return, Kohrin offered me his, which consisted of a set of extremely long, coarse fingers, no doubt callused from years of grabbing hold of rocky outcroppings. I shook it, trying not to wince at his painfully powerful grip.

"I heard you two speaking of my kind," he said, pulling his otherworldly eyes to mine. "Would you like to know more about us, Vega Sloane?"

"I…I don't want to be rude, but yes, I would," I confessed.

I wasn't sure if I imagined the smile that appeared to pull his lips up at the corners.

"Legend claims that Grells came to be when time froze here in this part of the Otherwhere, on what they call the *Longest Day*. It was many centuries ago now, and few are now living who remember it. The story tells that a great sorcerer stopped the world so he could move through it unseen. In this part of the Otherwhere—the land known as Balvenor—everything came to a standstill—humans and animals alike."

I shuddered as I recalled how, on my birthday, the same thing had happened to my hometown. Everything had stopped moving —cars, birds. Everything, that was, except for me and Charlie, the homeless man who—accompanied by his dog, Rufus— had first given me the dragon key.

Of course, *that* had been the work of my grandfather, not some evil sorcerer.

"Something strange happened during that freeze," Kohrin continued. "Many of those who had both animal and human inside them—shifters, they are called these days—became one entity, made up of both species. As you might guess, my own ancestors took on the characteristics of a human and a mountain goat."

I nodded, fascinated.

"Purebred humans," Kohrin continued, "were horrified by my kind. They rejected us, and so the Grells moved out of the towns and cities, building dwellings in mountainsides and caverns. We were not welcome to live near their kind."

"That's awful!" I blurted out.

But instead of agreeing with me, Kohrin smiled. "It probably was, for a time. But after years passed, some humans began to accept us. We found homes and work in the cities of the Other-where—that is, until recently, when the Blood Queen began to drive our kind out again."

"The Blood Queen?" I asked.

"The one you call Usurper," Kohrin said. "We call her the Blood Queen, because she brings death and seeks blood wherever she goes. Her Waergs thrive on cruelty and have killed many of our kind." He let out a sigh. "But the truth is that, in spite of being banished, I am happy where I am. My home is beautiful. I was not built for city living, after all." He gestured to his feet, and for the first time I noticed that his leather boots didn't have soles. Instead, I could see the rough bone-like structure of hooves jutting out at their base. "Cobblestones are torture for me, as you can probably imagine."

I frowned. "Well, even if you don't want to live among them, I'm sorry humans are so awful to you."

"The truth is, I don't see many purebred humans, so it's not a concern of mine. Speaking of which," he added, looking to Callum, "what news do you bring from the Lower Lands?"

"The search is on for the Relics," Callum replied. "The queen has one in her possession, though it sounds like she didn't exactly acquire it honestly. She's up to her old tricks, it seems."

"Not surprising. We've seen some of her eagle and drones above the mountains, as well as spies down below." Kohrin pointed to the sky with one long, stick-like finger. "The Blood Queen likes for us to feel threatened and scared."

"I'm sure she does," Callum said. "But you say you've seen spies below, as well?"

"Patrols, yes. Waergs, stalking in the hills below the mountains as they haven't done in many years. We think they're assessing our numbers. Trying to figure out how strong we might be. The mountains have always been a haven for our kind, impassable for theirs. But they are seeking a way. They want to take all of the Otherwhere for themselves. If the Blood Queen acquires all the Relics, I fear our time in this world will come to an end."

"I promise we'll do our best to prevent that from happening," Callum assured him. "In the meantime, if you see anything out of the ordinary—anything that you think might cause panic—have your messengers come find me at the Academy. The Queen has the upper hand right now, but we can't afford to let her win the coming war. I need all the Watchers I can get my hands on, and your eyes are keen."

"I will help in any way that I can. But there's one thing you need to understand."

"Oh? What's that?"

"The war is not *coming*, Lord Callum," Kohrin said, shaking his head slowly. "It has already begun."

Kohrin went on to explain to us about how some of the Grells had already found themselves engaged in bloody combat several times in the woods on the other side of the mountains. But, he said, they'd managed to drive the enemy's limited forces back.

"I suppose that's good news," Callum said. "But it reinforces our need to keep the Relics of Power out of the queen's hands."

Kohrin nodded his agreement. "The Relics will bring strength to the Academy and its allies," he said. "But even without them, the queen has powerful allies of her own." With that, he looked me in the eye, and as if someone had flicked a switch inside my head, the image of the man with the silver hair flashed through my mind.

Somehow, Kohrin knew I'd seen him in the queen's Throne Room. He knew who and what that man was.

But he said nothing, and the moment passed.

"I must return home," he said at last. "My wife and children will be waiting."

"Of course," Callum replied, extending a hand. "I look forward to seeing you again."

"And I you."

With one final bow of his head to each of us, the Grell sprang off and disappeared over a jagged wall of black stone.

# HOMEWARD

"We should get back, too," Callum told me with a frown. "As much as I want to stay out with you forever, if our 'lesson' goes on for too many hours, we both know tongues will start wagging."

"I guess you're right," I replied with a heavy sigh. "Well, I've got to say, this has been the wildest date I could ever have imagined."

"Wildest as in good, or as in horrifying?" he laughed.

"Good, of course. Exciting. Strange. Bizarre. Not that I have anything to compare it to. It's not like I ever, you know, dated anyone in Fairhaven. But I can say with confidence that most girls don't find themselves standing on mountaintops staring at armored cats or having casual chitchat with Grells about war."

"The Otherwhere is full of surprises. Some are pretty amazing, others can be terrifying," Callum said, slipping his hands onto my waist. The way he was staring at me filled me with all the soothing warmth of a roaring hearth on a cold winter day, and I wanted to press myself into his chest, to absorb the feeling into my skin. "I just hope this wasn't disappointing for you."

"I could never be disappointed by you," I told him.

He kissed me then stepped back. "Let's hope you're right," he said. "But for now, I guess it's time to fly back."

"We don't need to fly, silly," I replied. "Don't forget—I can summon doors."

"You're not too tired? I thought maybe…"

"I'm fine," I replied with a shake of my head. "I'll admit the thing with the razorbeak took a lot out of me, but I seem to have recovered quickly. I'm sure I can find the energy to summon a Breach."

Callum swung his arms open, sweeping the air between us. "Then summon away, Seeker," he said with a grin that made me wish I could stay on the mountain forever, kissing his extremely appealing lips, his neck, his hands.

Slightly deflated that our wondrous time together was coming to an end, I called up a door to lead us back to my bedroom in the Academy's tower. We slipped through without incident, with the Breach fizzling away behind us.

I plopped down on my bed, grateful at least not to have crevasses to worry about. "Home sweet home," I sighed.

"You've got mail," Callum said, stepping over to reach down and grab a folded piece of paper that someone seemed to have slipped under my door.

"I hope it's not a letter of reprimand from my Headmaster-grandfather," I said as he handed it to me. "Though I can't say I'd blame him if he barked at me for leaving again. Even if it *was* under the protection of the mighty Callum Drake."

As Callum let out a chuckle, I unfolded the paper and read out loud:

---

*Tomorrow.*

*First light.*

*Training in the Eastern Courtyard.*

*Get some good sleep, Vega. You'll need it for what the morning has in store.*

*M.*

---

"Ugh," I grunted, remembering that Merriwether had ordered me to muck out the Academy's stables. It probably wasn't even 8 p.m. yet, but already the thought of how early I'd have to get up exhausted me.

"Bad news?" asked Callum.

"Just that I'll be back to making an ass of myself tomorrow morning," I said. "I suppose you'll be there to see it?"

"I will. But you won't look like an ass. You couldn't possibly."

"I can, and I probably will. But I'm glad to know you'll be there to witness my failure."

Callum shot me a disapproving look. "Listen, Miss Self-Deprecating—are you willing to take a little advice from your tutor?"

Wincing, I nodded. "Sure. Fine. Do your worst."

"As I've said, don't worry about swords or daggers. Your weapon is your mind. You need to learn to use it offensively—which means learning to use it *defensively.* Don't forget what you learned today. Your instincts were spot-on. You know how to protect yourself and others."

"All I did was summon a couple of shields."

"Shields save lives. It's why people have used them for centuries."

"Can't I just scream deeply offensive curse words at my enemies? Maybe their hurt feelings will make them collapse into useless heaps?"

One corner of Callum's lips pulled up into an adorable, crooked grin. "Come on, Sloane. That incredible brain of yours is good for more than swearing." He crouched in front of me, took my face in his hands, and kissed my lips gently. "Get some sleep. I'm going to head to my room to let you get some rest."

"You're really leaving?" I moaned.

It was too soon for him to take off; I felt like we'd only just found each other again after my torturous days of incarceration.

"Don't worry, I'll be right next door if you need me. But Merriwether's right. You should get a proper night's sleep, and that won't happen if I'm taking up most of your very small bed."

"Fair enough," I said with a yawn and a stretch. Much as I would have liked him to stay, I couldn't deny that he was right. My bed *was* tiny, and I was desperately in need of a good night's sleep. "Then I'll see you first thing in the morning?"

"Of course. But we'll probably have to go back to pretending we're not, you know, two people who spend their free time hanging out in fruit groves or at the summits of forbidden mountains. We don't want to provide fodder for the Academy's gossips."

"I know," I replied, expelling an exaggerated breath. I stood up and headed toward the door to see him out. "You're Callum Drake, and I'm just a lowly aspiring Seeker."

"Don't say that." He grabbed my hand playfully and spun me to face a round mirror that hung on the wall. Standing behind me, he pressed his chin to the top of my head. "You're so much more than you think. Look at yourself, Vega."

It had been a while since I'd really stared at my reflection. At the once dull hazel eyes that had brightened significantly since my seventeenth birthday. At my cheekbones, which had grown more prominent over the last weeks, giving me a strange air of maturity I didn't quite recognize. At the tight ringlets of dark hair framing my face like out-of-control vines.

"You are very beautiful, you know," Callum said, his voice vibrating down my spine.

I smiled, more out of embarrassment than flattery. "I'm not

staring at myself because I think I'm beautiful," I said. "It's only because I don't quite recognize myself these days."

"Well, maybe someday soon you will." He kissed the top of my head before heading to the door. "I'll see you in the morning, Seeker."

"See you then, dragon shifter."

# TRAINING

I woke up to the sound of a trumpet—or maybe it was a dying cat —blaring in the courtyard below the east tower. The first rays of sunlight were already beginning to illuminate the Otherwhere, and I remembered with a panic that I was supposed to muck out the stables before the morning's training session.

I dressed quickly, raced down the spiral staircase outside my room, and sprinted to the far end of the Academy.

But when I reached the stables, I found them dark and uninhabited by humans or horses. I stuck my nose over the first stall door I saw, only to see that it was pristine, a new bed of straw laid over the floor.

"You looking for someone?" a voice asked.

I spun around to see a tall woman in riding pants and boots that looked like they'd never been anything other than a fashion accessory.

"I'm supposed to muck out the stables," I told her.

"Are you, then?" she asked with a strange smile. "That's interesting."

"Why's that?"

"There's nothing to muck. Hasn't been for days. The Rangers have all the horses out on patrol."

"When will they be back?"

"Not for days yet. I'd say you should come back in a week or so."

"Are you serious?" I asked. "Does…does the Headmaster know about this?"

"Well, he's the one who sent them out on patrol, so I'd say he does."

I wanted to curse under my breath, but instead I smiled. My grandfather had managed to officially punish me, *not* punish me, and play an excellent practical joke on me, all at the same time.

"Okay," I said. "Thanks for your help."

With that, I jogged back toward the Academy's central corridor, hoping to grab a quick bite before the training session was to begin.

There was no sign of Callum in the Great Hall—in fact, very few of the school's denizens were sitting around, which told me those who were participating had already made their way to class, while everyone else was smart enough to have stayed in bed.

The moment I had a warm buttered bun in my hand, I sprinted toward the Academy's eastern wing, taking swift bites as I went. It wasn't the healthiest breakfast, but at least it was enough to keep me from fainting from hunger.

When I arrived, most of the Seeker Candidates were already standing around the courtyard, dressed in their silver tunics. Among them were an assortment of Zerkers and Casters, including Niala, who had Rourke sitting at her side in his Husky form, his eyes piercing fiery blue against his dark fur.

Callum was off to one side of the courtyard, chatting with Merriwether. I was surprised to see the Headmaster up and about so early in the morning. It wasn't like he had to attend the session.

But I was even more surprised when he marched straight toward me.

"How are you this morning, Miss Sloane?" he asked, slouching over me like a friendly vulture.

"I'm...fine," I replied. "Thank you for asking."

"Good to know." He leaned in close and whispered, "I hear you and Mr. Drake had an adventure last evening."

"We...I..." *Don't lie. There's no point.* "Yes, we did."

"Well, your tutor informed me that you worked on some drills and honed your talents. So I suppose I can ignore the fact that you seem quite addicted to leaving the Academy."

Ah, so *that* was what why he'd shown up so early.

I opened my mouth to reply, but my eyes were drawn to Callum in the distance, who shook his head almost imperceptibly, as if he could tell what was about to transpire.

"I—" I began, swallowing the excuse that I'd been on the verge of spewing at my grandfather. "I'm sorry. I probably should have told you we were going."

"It's fine," Merriwether chuckled, shooting a look at Callum. "You were in good hands. Besides, as with all your ill-advised adventures, your little act of rebellion may serve us well in the end. I hear you met an old friend of mine."

"Kohrin?" I asked. "You know him?"

"Yes. A very excellent Grell, that one. A valuable ally. Mr. Drake was just telling me that his Watchers are on high alert for our enemies' movements. They will keep us apprised of anything suspicious."

"Yes, they seem to be on top of things," I replied, hoping that was all the Headmaster had to say to me so I could get back to freaking out quietly.

"You will let me know if you hear anything?"

"Of course."

"Speaking of the enemy," Merriwether said, eyeing the sky,

"Do you remember what happened last time you participated in an outdoor training session?"

I looked up nervously, my memory swirling with the buzzing of the queen's drones, sent to attack me during a sparring match. "I remember," I said.

"Don't worry. I've seen to it that nothing will disrupt today's class."

I wanted to ask what he'd done, but I was interrupted by the booming voice of Mr. Strunk, the instructor taking charge of the session. The last time I'd seen him was when I'd escaped from the queen and summoned the dragons to the Academy.

And I got the distinct impression that he didn't like me much.

"Candidates!" he shouted. "Today, you will be tested on your battle instincts, with the help of some of our more experienced students. Gather around in a circle and I'll explain what I mean."

"Excuse me," I said, bowing my head reverently toward my grandfather.

"Of course. Good luck to you. And don't beat yourself up over what's about to occur," Merriwether replied mysteriously. "Everything happens for a reason." With that vote of confidence, he headed inside.

I joined the others in a large circle, only to find myself standing opposite Raff, who was once again dressed in the uniform of a Seeker Candidate.

It was so strange—I'd all but forgotten about the boy who'd come to be a much-needed friend in my prison cell. I raised an inquisitive eyebrow in his direction.

But instead of acknowledging me, he grimaced and looked away.

*Okay, that was...weird.*

Well, whatever the reason for his hostility, it didn't matter now. We had a class to focus on. I shook off my concerns and focused on Mr. Strunk, who was explaining the drills we'd be participating in over the next few hours.

"Seeker Candidates, listen up! This will be much like your usual sparring sessions. As always, you aren't allowed to try to murder one another, tempting though it may be," he said, pulling his eyes to me. "Yes, I'm looking at you, Miss Sloane. We haven't forgotten what nearly happened to you several days back."

I felt my cheeks flush as everyone's eyes turned my way. I had no doubt everyone knew the incident he was referring to, when a Seeker Candidate called Freya had flung a large rock at my head. I was a victim in that particular conflict, not an instigator—not that Strunk seemed to care.

"I'll try my best to avoid being slaughtered," I replied in a tone more snide than I intended.

"Good. See that you don't."

Strunk went on to explain that we would be working in groups of three. "In some cases, you'll find that your two opponents have ganged up on you," he said. "Which is a tactic I fully encourage. Waergs don't attack you one at a time, waiting politely for their chance to pounce. So it's up to each of you to figure out how to stay alive. The purpose of this drill is to test how quick you are on your feet and how honed your survival skills are."

I shot Callum a look, my eyebrows raised, and he gave me a quiet nod as if to say "See? Told you so."

"I am *not*," Strunk continued, "here to watch you do serious bodily harm to your opponents. Defend yourselves. Stay alive. But I warn you: I will only consider you a winner in your bout if you manage to gain the strategic advantage. Remember that the true enemy—the one outside the walls of the Academy—will not be merciful when the time comes. You need to work out how to keep yourself alive. If a student's speed is too great, find a way to slow them down. If a magic user hurls a bolt of lightning at you, you are to dodge or block it and return the favor with an attack of your own."

"Wait—you're telling us we're going to get hit by lightning?" whispered Desmond, who was standing to my right.

"Not if you're even remotely competent," replied Crow, who was positioned on his other side.

I'd first met Crow when he was hanging out with Niala and Callum in Fairhaven on the evening of Midsummer Fest, a night that now seemed like it had taken place decades ago. He was a Zerker. Tough as nails, he'd taken part in his share of fights during the course of his life. As if to prove it, he wore an angry scar on his right cheek like a badge of honor.

"Great. So I'm about to be burned to a crisp," Desmond replied.

"Do you have something to say to the group?" Strunk snapped at him.

"No, sir. Only that I'd like to formally request that someone tell my parents I love them when you send them my ashes."

"That can certainly be arranged." With a guffaw, Strunk addressed us all once again. "On a serious note, Casters are—of course—not to use your most deadly spells. It's one thing for students to wind up in the infirmary because they've got a few bruises or a cut. It's quite another for us to have to haul corpses out of here." With that, he pivoted to address a few of the meeker-looking Seeker Candidates. "If you cannot bring yourself to finish your bout, simply raise a hand and announce that you're done, and you will be free to leave the ring. It may not be the most honorable way to end a match, but it's often the safest. Now, I'll read off your groups, and you can prepare yourselves for the onslaught."

Strunk began to list groups of three students, beginning each one with the name of a Seeker. Meg was with a Zerker and a Caster. Niala was up against a Seeker and a lanky Zerker, neither of whom I knew well.

When my turn came, I was horrified to hear that I was going up against Larken, a Zerker whose specialty was trying to set his enemies on fire. He'd been looking for an excuse to kill me since my first day at the Academy, and now, much to my dismay, he had his chance.

Oddly enough, my other opponent was Raff.

"I thought it would just be one Seeker per group," I said, turning to Niala, who'd crept over to stand beside me.

"I did, too," she replied. "Maybe Strunk's put you with Raff so he can follow your lead. Remember, you've had more training than he has."

"Barely," I protested. "I was in prison while everyone else was training here. Raff would be better off with literally any of the other candidates."

Niala shrugged, and I shut my mouth. There was no point in protesting. Maybe this was Strunk's way of punishing me for my disappearing act.

If so, whining about it wasn't about to make matters any better.

I searched the crowd for Larken, only to see that he and Raff were huddled together with their eyes fixed on me, malicious smiles on their faces. If I hadn't known better, I would have guessed they were old friends sharing a joke at my expense.

When the first bout was set to begin, I moved out of my position and edged around the makeshift fighting ring at the courtyard's center until I found myself next to Callum.

"Not sure how I'm going to contend with my opponents," I whispered out of the side of my mouth. "I'm not so worried about Raff—he's been in prison all his life so it's not like he even knows how to fight. But Larken hates my guts. He'll be chomping at the bit to burn my face off."

"You'll find a way," he replied, arms crossed, eyes focused directly at the center of the ring. "You always do. Just remember what I said yesterday. And if those two give you any trouble, don't forget that you can always submit. And you *should*, if it comes down to protecting yourself. I—*we*—can't afford to lose you, especially not like this."

"Gee, thanks for the vote of confidence."

"You know what I mean, Vega. This is a new experience for all of you. It's one thing to protect some razorbeaks from a cat. It's another to deal with teenage boys who think it's fun to intimidate and wreak havoc. Don't underestimate them."

He gave my hand a quick, surreptitious squeeze before taking off to help a frustrated student with their sword's grip.

I found myself growing more and more tense as I watched the first few sparring matches. Meg, whose gift was lightning speed, spent most of her time deftly dodging attacks but ended up losing when her two sword-wielding opponents quietly teamed up to trap her in a corner of the ring. Unable to push her way between them without risking injury, she surrendered.

Niala won her bout, mostly thanks to the fact that Rourke transformed into a bald eagle and flew at one opponent's face, distracting the Seeker Candidate in the ring long enough for Niala to get behind him and wrap her narrow leather belt around his neck.

When the time came for my bout to begin, I caught Raff standing on his own, staring at me from across the ring, only to see the same look of disdain that he'd shot my way several times since our arrival at the Academy.

In that second, the last of my confidence in our tenuous friendship crumbled into a wretched pile of dust and disillusionment.

Something told me the moment I crossed the threshold into the ring, I'd need to focus every ounce of energy on keeping myself alive.

# THE BOUT

LARKEN WASTED no time making his intentions known.

The second he set foot in the ring, he summoned a fireball and hurled it directly at my face. I managed to duck out of the way just in time to see Raff standing in the opposite corner with a gleaming, sharp-looking sword in hand.

"What the hell?" I yelled at Larken. "What happened to 'you're not supposed to kill each other?'"

"Don't worry, Sloane!" he shouted back. "I'm using the *gentle* setting on my fire. Sure, maybe you'll suffer a second-degree burn here and there, but it's nothing a little skin graft can't fix." He called up another ball of flame that hovered in the air above his palm, rotating slowly. With a vindictive smirk and a sideways nod toward Raff, he said, "Good luck dodging *both* of us."

As if on command, Raff darted toward me with the sword raised over his head, a look of unmitigated rage on his face. As he brought his weapon down directly where I stood, I dodged out of the way, only to have him come at me again.

"Seriously?" I cried, my eyes darting from one opponent to the other before landing on Mr. Strunk, who simply shrugged, the half-smirk on his lips telling me he was enjoying bearing witness to my misery.

It was entirely possible that Larken was just toying with me. But there was no question in my mind that Raff was trying to hurt me.

Or possibly even kill me.

Raff lifted the sword a third time, his intent heavy on the air around me. Once again, he was set to strike. And this time, he didn't intend to miss.

Desperate, I shut my eyes, wincing from a potent combination of fear and desperation.

"Vega! Look out!" Niala shouted from the sidelines. I could hear the panic in her tone.

What happened in the next few seconds felt like an out of body experience.

Opening my eyes, I raised both hands toward the sword, mumbling words in a language I neither knew nor understood. Maybe it was just gibberish. Maybe it was something from the far reaches of my subconscious. But it didn't matter. It all happened so fast I didn't have time to think.

As I pushed my hands upward, a crystalline shield formed in the air between the flying sword and my palms, much like the barrier I'd created in the valley the previous day.

When Raff's sword came crashing down, I felt the blow vibrate through my muscles and bones like a rumbling crash of thunder. But at least I wasn't bleeding.

I heard him curse under his breath as I drew the shield to my side and backed away, chin down, eyes glaring.

"What's gotten into you?" I asked, my chest heaving. "Why do you want to hurt me so badly?"

"Come on, Vega—I'm just here to learn," he said with a strange, awful grin. "I thought we Seekers were here to study. Isn't that why you brought me to this place?"

"Well, yeah," I replied. "But we're not supposed to *kill* each other. We're supposed to be working on defensive moves. Besides, I saved you from that prison, remember? I thought we were on the same side."

My words seemed to irritate rather than appease him, and he raised the sword once again, just as another fireball flew my way. I'd forgotten about Larken, who had apparently been watching from a distance, entertained enough by our tense conversation to leave me alone for a few seconds.

I managed to twist around, shoving my summoned shield between myself and the projectile. As the flame hit, it sizzled and smoked like it had met a wall of melting ice, then faded into a small cloud of dark smoke.

"You're lucky I'm not allowed to call up the real stuff, Sloane!" Larken shouted. "It would tear through that shield of yours like it's paper."

"I'm sure it would," I yelled back, my eyes locking once again on Raff, who was circling me now, a look of insatiable, disturbing hunger in his eyes.

"Aren't you going to summon something else?" he asked. "A sword of some kind? Or is that chain around your neck the only weapon you know how to use?"

Confused, I stared at him. I hadn't told him a thing about my altercation with the Usurper Queen. In fact, I hadn't told anyone except for Merriwether how I'd managed to take the amulet from her.

And there was no way the Headmaster had told Raff.

"How can you possibly know…" I began to ask. But Raff leapt at me with a fierce growl, interrupting the question.

I thrust the shield between us to absorb the blow, which sent me reeling backwards and tripping over my own feet.

"Did you enjoy it?" he snarled. "Did you like holding that much power in your hands? The great Vega Sloane, killer of the Usurper Queen. You could have had all the glory. But you choked. You ran away like a coward."

"Stop it!" I cried out, drawing my small dagger from its sheath at my waist, holding it up as threateningly as I could.

In that moment, I hated everything. The anger I was feeling, the hostility in Raff's eyes. I hated that the Academy pitted us against one another like we were raging animals lusting for one another's blood. I hated that a crowd made up of friends and enemies was watching me fail this challenge in every conceivable way.

All I wanted was to go back to the friendliness I'd so enjoyed the first few times Raff and I had spoken. Now we were nothing more than rivals who were beginning to despise each other, both of us desperate for a prize we may never win.

"That dagger's not going to do you a lot of good," Raff said with a laugh, swinging wildly with his sword as he advanced. He'd nearly pushed me all the way into the corner of the ring by now.

"Focus, Vega! Remember—your mind is your weapon!"

It was Callum's voice that shouted the words from somewhere behind me.

"I'm trying!" I called out, my voice trembling with an all too potent cocktail of emotions.

As I cowered against the ropes of the sparring ring, another fireball crashed against the shield, followed immediately by Raff's sword.

By now, my arm was a shaking mess, alternating between intense pain and tingling numbness.

Staring through my conjured shield at the two boys who both seemed to despise me with every fiber of their beings, I could easily have wept. Instead I crouched, shaking, my back pressed against the corner post.

I pulled my eyes down to the dagger clutched in my right hand and frowned. Raff was right. The blade was useless.

I dropped it to the ground, raised my free hand, and called out, "I submit! I submit!"

I loathed the sound of those words coming from my own lips. An admission of defeat. Worse still, an admission of inadequacy.

But I had no choice. There was no way for me to combat such potent, raw rage. Even the queen's Waergs hadn't been so cruel when they'd had the chance to hurt me.

Strunk raised his hand and called out to the other two to stand down.

"Back away," he ordered, apparently aware of their desire to murder me. "Let her out. And you two had better play nice from here on in. You were approaching dangerous territory with Vega."

"*Approaching?*" I muttered. "Tell that to my arm."

Strunk nodded to Niala to help me climb out of the ring, and I was grateful to let the summoned shield fade to nothingness as I picked up my dagger and extracted myself from my living hell.

"You all right?" Niala asked quietly as I made my way to the back of the still-watching crowd. Rourke, who'd shifted into his house cat form, rubbed himself affectionately against my calves.

"No," I admitted in a strained voice. "That was totally screwed up. I expected Raff to be on my side—or at least, not to be in full-on kill mode. I have no idea what I did to upset him so much."

"Maybe he thinks Merriwether will send him back to the queen's castle if he's not good enough? He might just be trying to prove himself."

"Merriwether would never send him away, not like that!" I hissed in response.

"I know that. But Raff doesn't. He hasn't been here long, remember. He probably doesn't trust any of us—not even the girl who saved him. Chances are he's wary of you, as well as the rest of us. You said he's been in prison most of his life. I wouldn't be surprised if the experience has played with his mind. I hate to say it, but you might need to be patient with him."

I wasn't convinced, but it was a fair point. Desperation led people to do all sorts of crazy things, and Raff was probably no exception. I told myself to calm down and try to see things from his perspective. I had no idea what his time in prison had done to him. After all, *I'd* only been in a cell for a few days, and I'd fallen deep into hopeless despair. What would *years* in the place have done to me?

"Whatever the case, Vega, you didn't deserve that mayhem," Niala added as Rourke transformed into his Husky form and licked my hand. "See? Rourke agrees with me."

"Thanks, you two." I began to breathe lighter. "I feel stupid. I was so confused in there. I didn't even try fighting back. I guess I let my emotions get to me."

"You felt betrayed by someone you thought was an ally," Niala said. "It's not surprising you were in shock. But it's actually a good lesson to learn in here. You might be surprised to discover how often people betray each other in times of war. Sometimes you have to put blinders on and remember that in the end, you only have yourself to rely on."

"It sounds like you're speaking from experience."

Niala looked away and chewed briefly on her lower lip. "I've been involved in some fights I wish I could erase from my memory," she said. "Let's just say I know what it feels like to be betrayed."

I nodded and turned away, searching the crowd until I spotted Callum. He was standing on the other side of the ring, his eyes locked on Raff, who was busy playing a game of cat-and-mouse with Larken. The two opponents were circling each other with equally menacing grins on their lips, but neither seemed particularly intent on hurting the other.

At least, not like they'd wanted to hurt me.

The look on Callum's face was oddly focused, like he was in the midst of trying to solve a puzzle. I could see that his hands were balled into tight fists, tension stiffening his entire frame. I wished more than anything that I knew what he was thinking.

But after a moment, his eyes met mine and he relaxed, even

going so far as to offer me a slight smile as Larken delivered a fiery blow to Raff's shoulder, scorching his tunic and eliciting a cry of pain. It was enough to win the bout.

AFTER A BRIEF LUNCH BREAK, training resumed. Anyone who wasn't a Seeker Candidate was dismissed to train elsewhere, and the rest of us were paired off with other Candidates to run slow-motion drills meant to hone our skills.

Fortunately, Raff was nowhere to be seen. I wanted to ask why, but Callum had disappeared after the morning session, and I had no desire to ask Strunk, in case he found a way to shift the blame onto me.

I ended up working with Meg on a series of methodical training exercises. Slow motion proved difficult for a girl whose strength was lightning speed, but over the course of two hours she gained the ability to control her quick dashes, to the point where she and I invented an amusing game where I summoned temporary transparent blockades, and she darted around them. In the end, our part of the courtyard looked like a small labyrinth of glass.

We both wound up doubled over laughing when she slammed face-first into one of the clear barriers, which I promptly removed only to have her then fall in a heap into a pile of gooey mud. It felt so good to be ridiculous for a few minutes.

But the moment the class ended, the feeling of failure began to eat away at me again.

I tucked myself away in my room at the top of the eastern tower, skipping dinner. I needed to be alone with my thoughts, to process what had occurred that morning. Raff's face, his laughter, the strange, malicious glint in his eye...none of it made sense, despite Niala's assessment of the situation.

*Maybe I should find him and talk to him. Tell him I'm not his enemy.*

I was just thinking about getting up to go find him when a knock sounded at the door.

"Who is it?" I called out.

"Callum."

I slipped off the bed and trudged over, pulling the door open. Much as I should have been delighted to see him, I couldn't fight off the veil of embarrassment that had already settled on the surface of my skin.

"How did things go this afternoon?" he asked, deliberately dodging any mention of the horrible morning session.

"Okay," I replied, my eyes locked on his chest instead of his face. I couldn't quite find the strength to meet his gaze.

"I'm sorry I disappeared. I had a meeting I couldn't get out of."

"It's okay."

"May I come in?"

I backed away, gesturing him inside.

"If you're here to lecture me on how poorly I did this morning, I don't think I can take it right now," I warned him, my voice breaking as I choked back a sob. "I really did try, but I was so shaken, I…"

But instead of answering, he grabbed me by the front of my tunic and pulled me to him in a tight embrace. I felt the tears come then, staining his sweater and soaking my cheeks. The release was like a valve opening inside me, letting out the agonizing pressure that had suffocated me for most of the day.

I held him as long as I could, not daring to pull back for fear that he'd see my blotchy face and red eyes. More signs of weakness.

"You don't have to win everything, you know," he said softly. "Today was a lesson. Nothing more. Larken and that boy—that *Raff*—they didn't learn a damned thing. But you did, and that's all that matters."

I pulled back, chuckling as I wiped my cheeks with the backs of my hands. "You sound so much like Merriwether sometimes, you know. Wise dragon lord that you are."

"I don't mean to sound patronizing. I just want you to know you didn't do anything wrong. Your opponents did. And Strunk should have stopped them, but he's a jackass who thinks he's an alpha male of the highest order."

"It's okay. I know I should have a thicker skin by now, after years of the Charmers…"

"Pain comes in a lot of forms, Vega. It might be a fireball or a cruel insult; it doesn't matter. It all hurts. It's okay to be upset, you know. It's okay to be angry."

With a sigh, I spun around and strode back over to my bed, where I plopped down onto my back, my knees bent. "I half expected you to tell me to suck it up, to be honest," I told him, turning my face his way. "I sort of thought you'd tell me to keep a stiff upper lip or something."

"Never." He stepped over and sat down, taking my hand and intertwining his fingers with my own. "A lesson I learned early on was never to dictate how anyone else should feel. It's not my place. Besides, I know how easy it is to lose control of my emotions."

"You?" I laughed. "You're the most controlled person I've ever seen. Even when I can see you're angry, you don't act on it."

"Give me time," he replied with a smile. "I'm afraid you'll see just how volatile I can be one of these days. But I can at least promise you one thing."

"Oh? What's that?"

"I'll try my hardest not to let myself take it out on you."

"Thanks. I appreciate it."

I rolled away from him onto my side, not so much in an act of defiance as the hope that he'd lie down and drape an arm over my waist. Reading my mind, he did so, pressing his chest to my back.

And like a soothing balm on my emotions, I bathed in the amazing warmth of his skin.

"Spend the night?" I asked, taking hold of his arm and kissing his hand.

"If you'd like."

"I would like it very much."

"Then your wish is my command, my lady."

# CONFUSION

EACH NIGHT, I slept next to Callum. We were both careful not to let things go too far. Mindful of the hurt we might both suffer soon, but grateful for the time we had together.

The morning training sessions went much the same as the first. Each morning, the Seeker Candidates were sent into the ring to spar with other students, and each afternoon we trained with instructors who explained why some of us had failed at the morning's lessons before teaching us how to do better.

We'd occasionally fight in teams of two, sometimes one-on-one, depending on Strunk's mood.

Fortunately, he didn't ask me to fight Larken or Raff again. It seemed Strunk had realized it wasn't a great idea to throw a student into a ring with boys who were intent on turning them into a smoldering, decapitated corpse. In fact, Larken had stopped showing up for any more of the classes. I could only hope he'd been reprimanded and sent to his room to think about what he'd done.

After a couple of days, I was surprised to realize I was no longer feeling vulnerable or embarrassed by my lack of skill. If anything, I'd begun to feel oddly grateful for the opportunity to fight, to learn, even to improve my magic-making abilities a little.

Perhaps even more surprising, I was growing to enjoy the fighting. Over the course of a short time, I'd learned to conjure everything from axes to helmets to projectile weapons that behaved exactly as I wanted them to.

During one sparring match, I even summoned a series of small throwing stars, which I managed to hurl at Desmond with extraordinary accuracy. Luckily for him, I had the foresight to ensure the temporary weapons were crafted from foam rubber, and we both laughed to the point of tears when they bounced one by one—with sponge-y plunks—off his forehead.

Strunk declared me the winner of that particular fight.

By the end of the fifth day, I'd begun to feel like a completely different person. I was stronger, more in control than I'd ever been. I was finally starting to embrace the full range of my summoning power. The fear that had haunted me since my return to the Academy had abated at last.

Perhaps it all came down to the fact that I'd largely avoided any contact with Raff since our strangely hostile altercation. We hadn't spoken once since then, and I'd avoided eye contact at every possible turn.

As much as I wanted to forget what had transpired, the stark emotional consequences of his betrayal still felt too raw, a pain etched on my mind and body.

When I closed the door to my room that evening, I examined myself in the mirror, convinced that I'd changed a little over the last few days.

My skin, usually a healthy mocha shade, had darkened from long hours spent in the sun. I also seemed taller, as unlikely as that was. Maybe it was just that I was standing with more confidence than ever before. I was evolving from *Vega the Slouching Wuss* to *Vega the Confident Warrior*.

Or, at least, *Vega the Doesn't-Think-She-TOTALLY-Sucks Warrior*.

I was snickering at the thought of a time when I'd despised mirrors when a knock at my door interrupted my nostalgic flashback.

Anxious to see Callum, I called out, "Come in!" as I twisted away from my reflection for fear that he would think I was embroiled in some narcissistic ritual of self-admiration.

Smiling, I turned toward the door.

But when it creaked open, I leapt backwards, shocked to see a familiar but unwelcome face.

"Raff?" I breathed as the tall boy stepped into my room. "How did you know where to find me?"

*Stay calm, Vega. He's not going to hurt you.*

*Hopefully.*

Inhaling a deep breath, I tried to keep my shoulders back, my head held high. I didn't want him thinking he could intimidate me. Even if he could—and did.

His behavior had been so erratic that the mere thought of being alone with him in a sealed room was terrifying.

"I asked around," he smirked. "Seems everyone knows you live in the special tower, away from all of us mere mortals. I guess that's what you get when you're the Headmaster's favorite, isn't it?"

"I'm not..." I was about to tell him I didn't receive special treatment, but I thought better of it.

*Let him think Merriwether keeps an eye on me. I'll be safer that way.*

I crossed my arms and leaned against the far wall, wondering if Raff was going to remain positioned between the door and me for the entirety of his visit. "So, what are you doing here?" I asked, my voice tense.

He puffed out a breath and leapt across the room, throwing himself onto my bed, a far too forward move that made me wince. "I suppose I was feeling bad," he said, pressing his fingertips into the mattress as if testing it for softness.

"About what?"

"About nearly killing you the other day. I thought it was time to make up."

"You didn't nearly…" I began, irritated. "I mean, I wasn't going to let you kill me."

"Still," he interrupted, sitting up, "the truth is, I wanted to hurt you, and I apologize. I let my anger get the better of me."

"I'm confused. What exactly did I do to make you angry? I mean, other than rescue you from a prison you'd been in for a decade?"

So swiftly that I barely registered it, he leapt to his feet and over to me. I'd never seen Raff move like that, and it freaked me out.

He was staring into my eyes now, his head tilted in a way that made me cringe. He was reminding me of someone, though I couldn't figure out who.

"You haven't done anything, Vega," he said, his voice suddenly sweet and lilting. "Nothing at all. It's all…my…fault." As he spoke the final few words, he reached out and caressed my cheek the way Callum so often did.

Only his touch was nothing like Callum's.

I shuddered, too petrified with confusion and fear to recoil, as much as I wanted to.

"Vega, you and I could make a good team. A *great* team…" Raff's hand was slipping down to my neck now. "I know you think so, too. We could be so good together. I knew it the second I set eyes on you in the queen's prison. I could feel in that moment that there was something between us."

I didn't know what to say or do. He was being so weird, so…intimate.

I felt nauseated.

I swallowed hard, my voice shaking and mousy. "Are you serious?"

"Of course."

He inched closer to me.

Too close.

I pulled away, twisting around him and hurrying over to position myself next to the door. "Maybe we *could* have made a great team," I told him. "If you'd seen me as an ally, or even just as a friend. But you've acted so weird ever since I got you out of that place. I don't know what to make of you at all. And to be honest, right now you're confusing the hell out of me."

In one long stride, he stepped across the room and grabbed my left hand, squeezing it hard enough to make me wince. "Someday you'll understand me. Someday very soon."

He was still holding onto my hand when a hard knock sounded at the door.

"Come in!" I called out, deliberately raising my voice as I yanked my hand away.

The door opened to reveal Callum standing in the hallway. His eyes moved immediately to Raff, who crossed his arms and stared, raising his chin high.

It seemed his attitude about Callum had changed since their first meeting. The boy from the prison had lost any hint of shyness or timidity.

"Are you all right, Vega?" Callum asked, never taking his eyes off the other boy. "I'm not used to hearing voices in here."

"I'm fine now," I said, stressing the last word. "Raff was just leaving."

"Yup," Raff said. "She's right. I have to go practice stabbing things. It's a very important skill to hone, you know. You never know when you might have to bury a sharp blade in your enemy's heart."

Without another word, he strode through the door past Callum, who stepped into the room.

I closed the door behind Raff and let out a breath for what felt like the first time in minutes.

"What was *that* about?" Callum asked.

"I wish I could tell you. I really don't know—but it was almost like..."

"Like what?"

"Like he was propositioning me. Which is *so weird*. I mean, he hates me."

"Propositioning you. I see. How did you feel about that?"

I stared at him, trying to gauge his mood. Was he jealous? Angry? Amused?

"Not good," I replied. "I don't like being in the same room with that guy, let alone my *bed*room. He just made himself at home, like he owned the place. He's become different ever since we left the prison. So...volatile. Honestly, he scares me."

"Well, he'd best stay away from you," Callum said. "Something about him feels...off. Though I can't quite put my finger on it. He feels like a poison on the air, if that makes any sense."

"Poison? That's a bit dramatic, don't you think?"

"Maybe, maybe not. Just be careful, okay? I just can't help remembering something Merriwether said to me when Raff first showed up here."

"What?"

Callum ground his jaw for a moment. "He told me the boy from the prison was meant to be here, despite the pain he would inevitably inflict."

"*Meant* to be here?"

"Merriwether has some strong notions about destiny and fate. I've always wondered if he sees things that the rest of us don't. *Knows* things."

I nodded as I took a seat in the small wooden chair positioned next to the room's solitary window. "I have no idea, really. My grandfather is pretty secretive."

"Don't I know it," Callum said as he sat down on the edge of my bed. "On another topic, are you feeling better about the training sessions? From what I've gotten to see, you look like you're almost having fun."

The truth was, I was feeling let down that he hadn't stepped across the small bedroom yet to kiss me. Come to think of it, he hadn't so much as touched me since coming in.

But instead of the truth, I simply said, "Other than Raff's uninvited visit, I'm fine. Good, actually. I feel like I'm finally starting to understand some things about my own mind. Then again, I felt like that during my first few days here, and I discovered pretty quickly that I was being over-confident."

"There's a fine balance between skill and confidence. People *learn* all our lives, whether we know it or not. But we're surprisingly good at forgetting that we don't know everything." He stared at me for a moment before swinging around to face the window.

"Speaking of knowing everything," I said, "I'd really like to know what you're thinking right now. You seem…distant."

Callum turned back to meet my gaze. "I'm sorry. I've been worried that I'm distracting you by coming here in the evenings. I suppose I've been feeling like I'm being selfish, taking so much of your time."

"Selfish? How could you say that?"

"The fact is that you're not really mine, no matter how much I may wish you were. And I'm being greedy, keeping you awake at night and invading your space, when you could be focusing on more important things."

Much as I understood his meaning, his words hurt. The last thing I wanted to hear was that he didn't consider our relationship important.

"But…"

He held up his hand. "I know," he said softly. "I know what you're going to say. And the truth is, you have my heart, Vega. You may not know it, you may not always see it, but you do have my heart. I think about you all the time. But I'm not talking about my feelings. I'm talking about *yours*."

He strode over to the window and pressed his hands to the wooden sill, staring out toward the horizon in the far distance beyond the Academy's walls. He was close enough now that I could have touched him, but something told me I shouldn't. I could feel him putting up a barrier between us, a wall preventing me from fully understanding whatever it was that he was feeling.

Something was eating away at him—something I *hoped* had nothing to do with me.

"There's a war being fought out there," he said quietly, "and we're both important players. I need, at least sometimes, to give you time to train, to think, to work on your skills. You have a part to play in all this that only you can control." Turning to look down at me, he asked, "Does that make any sense?"

"It does, I suppose," I said. "And you're probably right, at least in one way. I've been feeling really good about my skills these last few days. I feel like I could take on anyone—even if I know it's not true. I've always relied on other people. My parents when I was little, then Will. I've always felt sort of helpless, but I'm starting to see that I'm not—even if self-doubt creeps in here and there."

"I'm glad. I hated watching Raff and Larken have a go at you the other day. It made me sick to my stomach. It was hard not to jump into the ring, truth be told."

"I know. I remember the look on your face afterwards." I inhaled a deep breath and summoned the courage to ask, "What exactly were you thinking?"

"I'm not sure you want to know."

"Try me."

Callum strode over and sat on the bed again, clutching the

edge of the mattress, his fingers white-knuckled. "I wanted to murder them both. Larken, for being an absolute plonker, as the Zerkers tend to be."

"And Raff?"

"Raff…" Callum muttered. "I wanted to do *worse* than kill him. And if I'd been leading that class, I might have." In a flash of blazing color, his eyes altered, red and orange flames dancing across his irises as though a fire had set itself inside his soul.

I felt the presence of the silent, terrifying threat that came from a place so deep inside him I couldn't begin to fathom it. This wasn't just *Callum's* rage—this came from the dragon who lurked far beneath his skin. The dragon who had seemed so calm, so gentle just a few evenings ago.

"Niala thought Raff was only trying to prove himself," I said, hoping to soothe him at least a little. "She thinks he's desperate to stay here—to win Chosen Seeker so he can avoid the risk of going back to Uldrach."

"And what do *you* think?" Callum asked.

"I'm not sure. He's definitely desperate, but I couldn't tell you what his endgame is. Like I said, he's volatile and unpredictable. He confuses me."

"Well, not that you asked—but I don't think he cares a bit about the Trial or the results."

I stared at him, puzzled. "Then why do you think he—?"

I was interrupted by a loud thud coming from the direction of the window.

I leapt to my feet, shaken, my breath temporarily imprisoned in my chest.

"What was that?" I asked through a surge of adrenaline. "It sounded like…"

"Like something slamming against glass."

# A MESSAGE

CALLUM PULLED THE WINDOW OPEN, leaning out to see what collided with the glass. A small bird was hovering just outside, its wings beating frantically.

"A razorbeak," Callum said, backing away. "There's got to be a reason he's so far from home. Let's let him come closer."

Backing away, I watched as the bird, a small metal tube in its beak, landed on the windowsill. Tucking its wings against its body, it dropped the tube to the stone floor below, where it clattered and rolled to my feet.

"What is this?" I asked, picking it up and turning it over in my hand.

"Message!" a high-pitched voice replied. "Important!"

The last time a razorbeak had communicated with me, I'd heard its voice inside my mind. But this time he was squawking the words out loud, as if mimicking sounds someone had taught him.

"Thank you," I replied, shooting Callum a slightly embarrassed look when I realized I was once again speaking to a bird.

"Welcome!" the razorbeak chirped before launching itself out into the night air once again.

I rotated the small tube in my hand, looking for words on its surface, but it was smooth, devoid of so much as a scratch.

"I don't understand," I said. "Is this supposed to mean something to me?"

"Not sure. Bring it over here," Callum replied. He clicked on the lamp above my nightstand, and the area around him was instantly bathed in white light.

I stepped over with the tube in hand, rotating it again until I noticed a hair-thin line running around its middle.

"Is that a seam?" I asked.

"Try unscrewing it."

Grabbing each end between my thumb and index finger, I twisted the two halves until the cylinder began to ease apart. Finally, I managed to pull one half away, revealing a small piece of paper rolled up tight inside the case.

I drew it out, unraveled it, and scanned the words.

"It's from Kohrin, I think. He wants to meet."

"May I?" Callum asked.

I nodded and handed it over.

> *Find me by the old oak.*
> *Please come quickly.*
> *—K. I.*

"The old oak?" I asked. "He wants us to find a tree? But there are millions out there."

"I know which one he means," Callum replied. "It's some distance away, but we can get there fast."

"How? I can't summon a door unless I can picture the spot. If I just call up a Breach to a random oak tree, we could end up almost anywhere."

"Don't worry." Callum took my hand and kissed it. "Trust me?"

"Of course."

"Good," he said, twisting around so he faced the open window. "Then hop on my back."

"Wait—seriously?"

He nodded. "Seriously."

Grabbing hold of his shoulders, I leapt up and wrapped my legs around his waist. "Um, this feels a bit…weird," I laughed. "I haven't had a piggy-back ride since I was about seven years old."

"Just wait. It'll get even weirder in a second."

I was beginning to wonder what he meant when he jumped onto the windowsill, grabbing hold of the wooden frame to either side.

I shrieked as my eyes took in the courtyard far below us. "Wait—your brilliant plan is to jump out the window? That's a ten-story drop, at least!" I protested, trembling as my gaze veered to the ground. I was already beginning to wonder if I'd be able to summon a mattress soft and thick enough to break our fall at the bottom.

"Hey—you said you trusted me, Sloane. You know I wouldn't do anything that would endanger you."

"Yeah, I know, but…"

"No *buts*. Just hold on tight. You're going for a ride."

With that, Callum leapt off the sill into the night, spreading his arms wide. I stifled the scream that wanted desperately to make its way across my lips, slammed my eyes shut, and held on for dear life.

And then we were surging upwards, and my arms were no longer around Callum's neck, but something jagged and smooth at once.

A deep voice rang through my mind. "We'll be there before you know it. Promise."

I opened one eye then the other, relieved to feel the gently undulating rhythm of Callum's dragon under me, swooping away from the Academy to begin his descent toward the woods.

In no time, we were landing in a small clearing to the west of the Academy's grounds, empty except for a solitary, thick-trunked oak tree.

I hopped off the dragon's neck and planted my feet safely on the ground. Callum shifted into his human form and let out a low hoot, which was answered a few seconds later by a high-pitched series of crow-like caws as a figure emerged from behind the tree. He strode rapidly toward us on legs that made him move more like an upright puma than a man.

"Kohrin," Callum said, "What's happened to bring you all the way here?"

"I'm afraid it's bad news," he replied, his bright eyes unreadable as always. "Lannach sent word that a large army of Waergs left the Usurper Queen's castle yesterday. They're heading this way."

"Who's Lannach?" I asked.

"A wizard," Callum replied. "In Merriwether's Order."

Kohrin nodded. "He says there are no deaths reported...yet. But rumors are circulating that the Blood Queen's Waergs intend to do to our land what they did to Kaer Uther. They say the queen has commanded her beasts to kill anyone disloyal to her and to burn their homes. Lannach fears she intends to go on a rampage."

I grabbed Callum's arm, barely holding in the cry of despair trying to make its way up my throat. "This is all my fault," I choked out. "I made her angry. She wants revenge."

"Who saw this army?" Callum asked, pressing a calming hand to my back.

"Lannach's flying sentinels. The ravens and the hawks. They informed him the queen's soldiers are moving in the Academy's direction. Death and flame can't be far behind. There are many villages between Uldrach and this place."

"So," Callum replied, "Isla has gotten desperate, and she's going to take it out on the innocent. Something needs to be done, or she'll burn the Otherwhere to the ground."

"How can we stop her?" I asked. "What can we possibly do?"

"We need to talk to Merriwether. We have to tell him about this as soon as possible." He turned back to Kohrin. "You have my word that we'll do everything in our power to halt her in her tracks."

The Grell nodded. "I feel a fear deep in my bones. A brutal frost will fall on us, and it will be worse if the queen is not stopped. She means to end this land from the bottom up—not only the towns, but our homes in the mountains, too. If not today, then soon."

Callum clapped a hand on Kohrin's shoulder. "Thank you for coming all this way. Now, go home and look after the mountain-folk, would you?"

"Of course," Kohrin replied. "Be well, and stay safe," he added, nodding my way before turning and bounding deep into the woods. A few seconds later I watched a creature take off into the air with the Grell's distinctive silhouette on his back.

"What was that?" I asked, bewildered. "It didn't look like a dragon…"

"A griffin," Callum replied. "They're rare these days, and they prefer to keep hidden."

"Griffin?"

"Part eagle, part lion. One day, if we're very lucky, I'll introduce you to one. But now we need to go." Callum took my hand and led me toward the clearing. "I'll shift and fly us back up."

"No," I said, taking him by the hand. "I can bring us straight to Merriwether's office."

Callum nodded. "Yes, of course you can."

As he looked on, I summoned a door. But a second later, a spell of dizziness overtook me, images swirling indistinctly through my mind.

"Wait," I murmured, holding the key in my trembling hand.

"What is it?"

"I suddenly have a bad feeling. Like I know something awful is going to happen."

"I wish I could tell you not to worry, but..." Callum pulled in close to kiss my forehead. "I'm afraid you're right. My sister isn't one to act spontaneously—at least not like this. She usually plans, she schemes. But this move—this is an act of pure, almost random destruction. It's reckless. Honestly, it doesn't make any sense at all. I'm afraid for this land, but even more than that, I'm confused."

"So why is she doing it? What are they trying to accomplish? Why burn the world to the ground if you're intending to rule it?"

"That might be the best question I've ever heard. I wish I knew the answer. Come, let's see what Merriwether has to say about all this. Then we'll figure out the rest."

# WARNINGS

"THIS IS GRAVE NEWS INDEED," Merriwether said when we'd relayed Kohrin's message to him, his forehead pinched into a deep frown. "Icewalker is no alarmist. He wouldn't have made the trip all this way unless he had major cause for concern."

"We need to do something," Callum replied, his voice stretched thin. His eyes were glowing bright, and I could feel him fighting back the beast inside him as he spoke. "We need to mobilize our best warriors, cut the queen's forces off before they can do any serious damage."

Merriwether nodded. "I'm afraid you're right, Mr. Drake. But I have to admit…I'm puzzled as to why I didn't see this coming…" He sounded exhausted and suddenly ancient, his voice fracturing as he spoke. "Well, we have no choice. I'll contact Lannach and tell him we're heading out in the morning. Perhaps he can assemble some of his own allies to help. But I'm afraid that even with our combined forces, we will be no match for the queen's army of Waergs."

"So that's it? We're going to war?" I asked with a jolt of excitement. The thought of taking on the queen again, as repulsive as it was, invigorated me.

"No. *We* are doing no such thing, Seeker."

"But why not?" I asked. "There are some good fighters among us. Oleana can do serious damage, and Meg has gotten really skilled at evasive maneuvers, to name just two."

"The answer to your question, Vega, is that a Seeker's value lies in their mind, not their combat skills," Merriwether said. "If we lose you lot, we lose our chance to retrieve the missing Relics. It's a risk we can't afford to take."

"He's right," Callum interjected. "You and the others need to stay alive long enough to find the Relics. Without them, we've already lost."

"But we haven't even chosen a Seeker yet," I protested. "And the queen already has the Sword of Viviane. How are we supposed to find the remaining Relics if no one's even been selected to search for them?"

Merriwether pulled open a drawer in his desk and extracted the Orb of Kilarin, which hovered briefly over his hand before losing its energy and sinking back into his palm.

"The Seeker will be chosen very soon, but there will be no Seeker's Trial this year—at least, not in the traditional sense. The Orb has told me as much."

"What do you mean?" I asked, wide-eyed. "Isn't that why we're here at the Academy? To prepare for the Trial?"

"All I can tell you is that the Candidates will be put to the test in a way that no Seeker has ever been before. There will be danger...and there will be loss. The true test will come in a different form than any of us ever imagined."

"When?" I asked. "Where?"

But Merriwether shook his head. "I don't know. My mind is distracted by thoughts of war, and the Orb is too weak now, too clouded over to offer me any insight. It will be gone within a day, or perhaps merely a few hours. Disappeared from the Academy, off to find its new hiding place." He pulled his eyes to mine, shooting me a disconcertingly sympathetic look. "You, Vega, will soon find yourself making a choice—a difficult one. Doubt will consume you. But you cannot allow it to win. You must do what's right. You must listen to your instincts, just as you've done before."

"I don't understand," I whimpered, sinking into a chair.

"I know." In my grandfather's eyes I could see a helpless agony, as if he wanted to reach for me, to save me from what was coming. "But I have faith that you'll do what's best." Without further explanation he turned to Callum. "Tonight, I will gather seventy fighters, and we will head out at dawn. We'll leave a few instructors and Niala to watch over the Seeker Candidates as well as the remaining students. The Academy will be sealed. No one is to come or go through its gates so long as we're gone… unless they have no other choice."

"You're leaving so soon?" I croaked out, instinctively reaching for Callum, who was standing next to me. But I drew my hand back and tucked it into my lap. "Both of you?"

"Mr. Drake is the most powerful weapon the Academy has," Merriwether said. "Much as I'd love to leave him here, I'm afraid we'll need his help."

Callum's voice deepened into an inhuman growl. "My *dragon's* help, you mean."

I twisted around to see his face contorted into a knot of rage.

"Callum? What's going on?"

"Nothing at all," he replied. "I have a nuclear weapon inside me that's just itching to go off. But don't get me wrong—I'm ever so glad to be of service."

His eyes were like fire, but his voice was even more terrifying. I felt like I was listening to a wild, cornered creature, one who ached to lunge at me, to strike out with razor-sharp talons.

Without another word, Callum strode over to the door and turned to face Merriwether. "Is there anything else, Headmaster?"

Merriwether shook his head. "I'll see you in the morning."

Callum nodded gravely and stormed out, leaving me behind.

"What was *that* all about?" I asked.

"He's not entirely himself right now, because he can feel what's coming. I'm afraid that knowing one's fate can sometimes be more of a curse than a blessing."

"What's *coming*? Is this about the prophecy?"

Merriwether looked at me curiously. "What do you know of it?"

"The other Seekers told me something about it a while ago. They said the heir to the Otherwhere's throne would one day claim what was rightfully his...which seems like a good thing, given who's ruling now."

"Yes, yes," Merriwether replied. "Well, if that were all there was to the prophecy, I suppose there would be nothing much to worry about."

The muscles tensed in my neck and shoulders. "What do you mean?"

"It is said that the heir will retake the throne...but also that he will unleash chaos and devastation on this land. Towns destroyed. Countless dead. The heir, the prophecy foretells, will become a tyrant worse than any we could possibly imagine. Worse, even, than the Usurper Queen. Unless..."

"Unless?"

"Unless he finds the *Ulaidh*—the Treasure."

My brow wrinkled with confusion. What the hell did *that* mean?

"Treasure?"

"I'm afraid I don't know any more than you do about the matter," Merriwether said with a tone of finality. "But now, you should go after Mr. Drake, Vega. He needs you."

"Yes," I said, my brain overloaded both with information and a total lack of it. "Of course."

He was right. It didn't matter what some ancient prophecy predicted. Right now, Callum was hurting, and I needed to make sure he was okay.

I leapt to my feet and sprang over to the door.

"Wait!" Merriwether called out. "One last thing. Very important."

"Yes?" I asked, twisting around to look at him.

"Whatever may happen, don't get yourself killed while we're gone."

"I'll try my best not to."

AFTER A FEW MINUTES, I managed to catch up with Callum at the far end of the Academy in the hall that led toward the eastern tower.

"Are you okay?" I managed, my breath heaving as I jogged along at his side.

"Sure," he replied through gritted teeth. "Why wouldn't I be?"

"Come on. I could see the look on your face back there…" I said, before noticing two curious Zerkers looking our way. "When you mentioned your…*dragon*," I concluded under my breath.

"It was nothing," he said. "It's not important."

"I'm not stupid, Callum."

He stopped and turned to me, not seeming to care about anyone who might be listening. "Fine. You want to know what's upsetting me, Vega? I'm a walking, talking weapon of mass destruction. So I go where I'm needed. That's my lot in life—for *now*. See, weapons of mass destruction are always valuable…until they explode. Which is just one of the many reasons I'll never be able to…"

He stopped, glared at the floor, then resumed his walk without another word.

Against my better judgment I pursued him all the way to base of the tower that housed our living quarters. I reached out and grabbed his arm just in time to stop him from heading up the spiral staircase.

"You can talk to me, you know," I said. "You can tell me anything. I'm…I'm here for you."

"Yeah? Well, did it ever occur to you that maybe you shouldn't be? Or that maybe you should just let me go and forget you ever knew me? Because I'm not good for you, no matter what fairy tales you might concoct inside that mind of yours. I'm not the good guy. I'm a ticking time bomb, just biding my time until I go off and take everyone I care about down with me."

"But I—"

Callum held up a hand. His jaw tense, he nodded toward a narrow slit of a window to his left. "There's a one-sided war being fought out there. Nothing else matters right now. Not you, not me. And we're not doing ourselves any favors by pretending our little fling is even remotely important in the grand scheme of things. So just…forget about me. You'll be better off."

When he turned away from me to stomp his way up the stairs I collapsed against the wall, tears streaming down both cheeks. I felt like the air had been knocked out of my lungs.

The person who'd just spoken to me—the boy who'd just taken an axe to my heart—that wasn't the Callum Drake I knew and loved. It was something lurking deep within him—something that frightened him even more than it frightened me.

Something cold as ice, yet as violently destructive as the hottest flame.

# VISION

ALL NIGHT LONG, my mind shot itself back and forth in violent waves between "Go knock on his door" and "Leave him alone. He doesn't want to talk to you." My head reeled with destructive thoughts.

*Maybe he never really cared about me at all.*

*Not that it matters.*

*It's over now.*

I tried to soothe my injured feelings, to tell myself that after all, he was right. My bruised pride didn't matter, not in the grand scheme of things. My purpose in this place was bigger than a relationship with a boy I'd only known for a few weeks.

But the wretched emotional state brought on by my insomnia and heartbreak wasn't exactly helping me to think rationally.

When dawn finally came and I heard the creak of Callum's door opening, I perched on the edge of my bed, waiting to see if he'd pay me a contrite visit.

But the next sound I heard was his boots hitting the stairs, the rapid thump of his footfalls growing quieter over the course of several seconds.

With each thud, I felt a piece of my heart break away until it seemed like nothing was left.

If I hadn't been certain before, I was now. What we'd had—our fling, our torrid love affair, whatever we did or didn't call it—was at an end.

*He's not the man—or even the boy—I'd hoped he was.*

Unfortunately, condemning myself for daring to feel emotions proved an ineffective strategy. I felt like I'd swallowed a sack of stones that were now weighing me down, preventing me from moving a muscle or even standing up.

The air felt as heavy as I did, as if it had changed into a thick, toxic gas bent on incapacitating me. Nothing made sense anymore. Not my feelings and definitely not my purpose in this place.

Nothing.

After a time, I finally mustered the energy to stand. I headed to the window and opened it, leaning out to look far below into the eastern courtyard, where many of the Academy's troops were gathering.

At their center were two figures: a man with a shock of silvery-gray hair and a young man dressed in golden mail that glinted under the first rays of sunlight.

As I stared down at them, the young man in gold raised his head to look up at me, his bright blue eyes reflecting every ray of morning light.

Pressing his right hand to the left side of his chest, he stared up at me for a long moment, then looked away.

In those few seconds I finally allowed myself to feel something other than misery. I supposed it was hope. Hope that he wasn't so heartless as to reject me without good reason.

Hope that I'd see him again.

It was with that hope that I chose to go on, as I watched him transform into a golden dragon and take off into the sky while the warriors of the Academy marched in orderly rows through a broad set of open double doors.

THE REST of the day passed slowly. The Zerkers who'd been left behind roamed the halls, looking lost. Seeker Candidates whispered to one another, confused and frightened about the rumors of a war that they'd never expected to come so soon.

"What's going to happen to us?" I heard Desmond ask two other Seekers, who responded with shrugs. I wanted to answer him, to reassure him. But I couldn't even reassure myself. I was as lost as anyone, my entire life turned upside down by Callum's coldness and sudden departure.

There was no class that morning, and Miss Carlaw, the tiger shifter, announced at breakfast that in fact, sparring sessions would be suspended for the near future. "You may, of course, practice what you've learned in the Academy's various courtyards. But you must be responsible. Any students caught endangering others will be punished severely. This is not a time for horseplay or risk-taking. And you must always keep an eye out for the enemy."

Niala and Rourke were sitting with me in an uncharacteristically empty corner of the Great Hall. Rourke was in his panther form, stalking uneasily from one end of the table to the other.

"Are you all right?" Niala asked after watching me push my scrambled eggs around my plate for several minutes. "You seem...distracted."

"Hmm? I'm fine," I replied, mustering the weakest smile in history.

"No, you're not."

I chewed on my lip, remembering that Niala was a Healer, among her other skills. Not only could she help a person who was physically injured—she knew perfectly well if someone was suffering inside.

But there was nothing she could do to heal my current emotional state.

"It's Callum, isn't it?" she whispered after checking to make sure no one was close enough to hear us. "I figured you'd be sad he left. But this is something deeper, I can tell."

"Of course you can," I sighed. For a moment I looked at her, then at Rourke, who'd stopped his pacing to stalk back and press the top of his head into my thigh. The gentle pressure soothed my quaking insides. "It's just...something strange happened last night, and I don't know what to make of it."

I filled Niala in on my brief but brutal conversation with Callum. His unusual coldness, the dismissive manner in which he'd pushed me away and told me to forget him. Through it all, I struggled to maintain my composure, to keep my voice from betraying just how awful I really felt.

"He keeps insisting there are things about him I don't know," I said. "Things I wouldn't like. I can't help thinking they're just words, that it's just his way of getting rid of me. He's tired of me and can't figure out a better way to dump me."

Niala sat back and pressed her palms to the table, and I watched as her lips curled into the slightest smile.

"I'm so glad to know you find this amusing," I snapped. "I'm sure you think I'm an idiot for even thinking a guy like Callum could be interested in me."

"Vega, no!" she replied, her grin disappearing immediately. She reached for my hand and gripped it hard. "I wasn't smiling because of your pain. It's just...I know Callum, and I can guess what's going on in his head. And trust me, it's not what you think."

"What...what do you mean?" I stammered, a flutter of hope renewing itself in the far reaches of my mind.

"Well, for one thing, he's clearly in love with you."

I almost snorted. "Oh, yeah. I forgot that guys show their love by telling you you're better off without them, then leaving to fight a war without saying goodbye."

Niala shook her head. "He's protecting you. He's pushing you away because he doesn't want to hurt you."

"Why's he so convinced he'd hurt me? I mean, it's not like I haven't known all along we'd have to break up eventually. We both know our time together is limited. Why can't we just enjoy what time we have?"

"Because *his* time is coming," Niala said. "His dragon will come of age soon, and Callum is afraid of how it may change him."

"Come of age?" I asked. "What are you talking about?"

"It's easiest to explain if I can show you. Come with me."

Niala rose from her seat and took off toward the door with Rourke padding along behind her. Curious, I followed, and we skipped in a half-sprint down several hallways until we came to one I'd seen before, its walls decorated with hovering animations of the Crimson King in battle. I stopped to watch his red dragon take out a battalion of wolves before turning toward a series of small towns in the distance.

"How much has Callum told you about his dragon?" Niala asked, staring at the scene unfolding before us.

"Not a ton. He's said he can be unpredictable, hard to control. But I've never seen that side. Callum always appears to have total control over him."

"That's because he hasn't been fully tested yet."

"I don't understand."

"Watch," Niala said, gesturing to the floating scene before us.

I obeyed, observing as the Crimson King's dragon dove toward the villages, spreading his wings wide. A long stream of flame shot from his mouth, burning houses and barns as people ran screaming from their homes.

"What's happening?" I asked. "Are those his enemies?"

Niala shook her head. "Those are—*were*—his people. The people of the Otherwhere. It's an incident that occurred many years ago. It became known as the *Great Shame*."

She turned and walked away, and once again, I followed. "There are men in the world—and women, of course—who are strong. Powerful. But no human—not even the Crimson King—is as strong-willed as a dragon."

When we reached a stone bench some distance down the hall, we sat and faced one another, and Rourke lay down at Niala's feet.

"At first, the Crimson King ruled the Otherwhere with kindness. For many, many years, they say, he was well loved. He never killed unless he was at war, and even then, it was only the enemy forces who suffered, never civilians. But his dragon had other plans."

"What plans?" I asked with trepidation.

"There are two significant moments in a dragon shifter's life." Niala turned to gaze out the window beside us. "The day their human side comes of age, and the day their dragon does. Somewhere in between is when human and dragon first begin to co-exist."

"Callum told me it happened late for him," I said.

"Yes. His parents kept him trapped as long as they could, thinking they could inhibit the change. But a dragon is too powerful. It will eventually find its way into the world, just as Callum's did. That was nearly a hundred years ago now, not long after the day he turned eighteen."

If I hadn't been sitting down, I would have fallen to my knees. I'd always known Callum was older than I was.

But putting an actual number to his age was a shock.

"He's over a hundred years old..." I stammered. "I mean, I've always known he's been around a long time. I just didn't know it was *that* long."

"Sort of, yes—he's old, and yet not so old. The day his dragon came into the world, his human side stopped aging. He has spent every day since then learning to control the beast inside him. It's one reason Callum has kept to himself for so many years. He doesn't seek out relationships. Meeting you was like a curveball that threw him completely off his game. He's always been cautious for fear of hurting people. But with you—well, I think he found you too hard to resist."

I felt myself redden. "He's been single for so long," I murmured. "It's hard to fathom how lonely his life has been."

Niala nodded. "Still, he probably hasn't felt the years as you might expect. A shifter doesn't age like some of us do. Then again, no one in the Otherwhere ages the way someone from your world would expect them to. The point is, right now, Callum's concern is his dragon. He knows it's about to reach a milestone, and not an easy one. When a dragon hits its one hundredth birthday, its powers begin to truly develop, much as you Seekers find your powers around your seventeenth birthday. It's the day of his *Naming*, the day when his identity—his nature —becomes fully formed. It's then that the Dragon shifter is truly put to the test."

"When exactly does his dragon turn one hundred?" I asked.

With a frown, Niala shrugged. "Callum probably doesn't even know, given all his family did to keep the truth about his nature from him when he was young. But it's got to be soon. A few months. Maybe as little as a few weeks."

"Weeks…" I breathed.

"It doesn't mean the Callum we know will change, at least not right away," Niala assured me. "The Crimson King managed to keep his dragon at bay for centuries before the Great Shame. But Callum is afraid he won't be strong enough to hold his dragon in check once the day of the Naming comes. He's already had one or two close calls—times when he's fought Waergs in distant woods. He confided to me once that he felt it then, a sort of foreshadowing of the bloodlust that comes with fully sharing his life with a dragon. He's afraid he won't be able to rein the beast in, to live up to the Crimson King's years of goodness...that he'll simply prove too weak. It makes him fear closeness to another person, as you can imagine."

"But he's so strong," I said. "So even-tempered."

"Sometimes that's not enough. Imagine yourself trying to hold back a dozen charging horses who are far stronger than you'll ever be. Then replace them with a beast as powerful as a dragon. All the strength in the world isn't always enough."

"I can't even *begin* to imagine it," I said, feeling defeated.

"For the Crimson King's dragon, it was a sort of constant rage that eventually took over and led to mass destruction. Rage against those who'd betrayed him over the years—the civilians who doubted him, who had once wanted to keep him from the throne. Rage, even, against the armies who had once joined him as allies. So much rage the king couldn't hold the beast back when it decided to strike. He killed thousands before finally regaining control. But by then, it was too late."

"Oh my God. That's awful."

Niala nodded. "The king decided the only honorable course of action would be to surrender the throne. For a time, his nephew—Callum's father—took over. But he fell ill and surrendered the throne four years later, and then the battle began to determine who would succeed him. It should have been Callum, of course. He was the older child. The proper heir."

I stared at the white wall opposite where we sat. "But Callum's family didn't want him to take over. Because...?"

"Because they knew what he might eventually become. And, as much as I despise the woman, it wasn't the Usurper Queen's decision alone. Some part of Callum allowed the seat to be taken from him, knowing what might eventually come to pass. He could have fought for the throne. He could have killed them, if he'd wanted to."

"He would never do that," I said. My chest grew heavy,

drawing me down into a slouch as my eyes moved to the floor. "I've always wondered why he didn't fight harder for what was rightfully his, why he allowed his sister to steal the title. His family's story is so much more complicated than I ever knew."

Niala nodded. "Callum is the best of humanity. He would give his life to protect someone he cares about. Multiply that by tens of thousands, and you can imagine what he would do to protect the Otherwhere." Her lips twitched into a sad smile. "He would even break his own heart, if it meant keeping you from harm."

A sting settled into my eyes then, a sense of fleeting joy mixed with a raw, brutal pain unlike anything I'd ever felt. If Niala was right—if Callum was really on the verge of experiencing something momentous—I wanted to be there for him when the time came. But here I was, stuck at the Academy with no way to talk to him. No way to tell him I cared, that no matter what, I would be here for him.

Then, like a jolt, it hit me.

I rose to my feet. "I have to go!" I said.

"Where?"

"Merriwether's office. There's something I need to do."

"Vega…"

But I was already walking. "I know, I know," I called over my shoulder. "I promise I won't do anything stupid."

"Why do I get the feeling that's a promise you can't keep?"

# THE ORB'S LAST STAND

INSTEAD OF HEADING straight to the Headmaster's office, which I knew would be locked, I took a detour to my quarters. Once inside, I summoned a door and unlocked it, stepping through into Merriwether's familiar retreat.

His desk stood in front of me, beckoning. I darted around it and pulled open the drawer where he kept the flickering Orb of Kilarin.

Instead of extracting it from its hiding place, I knelt down and stared at the pale purple light emanating from inside.

"Show me," I said softly. "Show me where they are."

The Orb went cloudy, a swirl of purple mist twisting around inside before seeming to settle to the bottom, only to rise up to reveal bits and pieces of a confusing scene. I tried to decipher the image, but it was like trying to piece together fragments of a forgotten dream.

A golden dragon soaring through the sky.

Ruins far below.

Merriwether leading a small army.

A man beside him with a long beard.

On all sides, they were surrounded by armor-clad Grells, Zerkers, Casters, and Rangers.

In the distance, brandishing weapons, were men of various sizes flanked by enormous wolves, all led by Isla, the Usurper Queen, astride a creature that looked like a cross between a horse and a ram.

The war had begun.

Only it *hadn't*.

Not really.

No one was fighting. No one was even advancing. Our side looked confused, as though they were searching their way through a field of mist and illusion. They neither advanced nor retreated, and all I could gather was that they were too wary to choose a direction.

As I watched, Isla shouted something to her men, and they turned on their heels to run in the opposite direction. From what I could see, those in human form were laughing as they retreated.

If this was a war, it was weirdly jovial. At least, on the enemy's side.

"I don't get it," I muttered. "What are they doing? And where *are* they?"

The one thing I couldn't make out was the setting. Everything was a rolling fog, an uncertain blur that came and went in waves before the Orb finally turned completely dark, leaving me with nothing.

With a groan of defeat, I sank to the floor and pushed the drawer closed. It was stupid of me to think I could open a door to our army's location. Even if I'd been able to figure out where they were, there was no way I could have gone to talk to Callum. Merriwether would lose his mind. Not to mention that it could endanger our fighters—or me—if a Seeker showed up unannounced.

I wouldn't blame one of our own for putting an arrow through my chest, thinking I was the enemy.

I'd have to wait until they came back. I'd hold onto hope that they'd win the battle—if it ever actually took place. That they would return, and then I could tell Callum what I'd been feeling since the moment Niala had revealed his deepest fear to me.

I SPENT the rest of the day wandering aimlessly through the Academy's corridors. Rifling my way through books in my room. Pacing, restless, along the Grove's rows of fruit trees.

Through it all, I kept telling myself I would find a way to see Callum again, and soon.

After dinner I retreated once again to my quarters, tucking myself into bed early in hopes of making the following day come sooner. But my sleep was fitful at best, my dreams filled with visions of fire and fighting, of enormous fanged creatures embroiled in bloody combat.

I woke up in the morning to find myself breathing heavily, my sheets damp with sweat. I felt useless, helpless.

Trapped as we were at the Academy, the Seekers were contributing nothing to the cause. Surely there was something, anything, we could do to help bring Merriwether and Callum home?

The answer to my question came at breakfast.

# DECISIONS

IN THE MORNING, I found Niala and Rourke seated at their usual table in the Great Hall. After grabbing my meal of eggs and toast, I slid into the seat next to Niala, who was staring at the table of Seekers on the far side of the room.

"What's so fascinating?" I asked with a smirk.

"They're plotting," Niala said. "Something's up."

"Plotting what?"

"Who can say?"

I turned to observe the Seekers, who were seated around the table, leaning in conspiratorially. Raff was on his feet, speaking to them in hushed tones. The others looked intrigued, as if they were hanging on his every word.

Which didn't sit well with me.

"What's his deal, anyhow?" Niala asked me, nodding in his direction.

"I wish I could tell you. He confuses me constantly. He started off so great. I really thought we were friends. Then, the next minute..."

"Yeah, I know. He was trying to slice your head off. He's a strange one, for sure. Some of the Zerkers have taken a real liking to him, which is always a bad sign. And right now, he bears a striking resemblance to Rourke when he's in his cat form, about to pounce on a mouse."

"Well then, that would mean the other Seekers are the mice," I chuckled. "And they're about to get eaten."

Niala's voice dropped, and she stared over at Raff through a tight squint. "The question is, why would he be luring them in?"

With a sudden jerk of his head, Raff turned our way, said something to our peers, then strode over to our table.

"Vega," he called out, his tone cool. "Would you come join us? I have a question to ask all the Seekers, and I want you there."

I shot Niala an inquiring look. "Go for it," she said, pushing her chair away from the table. "I have to go find Miss Carlaw, anyhow. We want to arrange some activities for tomorrow in hopes of keeping everyone from going stir-crazy in this place."

Hesitant but curious, I followed Raff to the table of Seekers and sat down opposite him, while the others stopped whispering and focused their attention on us both.

"Now that Vega's here, I can give you all the details," Raff said, looking around as if to make sure we weren't being spied on, his voice barely above a whisper.

"Details?" I asked. "What's going on?"

"Raff has a plan!" Desmond blurted out. "To help Merriwether."

My heart bounced around in my chest. "Really? Help?" I asked. "How?"

Helping Merriwether meant bringing him back. Which meant bringing Callum back. Even if he didn't want to see me, I wanted—*needed*—him to be safe. The thought of him out there fighting the queen's loyal army of sadists was more than I could bear.

Raff leaned forward, interlocking both hands on the table. "The queen's armies have moved out of her castle, right?" he asked. "And by all accounts, she's with them."

My stomach turned. He couldn't—*wouldn't*—be saying what I thought he was saying.

"You're not about to suggest we head to Uldrach, are you? Because I—"

He shook his head and chuckled. "Of course not. Do you really think I'd ever want to go back there?"

"So, what then?"

He fixed his gaze on mine before looking around the table again. "The queen wouldn't leave the Sword of Viviane unguarded in the castle. So it occurred to me that she must have had it moved to a safe location. Somewhere far away. Somewhere secret."

Everyone at the table was staring at him, eager to hear the next part.

"Well, I might just know where it is," he said, leaning back in his seat.

I narrowed my eyes at him, trying to figure out if he was lying or just being cocky. "That's just a theory," I said, trying to mask my disappointment. "There's no way you could know."

"Now, now, Sloane, I was getting to that," he said with a crooked smirk. "I *do* know where it is, in fact. It's in the same place where we—I mean *I*—found it the first time."

"How could you possibly know that?" I snapped.

By now, the other Candidates were glaring at me, irritated that I was ruining Raff's intriguing plan with sensible questions.

"I just know," he said with an exasperated huff. "I'm a Seeker, remember?"

"So are we," I said, gesturing to the others. "But I'd be willing to bet no one at this table claims to know where the Sword of Viviane is. It's not like we're psychic."

For a second, Raff looked flummoxed, like I'd hit on something he didn't want to acknowledge. "Well, maybe *I* am," he said defensively. "Maybe it's one of my powers."

I sat back, my arms crossed.

"If you're psychic, what am I thinking right now?"

"That's too easy." Raff let out a snicker. "But I can't tell you on account of the fact that there are ladies present."

"Good guess. Fine. I'll humor you. Describe the hiding place for us."

A sly smile slipped over Raff's lips. "Of course. But not until you agree that we should all head there, together. We should go as a group, get the sword, and bring it back to the Academy."

"We can't, Genius. Merriwether wants us to stay put, or had you forgotten that small detail?"

"Since when do you care about rules? You're the one who went to the queen's castle without permission in the first place."

"Yeah, well…" I began. But he was right. I'd done nothing but break rules since my arrival in the Otherwhere. "Still, it's dangerous."

Oleana leaned forward to interject. "Raff does have a point. I mean, it's a secret location, so there probably won't be a ton of guards. And with the queen and her army out waging a war, we could probably just walk in and take the sword, even if there are a few Waergs around."

The others began chattering amongst themselves while Raff sat back, watching, a smug grin on his face.

"Vega could open the portal for us," Desmond said, having decided he was firmly in favor of the plan. "If Raff describes it to her." He turned my way. "Right?"

"I haven't even agreed to go!" I protested.

But it seemed the others had made up their minds. "Look," Meg said, "We're Seekers. It's our job to find the Relics. Raff's right—if we get our hands on the sword, we'll give Merriwether and the others the advantage. The queen will lose some of her power. It's a no-brainer."

I shook my head. "It's not as simple as you think," I said. "I walked into her castle like it was nothing. It seemed so easy. But it was a trap, all of it. She knew I was coming. She may see this coming, too."

"But we're not *going* to the castle," Oleana said. "They don't have your brother or your friend imprisoned this time. They won't expect us."

I sucked in a breath and looked around the table. Every set of eyes was staring me down, pressuring me to give in.

"You're sure it's not in the queen's castle?" I asked Raff. "You've…seen it?"

He nodded. "I'm positive. But if it makes you feel better, why don't you summon a door to the Throne Room so you can look for yourself? If I'm wrong, no harm done."

I hated to admit it, but he had a point. Looking through a door probably wouldn't put me or anyone else in danger.

I drew myself to my feet and stepped away from the table, calling up a Breach. When I opened it, instead of stepping through, I merely peered into the enormous Throne Room with its dome of stained glass, taking in the red and gold throne, the braziers, the colorful stained-glass windows…

But the sword no longer hung over the throne.

With shallow, rapid-fire breaths, I slammed the door and waited for it to disappear before turning back to the others.

"Let me think about the plan," I said. "I need some time."

"Fine," Raff said, pushing himself to his feet. "You have until nightfall. If you don't want to help by then, we'll just have to find our own way."

# THE CHOICE

AT LUNCHTIME, I found Niala at a secluded table in the Great Hall and told her we needed to talk.

"What's going on?" she asked when I'd planted myself next to her.

I filled her in on Raff's plan and the other Seekers' enthusiasm. How he wanted me to open a portal so we could retrieve the Sword of Viviane from its hiding place. "Everyone wants to contribute. I get it," I said. "I mean, I want to help Merriwether and…everyone who's with him…of course. But I'm not sure about this plan. It just doesn't feel right."

"Ah. So this was what he was conspiring about this morning," Niala replied. She seemed oddly unsurprised as she took a bite of her sandwich. "So, what are you going to do?"

I stared at her, stunned. "I was hoping you'd tell me. I thought Merriwether left you and the others in charge of the decision-making around here. Shouldn't you tell Miss Carlaw to expel me or something? Students aren't supposed to leave the Academy, remember?"

"Yeah, about that…" Niala peered around, waiting for a couple of faculty members to wander by before continuing. "Merriwether didn't *exactly* leave us in charge." A strange expression took over her cat-like eyes. "But he *did* say something odd to me before he left."

"Oh?"

"He told me not to let Miss Carlaw or anyone else know if you made any moves that were…out of the ordinary. He said I should support you in his absence, no matter what. I believe his exact words were, 'Look after her. Don't let her out of your sight. And when she chooses her path, help her, because she will need you like she's seldom needed anyone.'"

I crossed my arms and gave Niala my best "Give me a break" stare. I genuinely couldn't tell if she was kidding or not.

"It's true," she protested. "I know it sounds strange, but that's what he said."

"Maybe he did, but he was probably talking about something else entirely. I can't imagine he'd think it's a great idea for me to lead a bunch of novice Seekers into a potentially dangerous situation."

"He might, if that dangerous situation was for a good cause."

"What cause could possibly be that good?"

"How about the preservation of freedom, saving the Academy, and preventing the painful deaths of half the people living in the Otherwhere?"

"You're exaggerating."

"No, I'm telling you to ask yourself when you've ever known *Merriwether* to exaggerate."

I let out a prolonged, resigned sigh. "He did tell me I'd have a choice to make. I suppose this must be what he was talking about. It's just…much as I'd like to…"

"Don't you trust him?"

"Yeah. Of course I do."

"Then the only other important question is, do you trust yourself?" Niala asked.

"I guess. Well, most of the time."

"So weigh the pros and cons of your decision. Then commit to it."

"I think I already have," I said, a familiar nausea swirling its way through my stomach. "But Merriwether was definitely right about one thing. I'm going to need your help. The Seeker Candidates have skills, but it's not like any of us has ever actually fought a Waerg."

"Tell me what you need."

"I need you and Rourke to meet me here at dinnertime. If you come with us, I'll feel a lot better."

"What about the other Casters and the Zerkers? They could help in a fight."

I thought about it for a second. She was right, of course. Some of our classmates were good fighters. Disciplined and aggressive, bordering on ruthless. But if we were really going off to a secret location to retrieve the sword, this needed to be a stealth operation. Bringing a horde of students with us would increase our visibility, which meant exponentially increasing the danger level.

"No," I said after a pause. "That's way too many wild cards. At this point, the fewer people involved, the better."

"I'll get the instructors to set up a class for the Zerkers after dinner to keep them out of the way."

"Great," I said. "So, we'll meet here in a few hours?"

Grinning from ear to ear, Niala slapped both palms on the table and stood up. "Your wish is my command, your majesty."

Suppressing a chuckle, I muttered, "Don't you ever call me that again."

As promised, I met up with Niala and Rourke at dinnertime, and after we'd finished eating, we headed to the Seekers' dorm.

"The Zerkers are heading to the eastern courtyard," Niala told me as we walked. "We set them up with a class called *Stabbing 101,* which should keep them occupied for hours."

"Good call," I replied.

I was wearing a tunic of fine silver mail under my silver Seeker's gear, my small dagger sheathed at my side. I should have felt confident and prepared, but by the time we arrived at the dorm's door, my hands were shaking with anticipation and fear.

All I wished for in that moment was to be able to talk to Callum. To fix what had broken between us, and to ask for his advice.

His voice had gone quiet in my mind since he'd left, and each time I tried to reach for him, I was met with an anguished near-silence—the sound of wind making its way between the trees of a dying forest.

Despite Niala's reassurance about my relationship with him, I was all too aware of the deep gulf that had formed between us, one I was starting to think we'd never find a way to cross.

I tried to push him from my mind as I opened the door and stepped into the room to find all the Academy's Seeker Candidates sitting on their beds.

All, that was, except for Raff.

"Niala and I have talked it over," I said as the Seekers stood in unison to stare expectantly at us. "We're with you. But—"

My words cut off by Raff, who appeared in the open doorway behind me.

"So you'll help?"

I turned his way and attempted to smile. "We will. If what Merriwether says is true, the sword is too important for us not to take this chance."

"And it could be the only chance we have," Raff said, nodding his agreement and throwing me what appeared to be a genuinely warm smile. He scanned Niala and the Seekers before locking his eyes onto mine once again. "You can get us there, right?"

"I need you to give me a graphic description of the place we're going. The more detail, the better."

"Of course!" Beaming, he turned to the others. "Gear up, everyone. We're going through one of Sloane's famous doors."

The other Seeker Candidates giggled and murmured, excited to have something to do that sounded both vitally important and relatively painless at once.

"This'll be a simple mission," Raff said, his voice low and laced with intrigue. "We head to the location. Find the sword. A Seeker will have to grab it. And Vega will get us back here before anyone knows we're gone." He brushed his hands and snapped his fingers. "Simple."

"I'll believe it when I see it," I muttered, recalling what had happened the last time I'd headed off on what I'd *thought* would be a simple mission.

When everyone had dressed in their sparring gear, I turned to Raff once again. Niala was standing to my left and Rourke, in his black panther form, stood to my right.

"So tell me," I said. "Where, exactly, are we going?"

Raff's eyes narrowed as the other Candidates leaned in to listen. "Picture a tall, steep hill," he said. "A narrow path zig-zags its way up one side. At the top is a huge and very old sandstone castle. Its base is coated in thick green moss, and its west tower is half-collapsed. Its other three towers are ready to fall, too. Somewhere inside is a chapel."

"Chapel?"

"Technically, yes. But it's bigger than most chapels. It's a huge space."

"Like a gym or an auditorium?"

"Even bigger. With stone columns rising up to the vaulted roof. Wooden support beams. Stained-glass windows. Marble floor. Lots of dust and debris around the edges."

"Sounds cool," Desmond beamed from the far side of the dorm.

Raff shook his head. "It's not. It's dirty. It's also old, aban-doned, and probably ten seconds away from collapsing in on itself."

"But it's where the sword is," Desmond mumbled. "Right?"

Raff nodded.

"So, is that where Vega's taking us?" Meg asked.

"No. It's too dangerous to head directly to the chapel, in case it's already falling to pieces or something. It's safer to aim for the front of the castle. There's a set of large black wooden doors, but they won't be locked. They don't even close properly."

"Then that's where we'll go," I said. "Can you describe the doors?"

"They're big, as I said. Ten feet high. Thick. Heavy. They have iron hinges the size of my forearm."

"I need more. More details. More about the doors."

"They're old and splintered, but you can still make out the detail of the engravings." Raff glanced over at me out of the corner of his eye. "Wolves. And not the noble, protective kind. The engravings are twisted. Deformed. Deadly. They're ravenous. Feasting. They're swarming over piles of bodies and bones."

Desmond's eyes grew wide. "Bodies and bones?"

"Of dragons."

The room fell into a stunned silence as Raff shrugged. "What can I tell you? Those are the doors we need to get through before we find the chapel."

"All right," I replied at last, my jaw grinding under a sudden onslaught of nerves. "I'll see what I can do."

I shut my eyes and pictured the scene he'd described, tracing my mind over the the zigzagging trail leading up the hill, the castle with its crumbling towers, and the horrific description of the engravings on the doors.

At last, the hazy picture solidified in my mind. I could smell damp grass and stale air as I stared at an ancient structure with narrow, alabaster windows and half-ruined parapets. As the image grew more vivid, my focus zoomed in on the ominous black doors.

Something called to me from behind them…faintly…beckoning without words.

*The sword.*

I could feel its presence. Its call was one of anguish. Of pain. And of…urgency?

"We need to hurry," I said, my voice barely rising above a whisper. "We need to get there soon."

"She did it!" someone called out as I opened my eyes to see a door standing in the middle of the room. On its surface was an engraving of a beautiful castle, its banners waving in the breeze like something out of a fairy tale.

Something told me the place we were headed wouldn't look quite so idyllic.

"Really? *That's* where we're going?" Desmond asked.

"That's definitely it," Raff said. "And with any luck, we'll be back before anyone even realizes we're gone."

He threw me a nod, and I proceeded to unlock the door and step through with Raff, Niala, Rourke, and the other Seeker Candidates following close behind.

We found ourselves standing on a windy hilltop in front of the black doors Raff had described. The sun was setting in the distance, a canvas of purple and orange clouds decorating the sky. The air was heavy and cold, and I suddenly missed the welcoming shelter of the Academy's walls.

Rourke padded up next to me, his shoulder pressing into my thigh.

"What do you think?" I asked him. "Is it safe?"

He answered with a low growl.

"He's wary," Niala said, stepping over to his other side. "But he hasn't yet picked up any threatening scents."

"That's good, I suppose," I said.

Raff, his eyes glinting, swung around to face us. "Let's head in.

The sooner we get the sword, the sooner we can get back to the Academy and get some sleep."

Without waiting for a response, he pushed the castle's heavy front doors open and strode through with the rest of us padding along behind.

# MISSION

Following Raff, we pushed our way through the huge double doors and stepped into a vast, windowless foyer.

"It's very…dark in this place," Oleana said with a shiver.

"Can you get us to the chapel from here?" I asked Raff.

He swung his head from left to right, taking a second to examine the walls and the floors of the two low-ceilinged corridors branching out in opposite directions.

"I'm not sure. The hallways in this castle are like a maze. Maybe we should split up."

"I don't know…," I started to say, but Raff stepped in front of me, calling out to two of the Seeker Candidates to join him.

"Crane and Talia," he said, pointing to a boy who was almost seven feet tall and a short, dark-haired girl. I didn't know either of them well, though Crane was famous around the Academy for his remarkable height. "Come with me. A few of you should stay here, and the rest should head down the other corridor. Whichever group finds the chapel, send someone back to get the others." With that, he took off with his two companions.

I started to protest—after all, Merriwether had wanted me to make the decisions—but Niala, sensing my discomfort, gave my arm a squeeze. "Don't worry about it. The important thing is for us to find the sword, right?"

"Right," I sighed before turning to the others. "Olly, Meg, Desmond—come with us," I called out, gathering a small group together.

Leaving the others behind, we headed down the second of the two dark hallways, mindful not to stumble over the scraps of old armor, shattered stone, or weaponry that littered the ground. I watched as Rourke sniffed around, finding nothing and no one— which I supposed was as good a sign as I could hope for.

"The place does seem empty," I said after a time. "But something feels...I don't know...off. Like we're not supposed to be here."

"Agreed," Niala said, her eyes fixed on a spot in the distance.

By now, Rourke had trotted twenty or so feet ahead of my team, his nose to the ground like a hunting dog. With a sudden jerk of his frame, he stopped and pulled his head up, freezing in place.

"What is it?" I asked. I could feel the others cowering behind me in fear of what they might see.

"I don't know," Niala replied. "But if I were to guess, I'd say there's—"

A blood-curdling scream filled the air, cutting off her words like the plummeting blade of a guillotine.

# TROUBLE

"IT CAME FROM BEHIND US!" Meg shouted, pointing back toward the foyer.

Our group raced down the narrow hall, frantically leaping over the mounds of detritus strewn on the stone floor until we came to the black doors where the other Seekers were now huddled together, looking terrified. I was relieved, at least, to realize it wasn't any of them who had screamed.

"I...I think the sound came from the way Raff and the others went," said Estée, a blond-haired Seeker from France.

Rourke, who seemed to agree with her, was already stalking along the hallway opposite us, his nose close to the ground.

"Everyone, stay behind me," I commanded.

Leading the group, I followed Rourke down the corridor until a horrifying sight stopped me in my tracks. I froze, reaching for Niala's arm with one hand while holding the other up to keep my fellow Seekers from advancing.

"What is it?" asked Meg, who was already stepping around me to look. When her eyes met the scene before us, she gasped and stifled a sob.

Crane and Talia, the two Seekers who had accompanied Raff,

were lying on the floor, blood pooling around their torsos between the smooth cobblestones.

Niala sprinted forward and crouched down next to the unmoving Seekers.

"Are they...dead?" Meg asked, her voice filled with horror.

"No," Niala said, placing a hand over Talia's chest, which was soaked in blood.

The others and I watched, still as statues, as Niala recited a quiet incantation, her hand hovering over our fellow students' wounds.

Next to me, Meg was sniffling and shaking, her voice quaking into a high-pitched sob. "Were they stabbed? Shot? *What happened?*"

"Attacked by an animal, I think," Niala replied, shooting me a look of quiet terror, as if she'd figured out something she didn't want to share with the others just yet. "I'll try my best to heal them, but I can't make any promises."

The others and I watched, still as statues, as she recited a quiet incantation, her hand hovering over Crane's wounds.

"I'm starting to think," Desmond muttered, "we should all head back to the Academy."

"We can't," I replied. "Not without the sword."

By now, both Seekers were awake, moaning in pain as Niala and Oleana helped them to sit up.

"What happened?" I asked.

Crane gazed up at me through glossy eyes, his chest heaving hard. "Not...sure. Got...attacked. It happened too fast to see properly."

Talia grimaced in pain but managed a weak nod. "Whatever it was...I think...I think it got Raff."

Niala called Meg and Desmond over. "Help me get them to their feet."

"Is it a good idea to move them?" I asked. "Shouldn't they stay here and rest?"

Niala shook her head. "Do you really want to leave them here, when whatever attacked them could come back?"

I chewed the insides of my cheeks. "No," I replied. "Of course, you're right. But maybe they should at least go back to the Academy's infirmary. I can summon a door..."

But the two injured Seekers shook their heads and waved me back.

"No," Crane said. "If we go back—if they find out what we've been up to—they'll try and stop you. Then we'll have no sword, and we'll all be in a ton of trouble."

"But..."

"We *need* to get that sword," Talia said through an insistent grunt. "We're Seekers, right? All for one, and one for all?"

"That's Musketeers," I retorted, and Talia replied with a weak chuckle.

"They'll be okay," Niala said. "For a while. A *short* while. Hopefully it'll be long enough for us to grab the sword and get out of here."

"Then we need to get moving. And we've got to find Raff. If there are Waergs around..."

"Waergs?" Desmond shot out. I wanted to kick myself for uttering the word.

"Or something else," I said. "It could have been anything."

"You said *Waergs*. As in giant wolves."

"I'm sorry. I take it back. Now let's get on with things so we can head home in one piece, shall we?"

After silently agreeing to our plan, we made our way down the hall, looking for any sign that Raff had been dragged away by whatever had attacked the other two. But the floor, dirty as it was, was devoid of clues, and we only had Rourke's keen nose to guide us.

He led us down corridor after corridor in a disorienting zigzag—right, left, right, left, until we reached what looked like another enormous foyer, its stone walls half caved in on one side.

At the end of the next hallway, we reached a set of arched wooden doors.

"The chapel?" Niala asked.

"There's only one way to find out," I replied, trying to mask the nervousness fluttering inside my chest.

I pushed the doors open, and we stepped into a cavernous room with a towering vaulted ceiling that arched so high above us that I was convinced I was staring at the night sky...until I realized that I was. Half the ceiling had long since collapsed, leaving a series of gaping holes.

Narrow, elegantly carved stone pillars climbed for what looked like hundreds of feet between stained glass windows, and thick wooden beams ran in angled rows high above us. Some of the pillars had huge chunks taken out of them, as though someone had taken a battering ram to them for sport.

The room was exactly as Raff had described: massive, but ready to collapse at the slightest provocation.

Moonlight seeped in through the colorful, smoky glass of the windows, highlighting the exquisite designs on their surfaces.

The chapel was largely empty, its floor bare except for what looked like a large stone altar sitting on a low platform at the far end.

Hurrying, I made my way forward, only to realize what I'd been staring at wasn't an altar. It was a thick-walled stone coffin.

Its edges were chipped and crumbled, but the rest of its surfaces were clean and smooth.

As a few other Seekers leaned in to examine it, a hard, a thunderous *thud* echoed through the room, shaking the delicate windows in their frames.

When a panicked voice cried out, "Look! The doors!" I spun around to see that the entrance we'd come through had slammed shut.

"Open them! Hurry!" I shouted.

Meg, the fastest of us, shot over to yank on the doors' handles, but failed to move them so much as an inch.

"We're locked in!" she called out over her shoulder. "Someone's jammed them from the other side."

"You two!" I called to Desmond and Oleana, gesturing toward one of the chapel's dark corners. "We need to bring Crane and Talia over there until we're ready to leave. Until we know what's out in that hallway, they need to remain out of sight."

Together, we helped the wounded Seekers limp over and sit down against the cool wall, making sure they were comfortable.

"We'll work as quickly as we can," I assured them. "I need you two to stay put. Understand?"

They nodded weakly, and I could tell they were grateful not to have to exert themselves.

"Raff was right," I said, spinning around to face the stone coffin. "The sword is in this place. I understand now."

"I don't care about the sword," Desmond whimpered. "We need to go back to the Academy. Please, Vega."

"It's okay, Des." I turned to him and placed a hand on each of his shoulders. Staring into his eyes, I recited the verse I'd learned in the queen's prison.

*"On an ancient hill stands the oldest house*
*Where glass and stone conceal a prize.*
*Ancient as the world itself,*
*On a king's chest it lies."*

"What are you on about?" he asked, his cheeks flushed with fear, irritation, or possibly both.

"I've been trying to figure out why this place feels weirdly familiar," I said. "When I was in the prison, Raff told me that verse—he said it was the one that led the queen's servants to this place. This is where the Relic had been hiding. And it's where it's hiding again—though why it's returned, I can't say. All I know is I don't think the queen's men brought it here."

"So what do we do?"

I pulled my eyes to the coffin. "We need to open it. Now." I looked around at the others. "This is it," I said. "It's what Merriwether was talking about. *This* is the Seekers' Trial."

"But the lid's got to weigh a ton," Oleana protested. "There's no way any one person can open it on their own."

"So we do it together," I replied. "We work as a team."

Niala signaled several Seekers to come help. We gathered around the coffin and, with some effort, managed to pry up the lid and set it on its side on the floor.

For a few seconds, everyone kept their distance, staring at the open casket, too frightened to approach.

Summoning all my courage, I inched forward until I managed to peer over its edge. Inside were the skeletal remains of a man suited in tarnished silver armor. Sitting at an angle next to his skull was a helmet that looked almost like a crown.

"*On a king's chest it lies,*" I whispered.

Clasped in the man's bony hands was a long silver sword. The same weapon I'd seen suspended inside the queen's Throne Room.

The Sword of Viviane.

"You didn't belong with her, did you?" I said softly as I stared at the blade. "You found your way back here, because you weren't where you meant to be. You came back to wait for us."

"Can we just grab it and leave?" Desmond asked, clearly irritated.

Relieved murmurs of approval made their way through the small crowd. "We're finished here, right?" Meg asked.

My lips curled up in a smile. I was about to tell them we just needed to find Raff when a bank of torches flickered to life around the perimeter of the room, lighting the space in a shocking, unnatural manner.

"Finished?" a voice echoed through the chapel. "We're just getting started."

# BETRAYAL

I swung around, hoping I'd only imagined the voice.

When my eyes met those of the speaker, I reached out with both hands, desperate for support. But there was no one there. No one to keep me from falling. No one to tell me everything would be all right.

Those silver eyes had chilled my blood once before. And I'd thought of them a thousand times since.

I was surrounded by my classmates, yet I felt utterly alone, my heart hammering so loudly that I could scarcely remember what silence felt like.

"You," I mouthed, but the word came out like something halfway between a gasp and a sob.

As the man stepped forward, the chapel's torches seemed to take on new life, their flames glowing blue, then orange, then yellow, as if in excited reaction to his presence.

Niala edged over to my left side, her hand on Rourke's back as the panther crouched low, hissing, his ears flat back against his head. "You know this man?" she whispered.

"I've seen him once, in the queen's Throne Room." I lifted my eyes to meet his and raised my voice. "I was hoping never to see him again."

"Come now, Miss Sloane." The silver-eyed man clicked his tongue. "But where are my manners? I should have introduced myself the last time we faced one another. My name is Lumus. You are, of course, acquainted with my wife, Isla. I believe you refer to her as the Usurper Queen."

It shouldn't have surprised me, and yet it did, to think that horrid woman could have a husband. Or that this strange, terrifying man could have a wife.

"I believe you know my son as well," he added.

"Son?" I inhaled the word.

As if on cue, a tall, broad-shouldered young man stepped into the doorway to stand next to Lumus, his keen blue eyes narrowing with malevolent pleasure.

Nausea overtook me then. I struggled to keep myself from doubling over.

My throat was dry, my hands shaking.

"Raff? But…you were in the prison…"

Raff gave me a lip-sneer and a condescending eye-roll, but it was Lumus who stepped forward to answer.

"Come now, Vega. Raff may have been in the prison, but you know perfectly well that he was *never* a prisoner."

Behind me, the other Seekers were murmuring amongst themselves, as shocked as I was.

"Vega?" Desmond whimpered. "What's going on?"

On hearing his voice, Lumus shot him an angry glare. I put up a hand to silence him, terrified of what the silver-eyed man might do.

"Never a prisoner?" I asked, drawing his attention back to me. "Then what was he?"

"He was insurance, in case you turned down Isla's offer," Lumus boasted. "A key to grant us access to the Academy, and to bring all of its illustrious Seekers here, to gather in one place for an evening of entertainment."

My eyes shot back and forth between Lumus and Raff, too confused to focus on either of them.

Raff snickered with malicious satisfaction.

"But we *were* locked up," I stammered. "You were in that cell. I found you there. We escaped…together."

"Sure, I was in the cell. But technically," he snickered, "I was never actually locked up."

"I don't understand. That whole time we talked…you told me about your mother…about…" I balled my hands into fists, unsure whether I wanted to punch myself or him more. "It was all lies. None of it was true, was it? We were *never* friends."

"You were nothing to me," he shrugged. "A means to an end."

Burning tears of rage seared my eyes over a final betrayal by a friend who had never existed, not even during our best moments.

"You told me about the queen's amulet," I said. "You were hoping I'd try to take it from her. All so I could help you escape to the Academy. So I…" I looked around at the friends who were staring at me with confusion and terror in their eyes. "So I could help you walk the Seekers right into another trap."

"Well, to be fair, my mother and I both hoped you'd agree to her original proposal and join her. You could have been a big help, you know. Seeker to the queen herself. But you turned her down, because you're a selfish bit—"

"Raff!" Lumus's silver eyes glinted as he shot his son an angry look before turning back to me. "You're delightfully naive, Vega Sloane. And I must say, you deserve everything that's about to happen to you, if only for what you did to my lovely wife with that silver chain of yours."

I wanted to scream, run, fight. But all I could do was stand there, frozen, staring at him.

Lumus was right. I *had* been naive. Trusting. Foolish. Even in the moments at the Academy when I'd hated Raff, I'd never suspected him of this level of awfulness.

Shaking off the daze, I managed to turn to him and ask, "How did you know the verse? I don't understand."

Averting his eyes, he mumbled, "We had some assistance from—"

"Enough, Raff," Lumus snapped.

"But," I said, beginning to understand, "it wasn't a *Seeker* who brought the Relic to the queen. That's why the sword was flickering when I saw it in the Throne Room. It's why it came back here, isn't it? It rejected you. You failed." Against my better judgment, I allowed myself a smile as I pulled my eyes to Lumus. "The sword even rejected your precious *queen.*"

"None of that matters now," Lumus snarled. "Seekers are not the only ones in the Otherwhere who can claim Relics. I, too, have the power to take possession of the sword."

"So why did you bring us all here, if not to help you acquire it?" I asked.

Lumus lowered his chin. "Why do you think?"

As the venom in his tone laced its way through the air, my legs weakened under me. Every muscle in my body suddenly felt exhausted from the mere effort of standing.

Lumus folded his hands in front of him as casually as if he was waiting at a bus stop. "Assembling all the Academy's Seekers in one place, far from Merriwether's reach, was no small feat." His silver eyes sparkled with malicious delight as Niala and Rourke pulled in close to me, the Seekers gathering in a tight cluster behind us.

"What are you going to do to us?" I asked. My voice echoed back at me in the cavernous space, mocking me and adding insult to what I feared was about to be some very serious injury.

Instead of answering, Lumus narrowed his eyes. A second later, a piercing pain shot through my head as if someone had taken a hatchet to my brain.

I pressed my hands to my temples and shrieked with agony as Niala threw her arm around my shoulders.

"Stop!" she yelled as Rourke paced the floor in front of us, letting out a low series of growls and snarls. "Stop hurting her!"

Lumus obliged, and a second later the ache subsided. But he'd done something to me. I couldn't say what—only that it felt like he'd stolen a piece of my mind.

"What *are* you?" I panted, steadying myself with a hand on Niala's arm.

"I am a warlock," Lumus replied with a cool shrug. "A master of the magical arts. But I am much more than that."

"You're a Waerg," I said, recalling the regal silver wolf who had padded into Uldrach's Throne Room, seemingly walking on air.

"Not a mere Waerg, no. I am a shape-shifter. The wolf is only one of my many forms. You'd best hope never to acquaint yourself with the others. Then again, something tells me you won't have a chance."

He flicked a hand in the air, and on his silent command, a pack of gigantic wolves slinked through the dark doorway behind him and Raff. The snarling animals stalked around to position themselves in a defensive line between our tiny army and the enemy, whose eyes danced with the joy of victory.

Behind me, my fellow Seekers moved in even closer, pressing silently together, their fear palpable on the air. Crane and Talia were still huddled on the floor in the corner, watching like captivated shadows.

"Oh, don't worry," Lumus said. "I'm not *entirely* sadistic." He eyed my allies. "Draw your weapons, and fight for your right to live through the night. Show me what you've learned at that ancient, pointless institution of yours."

With shaking hands, Niala and the others obliged, drawing their weapons from their holsters, belts, and sheaths. But our tiny party was small and weak. Weapons or not, there was no way for us to fight off a warlock, his traitorous son, and a deadly pack of killer canines.

A dozen massive wolves now stood between us and Lumus, their hackles raised. The thick-shouldered creatures bared their daunting teeth, their heads lowered toward the floor, eyes scanning us like the prey we were.

"Keep back!" I called out to Niala and the others. "Stay close together! Don't make any sudden moves!"

"What do you mean, don't move?" asked Nevin, a boy with sandy-blond hair who was holding a gleaming short sword in one hand. "They'll kill us if we don't get to them first!"

"He's right!" replied another boy called Cairn, shifting his weight nervously from one foot to the other. "Come on, let's take them out!"

Before I had a chance to reply, they leapt forward, springing at the line of Waergs, who snarled and lunged in defense of their master.

Outnumbered and outflanked, the two Seekers were instantly pinned down by the wolves. Snarling through finger-sized fangs, the animals looked back at Lumus, who nodded his permission to complete the kill.

Frantic, I looked around for guidance or advice, only to see the faces of Seekers who were even more terrified than I was.

"Rourke!" Niala cried out, taking charge. "Leòmhann!"

Faster than I could blink, Rourke transformed from his sleek black panther form into a massive lion and leapt forward, tearing a paw through the air with a snarl that made even Lumus and Raff recoil in fear. The Waergs backed away, and Niala and Desmond ran forward to grab the wounded Seekers and help them limp back toward our group.

Raff stepped forward then, chin down, a look of pure hatred in his eyes. As he advanced, the Waergs pulled apart, allowing him room to make his way toward me.

Even as I drew my dagger, he sprang forward and, with a

fierce cry of rage, morphed in one smooth motion into a large, dark gray wolf. His huge front paws thundered when he landed, and he pressed his chest to the floor, the muscles twitching through his neck and shoulders as he prepared to lunge.

Fully in attack mode and with a guttural growl, the wolf surged forward.

I closed my eyes and waited for death to take me.

# ONSLAUGHT

A SINGLE LIGHTNING bolt of a word sizzled in my mind.

*Protect.*

A split-second later, Raff's wolf slammed into me, knocking me back and sending me crashing into the other Seekers.

But other than a throbbing pain in my backside and a confusing feeling of heaviness, I was miraculously okay.

I opened my eyes and looked around frantically to see that each member of my meager army—including myself—was tucked behind our own shimmering, transparent shield.

Each of us was also wearing a trim suit of silver armor with the image of a long sword—the Academy's sigil—etched into the chest piece.

Niala must have been reading my mind because she said, "Nice job!" as she stepped over hauled me to my feet.

"Um...Thanks?"

But there was no time for celebrating.

"Vega! Look out!" Meg shouted from somewhere to my right.

Still in his wolf form, Raff charged head-first into my shield again before crashing backwards to the ground, shaking his head in confusion and pain.

The impact staggered me back again, only this time, it was into three of the Seekers, who thankfully caught me with their shields before I hit the floor a second time.

Raff rose to his feet and lowered his head, growling. With my feet planted this time, I braced myself against his attack, but I could already feel my muscles giving out. It was an all too familiar feeling, one that I'd come to know in the sparring ring when Raff and Larken had decided to treat me to a few minutes in Hell.

But just as Raff looked ready to attack a third time, Desmond swept around in front of me, focusing his attention on a large brown Waerg standing a few feet away.

The huge beast stumbled forward, swinging its head back and forth on its thick neck. Baring its teeth, it turned and leapt at Raff, who twisted around and recoiled in startled horror.

I'd watched Desmond use his gift of mind-control in the sparring ring once or twice, in moments when he'd taken hold of other students' thoughts. But he'd always done it with kindness, taking care not to hurt anyone.

This time, however, he compelled the brown wolf to tear at his victim, digging his teeth into Raff's side hard enough to elicit a howl of agony.

I shouted out a "Thanks!" to Desmond, who looked more than a little pleased with himself as he turned to face me. I couldn't blame him for a moment of self-congratulatory smugness. It was our first real battle, and he'd managed to take full control of a Waerg.

But with one swift movement of his hand, Lumus strode forward and took over, sending the Waerg flying through the air into the stone doorframe, and the creature crashed to the ground, motionless.

Still in front of me, Raff shifted back into his human form and crossed his arms, staring at me with an arrogant smirk as his father stepped forward to join him.

Blood dripped from Raff's shoulder, but he looked like he had plenty of strength left to rip me limb from limb.

"Get back!" I shouted, and each Seeker ducked below their summoned shields, safe for now but terrified of what was to come.

"Your conjured shields won't hold forever, Vega," Lumus said. "They're only as strong as that weak mind of yours. And as you fail, I will take out your friends, one by one."

As much as I hated to admit it, he was right. It had taken half my strength to summon the shields and armor for everyone, and it was taking the rest just to keep them intact as the Waergs began to lunge and paw at them, snapping with their powerful jaws.

"You can't stop what's about to happen," Lumus said. "As amusing as it is to watch you try, I should really just put you all out of your misery. Come now. Lower your shields."

I wasn't sure if he was bluffing or not. But something told me not to test him.

"I'll lower mine," I called out, my voice trembling. "But only if you spare my friends."

Behind me, a scattered chorus of "No!" and "Don't do it!" rang out.

Lumus scanned the students before locking his eyes back onto mine. "I suppose I'll consider it. You're the one we need, after all. You've *always* been the one."

*The One.*

Callum had spoken those very words a few days earlier. Words that seemed so ridiculous, so dramatic.

So wrong.

But if I could help—if I could save the lives of my fellow Seekers right now by giving Lumus what he wanted—he could call me whatever he wanted to.

Stepping forward, I let my shield and armor fade until

nothing remained except a shimmering, wispy mist that quickly dissipated to nothing.

The only thing standing between the warlock and me now was a few feet of empty air.

"Don't trust him! He'll kill you!" Meg cried from behind her shield.

"Silence!" Lumus called out, raising his hand, palm out.

When I took another step toward the warlock, Desmond shouted, "Vega! Stop!"

Lumus's voice thundered. "I said, *SILENCE!*"

He flicked his right hand in a tight, quick circle, and in an instant, Niala, Rourke, and every Seeker but me stood frozen in place.

I twisted around, horrified to see that my conjured layers of protection—shields and armor—had disappeared, and my class-mates were motionless, a battalion of marble statues, petrified yet conscious and alert. Even Crane and Talia, their bodies squeezed together, sat frozen in the corner like hunched gargoyles.

The only sign of life was in their eyes, which shifted around, panicked, as they took in what was happening.

Defeated, I wanted to punch my fist through a wall.

This was all my fault.

I'd helped Raff set his trap. I'd literally opened a door that every single Seeker Candidate in the Academy had walked through.

The only thing to do now was hope that sacrificing myself would be enough to free them.

I turned back to Lumus. "What are you going to do?" I asked, my voice stretched nearly to its breaking point.

The silver-eyed warlock cocked his head to the side like a dog who was quietly trying to decide whether to play with me or bite my leg off.

"What do you *think* I'm going to do?" he asked with a twisted grin.

I knew the answer, of course. But the last thing I wanted was to say it out loud.

It was too horrifying. Too grotesque.

Too cruel.

"Please don't," I murmured. "Don't..."

But Lumus raised his hand, curled it into a fist, and pointed it toward Cairn, one of the Seekers who had attacked Lumus's Waergs minutes earlier. The boy's eyes were white with terror, his long dagger held high. As Lumus gestured toward him, he shot me a pleading look.

"Please," I moaned. "Please...don't..."

Smiling, Lumus opened his hand, splaying his fingers in a violent burst before slamming his fist shut. And with the horrific sound of a hammer smashing stone, the Seeker's body shattered in front of my eyes, crumbling to the ground in hard, rigid pieces that quickly faded to dust.

I fell to my knees, out of breath and sick to my stomach, tears burning my eyes.

"I will do that to every one of them," Lumus said. "Perhaps the boy with the rosy cheeks will be my next target..."

With that, he pointed at Desmond.

"No..." a high-pitched voice croaked out, and I wasn't sure if it came from my friend or me. All I knew was that the thought of Desmond's parents losing their son to such a malevolent creature pushed me to my limit. Rage scorched my insides like a stream of roiling lava. I lifted my chin to look up at Lumus, my eyes narrowing.

"Hurt him, and I promise you, when you die, it will be by my hand," I snarled through clamped teeth.

Lumus laughed a cruel, awful chortle that made me want to tear his head off with my bare hands.

"You really think you, a young girl with weak powers, can take on a warlock? You have so much to learn, Miss Sloane. It's almost unfortunate you'll never get the chance."

He surged forward and, before I had time to react, grabbed me by the neck and lifted me off the ground.

A searing cold blasted through my body, the burning sensation of instantaneous, agonizing frostbite. With my feet dangling, my throat began to close in on itself. My chest throbbed with each attempt at a breath.

Forcing my mouth open, I tried to cry out.

But no sound came.

"Arrogant girl, thinking you can actually defeat those who have laid claim to the throne of the Otherwhere. It's ours. The *Relics* are ours. The days of the Academy's Seekers are over, Vega. As of today, your kind is no more. I will end each and every bloodline in this room."

His grip tightened, and my hands reached for his arm, weakly clawing at him, grabbing his fingers and trying to pry them off my throat.

But I had no strength left to fight. Lumus was freezing me from the inside out and choking me to death, all at once.

I couldn't speak. I couldn't breathe. I could barely think. I only had strength enough for one thought:

*Find us.*

The words shot out of my mind like a pair of arrows.

I didn't know where their trajectory would take them. All I knew was that the world was about to end. Death would steal all of us away from our families, our friends.

I would never see Fairhaven again. Or Merriwether.

Or…

or…

*Callum.*

As the room began to spin, my mind swirled with the image of his face. And then his beautiful features disappeared as a burst of shattering glass and tumbling stone came crashing down around us.

With my last shallow breath, I pulled my eyes up to see a multitude of shadows swirling through the air above me.

Shadows that would either bring me swift death...or give me new life.

# HELPERS

THE SHADOWS PLUMMETED DOWN, flocking around Lumus in a screeching attack. The warlock let out a shriek and his hand opened, releasing me from his death grip.

Like a sack of sand, I dropped to the floor. I gasped for breath, my chest tight as I scrambled backwards.

With the warlock's spell broken, the world had begun to move again. Despite their lack of shields or armor, Niala and the others, enraged and no longer frozen under Lumus's spell, leapt forward. Waergs thundered toward the Seekers, who fought them back with swords and daggers.

Oleana flung missiles of ice, while Meg darted impossibly fast around the room, distracting a small group of Waergs long enough to allow a few of the Seekers to circle around into attack position.

Rourke, still in his impressively large lion form, was tangled in a growling, roaring fight with one of the Waergs. Blood and saliva sprayed through a flurry of gnashing teeth and slashing claws.

In front of us, a hundred razorbeaks were attacking Lumus, swooping up then down in a coordinated effort to keep him distracted. He tried to call out one of his spells, to recite an incantation, but the birds were too intelligent and too determined. They dove repeatedly at his head, slicing into the skin on his face and arms with their blade-like beaks.

Raff, in his gray wolf form, charged full-throttle at the birds, leaping into the air and snapping at them with his powerful jaws full of deadly, dagger-shaped teeth.

When the terrified birds flew upwards to regroup, Lumus managed to scramble to his feet, wiping at the blood on his face.

"What's happening?" someone on our side shouted. "Where did those birds come from?"

"They're friends," I croaked out, though I wasn't sure anyone heard me over the din of growls and enraged cries.

After a few seconds, I was finally able to haul myself to my feet, my head and neck still throbbing from Lumus's attack.

The Academy's fighters were somehow holding their own against the Waergs, pushing them back toward the twin doors they'd first come through.

Raff, desperate to protect his father, had shifted into his human form. Frantic and undisciplined, he waved a sword up at the razorbeaks in a weak attempt to defend Lumus from further attacks and keep the birds at bay.

Though he failed to take the razorbeaks down, he did manage to keep them far enough away that the warlock was able to gather himself, his cold eyes focused on our group of fighters.

It was only a matter of time before he cast another destructive spell, and I could only imagine how many of my fellow students this one would take down.

*Don't let him do it, Vega. Don't you dare let him win.*

The voice, so familiar and so welcome, swept its way first through my mind, then through my entire body, along my skin, deep into my bones.

I hardly dared believe he was speaking to me.

But I needed to. I *had* to believe it.

*You are the granddaughter of a wizard and a Seeker. You are a Summoner. You are a Shadow.*

*Summon them. Call them to your side. They will come.*

I pulled my chin up, my eyes fixed on the gaping wound in the chapel's ceiling and the stars above, twinkling far in the distance.

My one hope was out there somewhere, waiting for three words.

"Come to me," I mouthed to the sky.

# KNIGHTS IN SHINING ARMOR

THE EARTH SHOOK.

Chunks of dark-colored glass fell in plate-sized pieces to the stone floor, red and violet daggers crashing to the ground only to shatter into a million tiny shards. The chapel's windows were gone. The stone columns rising from floor to ceiling creaked, splintered, and threatened to tumble. Crane and Talia cowered together in their corner, mercifully unhurt by the falling debris that just managed to miss them.

Perspiration trickled down my lower back as the temperature skyrocketed inside the chapel. Ten, twenty, thirty degrees, until it started feeling like we'd been thrown into an oven to roast. The razorbeaks flew upwards, soaring out of the chapel as though they knew exactly what was coming.

I shouted with joy as five enormous silhouettes swept through the air in tight circles above the now nonexistent roof, descending rapidly to unleash missiles of flame at the remaining Waergs, who retreated in terror through the doors of the chapel, howling as they ran.

"The dragons!" yelled Desmond, bouncing up and down, his fists clenched. "Vega's dragons have come!"

With the Waergs fleeing, the dragons set their sights on Lumus and Raff, aiming directly for the two figures who now stood frozen in the doorway.

"Why are they still here?" I muttered, wondering why the father and son hadn't followed the Waergs out the door.

But a second later, I understood.

Dachmal, the blue dragon, twisted unnaturally in the air then came crashing to the ground, cracking the marble floor beneath him. He moaned, his head and wings pinned to the floor in a grotesque knot of splayed scales and twisted limbs.

I shot my eyes toward Lumus, whose hands were out, an incantation on his lips.

There was no longer any doubt in my mind as to how the queen had managed to cage the five dragons in her Throne Room. It was the work of the warlock—a man with the power to control the beautiful creatures against their very powerful wills.

The dragon Tefyr fell next, landing next to Dachmal. His head was wrenched sideways, his tail pressed to the floor. The dragons shrieked, their thick chests surging in and out as they struggled for breath.

Enraged, I stared at Lumus, feeling helpless against his power. The only weapon I had was my small dagger, and the warlock would have it melt in my hand long before I could ever reach him.

Oleana thrust her hands out and shot a bolt of ice at Lumus, who flicked a finger toward it, prompting the sharp missile to fizzle to steam in mid-air. Meg darted through the room at lightning speed, her blade drawn, but Lumus sent her reeling backward with another flick.

He was unstoppable.

*Unless…*

"The sword!" I said under my breath, spinning around. I ran at the stone casket. In a flash, I leaned over and snatched the silver blade from the bony hands of the long-dead man who lay inside. "Thank you for protecting it," I said as I slipped it out of his grasp.

For such a massive weapon, it was remarkably light, and I managed to lift it without much effort.

"No!" shouted Lumus, whose attention had shifted to me. "You don't know what you're doing!"

"I know exactly what I'm doing," I shouted. "I am a Seeker, and I have in my hands a Relic of Power—one that was stolen by people who had no right to it. I claim it now in the name of the Academy for the Blood-Born."

Lumus stretched a hand toward me and rattled off something in a language I'd never heard. A shooting pain blistered through both of my arms, and I dropped the weapon, which went clanging to the stone floor.

"You will not take it," the warlock growled. "I won't allow it. The sword is ours. It should never have left Uldrach."

"But it did, didn't it?" I snapped, too angry to let my fear silence me. "Because it was never yours to begin with. You know as well as I do that even if you take it now, it will just find its way back here. It rejected you, because even a freaking *sword* knows how horrible you are."

"Lies!" Lumus growled.

"Vega," Niala warned, "he's got the dragons pinned. He'll kill you—he'll kill us all, unless we let him take it. Please…we need to let it go."

"No." I shook my head, tears welling in my eyes. "If he takes the sword, he'll kill us anyhow. I can't let him win."

I was about to reach for the weapon again when a deep, familiar voice once spun through my mind like silk.

*Don't worry, Sloane. He won't win.*

With a sudden injection of hope, I twisted around, searching.

But there was no sign of him.

*Look up, Vega.*

Dropping down toward the ruins of the castle, a spot of light

—bright as the sun against the black sky—beamed in from above and careened down like a missile toward the interior of the ruins where we stood.

Only it was no missile.

As the golden dragon came in for a landing, the last of the razorbeaks circled the fallen chapel and flew off in a mass of screeching blackness. Taking advantage of the distraction, I reached for the sword just as Raff made a mad dash for it. A shot of blue-hot flame landed on the floor between us, and I knew without looking that it had come from the golden dragon's mouth.

"Stay out of this, *Uncle!*" Raff snarled, turning his angry eyes to Callum. "This isn't your fight."

With a quick flash, Callum shifted into his human form and marched forward with powerful, determined strides. He was still dressed in gold armor, his eyes shining bright blue in contrast. The look on his face was one I'd seen only once before, when Raff had attacked me in the sparring ring.

Pure, unadulterated rage.

"*Uncle* is a title reserved for family, and you and I are *not* family You're a traitor, a liar, and the worst kind of coward." He pulled his eyes to Lumus. "You know, I heard years ago about my sister giving birth. I'm sorry to see that my worst fears have been realized. Her son is a monster, just like her husband." Callum shot a fierce glare at Lumus, and the warlock winced liked he'd been punched in the gut.

"You're the only monster around here," Raff snarled through trembling lips. "You're just like the Crimson King. You want to take everything for yourself. You'll destroy this land."

"The only ones in the Otherwhere looking to claim our world for themselves are your parents," Callum said calmly. "You can't see it, because they've tainted your mind with hatred. I'm truly sorry for you, Raff."

"You shouldn't be. I'm about to take your life." Raff looked down at the sword that lay on the floor between us. "They say whoever wields the Sword of Viviane controls the Otherwhere," he snarled, bending down to reach for its hilt. "I will make sure it remains within Uldrach's walls from now on."

But when he tried to pick it up, he winced with pain and effort, as if the weapon was suddenly too heavy to lift.

"*You're* doing this!" Raff shouted at Callum. "Let it go! You have no claim over the Relics of Power!"

"I'm not doing anything," Callum replied with a shrug. "You may have fooled the sword once, but like all Relics of Power, it's waiting for a *Seeker* to claim it. Not a traitor."

"It should have been ours from the start," Raff snarled.

"I'm afraid you're wrong." With that, Callum turned to me and nodded toward the blade. "Vega, I believe you dropped something. Perhaps you should pick it up."

I reached for the sword, lifting it as easily as if it were a ballpoint pen. I held its hilt in both hands, its fierce tip pointed toward the stars above us.

"The good news for you," I told Raff, "is it's not like I'm going to use it as a weapon. We all know I'm terrible with swords."

"Vega!" Niala cried out from somewhere to my right. "Watch out!"

I jerked my head around to see Lumus, his silver eyes laser-focused, his lips muttering an incantation. Sparks of light flickered around him in strange, powerful bursts.

Callum growled at me to run, which I did, sprinting back toward the doors the Seekers and I had first come through.

Lumus, with Raff by his side, began following me, death in his eyes.

I whipped back around in time to see Desmond leap forward, positioning himself in front of our two powerful enemies.

"If you want her, you'll have to go through me," he said.

"And me," said Oleana, stepping up to join him.

"Same," said Meg, and then they were joined by a fourth and a fifth Seeker until Niala and everyone else in the room stood in a defiant line between Lumus and me. Even Crane and Talia had managed to extract themselves from their corner and hobble over.

With a blinding flash of light, Callum shifted back into his dragon form. He swung around to align himself with the Seeker Candidates, Niala, and Rourke in his lion form, all of whom had their sights—and their weapons—trained on Lumus and Raff, who stopped, frozen in their tracks by this sudden act of unified resistance.

The golden dragon arched his neck and huffed out a cloud of black smoke, followed by a jagged bolt of flame. A warning.

I wondered with horror if Lumus could take us all out at once. But when the golden dragon shot a second bolt of fire that hit the floor inches from Raff's feet, the warlock merely watched, a look of defeat on his cruel, otherworldly features.

"Enough!" he called out, his eyes darkening, the sphere of electricity around him fading to nothing.

His gaze focused on Callum.

"I would so love to kill you, Drake. To take out the other dragons, too. I want you to know that I would do it right now, if not for your sister's wishes."

Callum reverted to his human form, his eyes glowing with powerful flame as he shot a hate-filled look at his brother-in-law. "My sister has long wished me dead. I doubt if she would object."

"You're right," Lumus said. "She does wish you dead. But you see, she wants to kill you herself. She knows what you will soon become, and so do you. Killing you after your change will make your death all the more satisfying. Who knows? Our lovely queen might even come off as the heroine of the Otherwhere for taking down such a threat against its people."

Callum opened his mouth to speak, but seemed to think better of it. For a moment he looked as defeated as Lumus, as though the cruelty of reality had issued him a final blow.

"I look forward to the day when I can confront my sister," he finally said. "Please tell her so."

With a silent nod, Lumus ordered Raff out of the ruins of the chapel. A howling wind had begun to swirl through the air as if to remind us where we were, and that it was time to go home.

I handed the Sword of Viviane to Oleana and stepped over to Callum. I had no idea how he felt about me anymore. But I could see his pain. I could feel it. And I wasn't about to walk away, even if he wanted me to.

I also knew he was the only reason we were still standing. He'd saved us all.

Clenching his jaw, he nodded a silent promise. "It's time to go home."

By now, the pinned dragons had regained their mobility and managed to stretch their wings. They flapped over to position themselves along the perimeter of the wrecked and ravaged chapel.

"Are they all right?" I asked.

"They're fine," Callum replied. "Lumus didn't break their bones—he wouldn't dare. Though I'm sure they'd be perfectly happy never to see him again."

"That makes all of us."

"Everyone find a dragon," Callum called out to the Seekers. "Climb on. We're heading back to the Academy."

"What?" shouted Desmond. "You want us to get on..." He pointed over to the giant, scale-covered mounts and whisper-hissed, "*those* things?"

"I do. You'll find they're quite safe, not to mention fast." He shot me a look before adding, "Those particular dragons aren't as volatile as some of us. I promise, they'll protect you with their lives."

Eager to get home, the Seekers, Niala, and Rourke managed to clamber up onto the dragons' backs, and when everyone was accounted for, the five winged creatures prepared to take off.

"Wait," I said, swinging my head toward the massive pile of glass and rubble that was all that remained of the chapel's walls. "What about Cairn? We can't just leave him here."

"I don't think there's anything left of him," Niala replied, fighting back tears. Rourke was curled soothingly around her neck in the ferret form I'd first seen at Midsummer Fest in Fairhaven. "I'm so sorry."

"I'll see to it that Merriwether knows about his sacrifice," Callum said with a solemn nod. "We'll make sure he's honored."

The others, bowing their heads, seemed to agree that this was the best and only course of action. Meanwhile, Oleana, who still had the Sword of Viviane in hand, called me over to where she was seated with Meg on Dachmal's back.

"You should carry it," she said, handing the weapon down to me. "You deserve the credit."

Though I wasn't sure I agreed, I took the sword from her and promised I'd get it to Merriwether. "You all go ahead," I said with a weak attempt at a smile. "I'll see you back at the Academy."

When the dragons had taken off into the night, I turned to Callum, the sword in my hand.

"You were out there, watching over us. You came when I called."

"Of course I did."

My face damp with tears, I looked up at him, grateful when he stroked a thumb over my cheek. I closed my eyes, pressing into his hand and savoring the sensation I thought I'd never feel again. I threw my free arm around his neck and squeezed.

"Vega," he whispered, his chest tightening as he pulled me in close. "I'm so sorry. For the things I said...for how I left you..."

"I understand now," I breathed. "I can't say I liked it. But I *do* understand." I pulled back and drew my mist-filled eyes to his. "I know you thought you were protecting me from what's going to happen to you."

"I did think that, yes. But I was wrong to push you away so

coldly. I knew it the minute I did it, but I was afraid to come talk to you, to explain. I was afraid you'd hate me."

"I don't hate you," I half-laughed, wiping new tears away. "But don't ever push me away again, okay?"

He pressed his hand to his heart. "Promise."

I wiped my cheeks with the backs of my hands and let out another quiet chuckle. "I don't know what's going to happen, Callum. To us, to the Otherwhere…but I need to say something before we go back. Before we return to life as it was. You need to know—"

"Don't," he replied, holding his hands up. "Don't say it. You don't need to. Not after everything I've put you through. I don't deserve it."

"But I…"

"Vega," he interrupted, taking my face in his warm, perfect hands, "It's okay. I already know."

"I'm not sure you do, Callum. The thing is that I—"

With a finger to my lips, he reached out to brush a stray curl away from my forehead. "I love you, too."

# HOMEWARD BOUND

"You're tired," Callum said, cupping my chin in his hand. It was a familiar gesture, but one I never tired of.

Pure affection.

I nodded. "So tired," I said. "Honestly, I don't know if I have the strength to summon a door..."

"It's all right," he replied. "I'll shift, and we can follow the others. Let's get out of here before Lumus changes his mind and comes back to finish us off. I can hold him off for a little while, but he's strong, as you've seen."

"Agreed," I nodded, backing away to give him room to shift. "Let's go."

When his golden dragon reappeared, I approached with trepidation and slid my hand along his neck.

I climbed onto his back and held on with one hand while I grasped the sword with the other, confident that for tonight, at least, the dragon was under the control of his human counterpart.

We flew through the night, not saying a word to one another until we landed at the Academy. It was almost like we'd tacitly agreed not to let the dragon be party to our private conversation.

There would come a time when Callum would need to confront him—when they would battle internally for dominance. But tonight wasn't the night.

We landed just outside the Academy's grounds, where the last of Merriwether's exhausted troops were marching through the main gates. I slipped off the dragon's back, landing softly on my feet.

When Callum shifted, I went to hand him the sword, but he shook his head.

"You should be the one to present it to Merriwether," he said. "You're the one who found it. You've officially proven that you deserve to be the Chosen Seeker."

"I almost got everyone killed," I protested, looking around as weary Rangers and instructors made their way by us, hardly bothering to raise their heads and acknowledge us. "Speaking of which, what happened out there in the wilderness, when you went to confront the queen? I tried to see you in the Orb of Kilarin. But everything was so foggy…"

"My sister set a trap for us, just as Lumus did for you," Callum said. "Only it wasn't exactly a trap. More of an intricate illusion. I suspect it was also Lumus's work."

"What do you mean?"

"Do you know what a misdirect is?"

"Sure. It's when a magician draws your attention to one hand while he's doing something with the other."

Callum nodded. "*That's* what I mean. Isla emptied the Academy of its best fighters and its Headmaster."

"You're telling me the Usurper Queen—your sister—managed to pull that trick on *Merriwether?*"

"Well, she pulled it on Lannach—Merriwether's wizard friend —who was convinced enough by what he saw to warn Kohrin's people. I guess she knew word would get back to us. She lured us away from the Academy knowing it was the only way Raff could persuade you all to go with him."

I thought about it for a moment, then said, "Still, I'm genuinely surprised Merriwether would fall for something like that."

"Merriwether doesn't fall for *anything*," Callum replied. "He does what he needs to in order to ensure the best possible outcome. He doesn't always know exactly what will happen. But he trusts himself, and he has faith in the mental images he receives. He weighs the risks and keeps his mind focused on the final goal. In this case, he walked into a fake battle in order to give you and the other Seekers time to accomplish what you needed to." Callum eyed the Sword of Viviane, which I held onto with one hand, its tip digging into the grass. "The sword is where it belongs. Somehow, he knew this would be the end result."

"I suppose you're right," I said, twisting the blade around to let it glint in the moonlight, "He knew exactly what would happen, didn't he? Even the worst of it."

"You mean Cairn."

I nodded.

"Yes. I suppose he did." Callum's jaw clenched and the tendons in his neck pulsed. He tilted his chin toward the sword and took my hand in his. "Come on. We'd better get this thing to Merriwether."

# REUNION

CALLUM ACCOMPANIED me upstairs to the Headmaster's office. But when we reached the door, he halted and turned to face me.

"I'm going to leave you here," he said, and when I opened my mouth to protest, he added, "Only for now. This is a conversation you need to have with your grandfather. I'll come check on you in your quarters in a little while."

"Promise?"

"Promise."

After a vow-sealing kiss, he headed back down the hall toward the stairwell. I watched him go, confident he would never let me down again. That whatever happened, we'd be all right.

When Callum disappeared into the stairwell, I knocked on the Headmaster's door.

"Come!" a booming voice called out.

Merriwether was sitting at his desk when I walked into his office, leaning forward, the palm of his hand pressed to his forehead.

"Headmaster?"

He pulled his face up. He looked older, somehow, and tired beyond words.

"Vega," he smiled, rising from his seat. "I can't tell you how glad I am to see you."

The urge to rush over and hug him was almost too powerful to resist. But I wasn't quite sure what the proper granddaughter-grandfather protocol was at this point. All I knew was how happy I was to see him alive.

"You were successful, then," he said, eyeing the sword in my hand. "Not that I'm surprised."

"No, I suppose you're not. You know a lot more than you ever let on, don't you?"

He let out a sigh and turned his back to me, stepping over to the bookshelf on the far wall. "I know too much, Vega," he said, flicking a hand in the air. A projection appeared between us of the chapel where we'd found the sword, minutes before its walls collapsed. The image of Lumus, casting the spell that killed Cairn. "If you only knew how much I despised the thought of sending you into a situation that would cause so much fear and anguish."

"And death," I reminded him.

"If I could have avoided it, I would have. I need you to know that."

"Well, if it makes you feel any better, you didn't *send* us. It was our choice to go."

"And my choice not to stop you."

A hard lump formed in my throat. "I just wish you'd told me what was going to happen. Maybe we could've prevented…"

He pivoted to face me and lowered his chin, shooting me a skeptical look. "If I'd told you that you were about to embark on a deadly mission, would you ever have agreed to go?"

"I…No. Probably not."

His eyes flickered toward the sword at my side. "If you knew someone would die for that…"

"I wouldn't have gone." I glanced down and then up again,

willing myself to meet his gaze. "Unless I knew *I'd* be the one to die."

"That's why you were the perfect one to lead the others."

My eyes welled up, and my chest tightened. "I should have done more to protect Cairn. Summoned a better shield, or a door, or something."

"Nothing you could have done would have kept him from dying by Lumus's hand. I won't tell you it's just a part of war and not to worry about it. You *need* to worry about it every day for the rest of your life. Remember Cairn and what happened tonight. It wasn't your fault. But, as a leader, it will always be your responsibility. It's the price of leadership. It's the price of greatness."

"What if the price is too much?"

"That's something only you can decide. All I ask is that you also never forget the hundreds...the *thousands* of lives you saved today. You were truly heroic."

"I don't feel heroic," I sighed. "I kind of feel like a failure right now."

"But here you are, with the Sword of Viviane in hand—the first victory in what will surely be a long war, tragically, with many more casualties to come." Merriwether stepped over to his desk and opened the top right drawer, gesturing to the emptiness inside. "The Orb of Kilarin has vanished at last. It's as if it was holding onto its last morsels of life in order to give you time to find the sword and bring it back here. We now have the advantage against the queen. Our possession of a Relic means her strength is weakened, but it's by no means gone. Lumus's spells are powerful and will remain destructive. He is a threat to us, whether or not he has a Relic in his possession. Even that awful son of his is a threat."

"Did you know all along who Raff was?" I asked, not sure I wanted to know the answer.

He shook his head. "No. Not exactly. I guessed, of course, that he wasn't the boy he claimed to be when he hesitated before telling me his surname. But it took me some time to figure out exactly who he was."

"You felt it?" I asked. "You read his mind?"

Merriwether chuckled. "I wish I could boast that skill. But no. The truth is, I followed him one evening to a corner of the Academy, where he met with a Zerker—a boy you know. A Sparker named Larken."

"Larken," I sighed. "He hates me." A thought occurred to me. "I haven't seen him in ages, and Niala told me she hasn't, either."

"That's because he's been sitting in a cell in the Academy's dungeon," Merriwether said. "For sharing secrets with the enemy."

My jaw dropped. *"Larken is the spy?"*

"His father works in service of the queen, a fact he and his family cleverly concealed from us when he first came to the Academy. The night I followed Raff, I overheard him and Larken engaged in a rather enlightening conversation about the queen and about you. When I saw Raff's eyes flash silver…well, it wasn't hard after that to connect the dots. I knew for the first time who he was. It was impossible not to see echoes of his father's cruelty in him."

"So, you know Lumus personally," I said, my mouth grating against the name.

"I do, though not well. He is older than I am, although he appears quite young. He was once considered an ally and confidant to the Crimson King."

"Really?" I said with genuine surprise. "But he's so…well, for lack of a better word, *evil*."

"Evil is a very…*definitive* word, Vega. One that offers little room for hope. I'm not sure the warlock is deserving of such a designation."

"If you'd seen what I have…" I began, remembering that

Merriwether probably *had* seen it as clearly as if he'd been there. "I just don't see how there's anything in him but cruelty."

Merriwether's knowing eyes flashed bright for a second before dulling again. "As questionable as his methods are, Lumus fights for what he thinks is right. As we all do. He saw what happened to the former king. He saw the damage and devastation reaped by the dragon shifter. And now he wants to protect the Otherwhere from reliving that particular ordeal. Strange though it may seem, on some level he's motivated by a sort of twisted benevolence."

"Wait—you're not saying he's *right* to support the Usurper Queen, are you? Because trust me, she doesn't have the Otherwhere's best interests in mind. I've seen what she did to Kaer Uther."

"I'm not saying that at all. If I thought Isla was the best possible ruler for this land, I would lock the Academy up, throw away the key, and wish her well. But all I'm saying is that she once had potential. That believe it or not, she began her reign with noble intentions. But where there is power, there is almost always corruption. She didn't set out to ruin this world. In fact, she had every intention of protecting it."

"From Callum," I replied.

"From the unknown." Merriwether sat back down in his chair and eyed the sword. "Now, we have a little matter to discuss."

I lifted the weapon and laid it flat on the desk. "It's yours," I said. "Or rather, it's the Academy's. I'll be perfectly happy if I never touch it again."

He slipped his hands under the sword and raised it up to examine its blade. "I'll keep it in a safe place. I lack the queen's vanity and have no intention of hanging it up as some kind of trophy or decoration." He laid it down again before fixing his eyes on me. "But it's not the sword I wanted to discuss."

"You wanted to talk about the Chosen Seeker."

He nodded. "You know, of course, that it should be you."

I shook my head. "No, actually. I don't think it should."

"Why is that?"

"Because I didn't do this alone." I chewed my lip as I pondered my reply. "When we were in the chapel—fighting Lumus, Raff, and those Waergs—every single one of the Academy's Seekers risked their lives and contributed to the fight. They all helped me free the sword from its hiding spot. I didn't do it alone. I *couldn't* have done it alone."

"So what are you proposing, Vega?" Merriwether asked, his eyes glinting with warmth.

"I think we should *all* be named as Chosen Seekers. There are three more Relics to find, and who knows where they're scattered? It may take all of us to locate them, and we know how powerful our enemy is. It's too much to expect just one person to find them all."

"Your grandmother was the sole Chosen Seeker in her time. She found all four Relics herself. Are you saying you can't handle the same responsibility?"

"No. I'm saying the Seeker Candidates who've spent so much time here, risking everything to help the Otherwhere—well, titles suck, in general. But if the Academy is going to insist on giving one out, the rest of the Seekers deserve it every bit as much as I do. *All for one, and one for all,* as Talia said."

The Headmaster's eyebrows arched, and he drummed his fingertips on his desk. I swallowed hard, wondering if maybe I'd stepped too far over the line this time.

"Well, it's out of the ordinary," Merriwether said at last as he stood up. "But then, so are you. Who am I to deny the wishes of the girl who brought me the Sword of Viviane? We'll announce it in the morning—as well as discuss a memorial service for our fallen Seeker. I know his parents well, so I will be the one to break the news to them. But now, you should head to your quarters and get some rest. You look as exhausted as I feel."

"You're right. I am. But there's one more thing I want to ask..."

"You want to know when you're going home."

I nodded. Part of me was eager to get back to Fairhaven. To talk to Will and see how he was doing in California. To go shopping with Liv and just have one normal day that didn't involve evil warlocks, horse-sized wolves, or a twisted assortment of near-death experiences.

But another part of me dreaded leaving the place I'd come to love...or the *people* I'd grown to love.

"I will tell you—all of you—tomorrow. But for now, try to sleep. And try not to worry."

"About what?"

"About your fate."

# THE TOWER

WHEN I REACHED the top of the Academy's eastern tower, I knocked on Callum's door.

He pulled it open after a few seconds, a crooked grin on his face.

"That's nice to see," I said. "Your smiles have felt like an endangered species lately."

"I've decided I need to be more positive. At least when it comes to you." He backed away and gestured toward the room. "Don't just stand there. Come on in."

"It's strange to be in your quarters," I said as I stepped inside. "I've always been hesitant about it, what with you being an instructor's assistant, and me being a mere student. I felt unworthy, somehow."

"Well, the good news is, I'd say you're higher ranked than I am in the Academy at this point," Callum said with a low bow.

"What do you mean?"

"Well, you *are* the Chosen Seeker, aren't you? There's no way Merriwether could have decided otherwise. That puts you a few steps above me in the Academy's pecking order."

With a laugh, I told him about my conversation with my

grandfather. "It didn't seem right, somehow," I said. "I didn't do any of it on my own. I mean, even the razorbeaks deserve some credit for saving our lives. Tiny little medals around their necks, or something."

"Don't change the subject," Callum chastised as he poured two glasses of water from a pitcher on his nightstand and handed one to me. "You *do* deserve the title. But of course, you're not egotistical enough to see yourself elevated above anyone else."

"I don't want to be elevated. I don't want attention. I just want to help, to be a part of something. And I want..." I cut myself off, my eyes darting around to everything but Callum's own. "I want to stay close to you," I said at last. "I don't want this to be a fling, Callum. I don't want to reduce it to 'nothing important.' I don't want to look back years from now and regret that I didn't at least try to be with someone I cared about as much as I care about you."

Callum took me by the hand, and we both plopped down onto the edge of his bed.

"I feel the same." He leaned back, his glass cradled against his chest. "You're so good. Not only to me, but to all the people you're constantly trying to save. It'll probably get you killed one of these days. And then what will I do?"

"Probably rejoice because your life just got a whole lot easier?" I said with a chuckle before taking a swig of water.

"Never." He set his glass down on the nightstand and gestured for me to do the same.

I did and then twisted around to face him.

His eyes were bright, devoid of any trace of the dragon who tormented him so much. He looked genuinely relaxed and happy for the first time in ages.

"What are you thinking?" I asked, reaching a hand up and playfully dragging the backs of my fingers along the stubble on his jaw.

"I'm thinking about how badly I screwed up. I wanted to push you away—no, *needed* to. I figured it was the only way to protect you. But I forgot that's not who you are. I should have remembered how much you really want to help—to support me, regardless of how broken I may be. I should have let you in. I should have let you know my fears about the future. *All* of them, no matter how bleak."

"I can hardly be angry with you for trying to spare me from getting my heart broken," I said, pulling my eyes down to the floor. "But I will admit…what you said to me hurt a lot more than the truth would have."

"I know."

I lifted my face again, mustering the courage to look at him, my lips defying me and curling into a slight smile as I saw the apologetic affection in his eyes.

"I want to kiss you so badly," he said. "But I don't feel like I deserve to."

"So let me kiss you, then."

Easing toward him, I cupped his chin in the way he so often did to mine and pressed my lips to his.

My intention was a quick, innocent peck, but once again, I found myself overcome by a fierce, insatiable craving. Before I knew it, my hands were on his neck, and I was pushing him down onto the bed, my hands pressed to his chest, kissing him with a wild abandon.

He grabbed me by the waist and flipped me over, and in an instant, we were tangled so I no longer knew which way was up. Gravity seemed to disappear. All that mattered was that we were falling together into an abyss from which we may never be able to escape.

Not that I wanted to.

Callum's lips were on my neck, my jaw, my cheekbone. His skin was warm—hot, even, as his fingers reached for the bottom seam of my tunic.

And then he froze, and I did the same.

I pulled back to see that his eyes were orange with searing, sparking flames dancing in his irises. Pressing my hand to his face, I felt the heat rising through his skin, as if glowing embers lay just below its surface.

"He's in there, isn't he?" I asked softly. "Your dragon. He's pushing himself into your head."

Callum nodded, but I didn't take my hand away. Instead, I pressed my forehead to his, my breath coming hard.

"He won't win," I said. "He won't control you."

"How can you know that, Vega?" Callum breathed, wincing his eyes closed as if to will away the creature consuming him from the inside.

"Because you're Callum Drake. You're the strongest person I've ever met."

"I don't know if I'm strong *enough*."

"You are *so* strong, Callum."

He opened his eyes, patted his chest, and pressed his fingers to his temple. "So is he. How do I know I won't lose myself?"

"I'm not sure," I admitted. But then I laughed and pressed my cheek to his chest. "But even if you do lose yourself, I'm a Seeker. I can hunt Relics for the rest of my life...but it'll always be *you* I hope I find."

# CHOSEN ONES

I AWOKE in the morning with Callum next to me, his breath coming in deep, soothing waves.

It was easily the most beautiful sound I'd ever heard.

We were both fully clothed, having spent another mostly innocent night together. It was another of our unspoken agreements: keeping risk to a minimum while still enjoying the benefits of one another's company.

Even with a modicum of self-restraint, sleeping next to Callum was the most pleasant way I could imagine spending a night.

With the morning light pouring in, a rush of pleasure wound its way through my mind to watch him resting so peacefully. For what had seemed like a long time, a shadow had been hanging over him. Something untouchable, unseeable, a nebulous entity I couldn't reach. But now that it had cleared away, we'd both settled into a new sense of calm, despite the uncertainty of both our futures.

After a time, he popped awake, smiling when he saw me staring at him.

"Morning," he said with a stretch and a yawn.

"Morning."

"What are we up to today, Miss Sloane?"

"We're headed to the Great Hall. And the rest, I'm afraid, is a typical Merriwether mystery."

"Well then, let's get started. I love a good mystery." He spoke the words with an encouraging smile. And, rather than allow myself to be overcome with dread, I chose optimism.

After a quick kiss, I left Callum to shower and change into fresh clothes before meeting him back at his room to head down together to the Great Hall for breakfast.

The air in the Academy felt strangely fresh, as if a new season had come overnight and brought with it a cleansing of some kind. It wasn't until we'd sat down with our food, surrounded by what looked like almost every one of the Academy's students, that a heavy feeling fell over the place.

Almost no one was speaking, and anyone who did want to communicate did so by whispering. Looking around, I recalled with a feeling of deep remorse the horrifying reality that we'd lost a Seeker last night.

"Everyone's thinking about Cairn," I said to Callum. "I wonder when the service will take place."

"We'll find out in a second," Callum replied, nodding toward the doors.

Merriwether was making his way into the Great Hall, the floating lights around us dimming as he marched up to the front of the chamber. He was dressed all in black, the expression on his face grave as he turned to face the sea of students.

"Forgive me for interrupting your meal," he said as the buzzing in the room died down and faded away. "As you all know by now, we lost someone last night. A Seeker by the name of Cairn. He served the Academy well during his time with us. He was an exemplary student and a brave warrior, and his loss will be felt in this place for the rest of time. His family in Ireland has been notified. His grandfather was a Seeker, and his parents knew of his presence at the Academy. Needless to say, they are devastated, but they wanted me to convey…" with that, he pulled his eyes to mine, "…that Cairn was well aware of the risks of being a Seeker. His greatest wish was to attend the Academy for the Blood-Born." Merriwether paused, a lump rising and falling in his throat. "We will hold a brief memorial for him in a few hours. His parents will honor him in his hometown, of course."

I bowed my head, trying to shake the image of the boy, hardened to stone, crumbling to inhuman pieces on the ground. The ugly truth was, I would always question whether I could have done something to help him. I would always wonder if my weakness, my inexperience, or just my plain stupidity had contributed to his death.

Callum, seeming to sense my sadness, reached over and squeezed my hand. "It wasn't your fault," he whispered. "Don't ever think it was. Always remember who killed Cairn. It was Lumus alone."

I nodded, though I wasn't sure I entirely agreed. Last night, Merriwether had told me it was my responsibility, and somehow, "responsibility" felt like even more of a burden than "fault."

"Two others were injured," Merriwether continued, "but thanks largely to Niala's quick reflexes and her skill as a Healer, they'll be fine. They're in the Infirmary right now, actively resisting the nurse's orders to rest." The Headmaster paused for a round of applause for Niala, who was sitting two tables away from us with several other Casters. "Now," Merriwether continued, "I need to move onto other business, as we have little time to lose. Cairn did *not* die in vain. Like many others, he was on a mission—one that succeeded against all odds. Most of you know that we now have in our possession the Sword of Viviane—one of the four Relics of Power."

The Seekers, dressed in their silver tunics, shot looks at one another and exchanged quick smiles, as well as nods of silent congratulations. As I watched them from the table where I sat with Callum, a feeling of affectionate pride swept its way through me. In a matter of days, we'd become a family, in spite of everything. We felt pain and joy as one entity, and the success of one of us had become the success of all.

"It was Vega Sloane who brought me the sword," Merriwether added. "It should come as no surprise, therefore, that I fully intended to name her the Academy's Chosen Seeker."

As he spoke, every student in the room turned my way. Some Zerkers and Casters gave me the thumbs' up, while others scowled, annoyed at the very mention of my name.

But every single Seeker smiled encouragement in my direction. They seemed genuinely happy for me, despite the fact that they'd all spent far more hours in the training ring than I had and probably deserved the title far more.

"However," Merriwether bellowed, drawing every set of eyes in the room back to his, "Miss Sloane has refused to accept the title."

Stunned murmurs rose up through the room, and once again, curious eyes turned my way as Seekers whispered to one another. I caught Niala and Rourke, in his tabby cat form, peering at me curiously through narrowed eyes.

Merriwether held up his hands to silence the room. "Vega has, however, suggested that the title of Chosen Seeker be shared equally among herself and her peers. With that in mind, Seeker Candidates, I ask that you rise."

Exchanging wide-eyed looks, the table of silver-clad students rose to their feet. I sat stone-still until a steely look from Merriwether and a nudge from Callum urged me out of my seat.

"In the name of the Academy for the Blood-Born, I hereby name you—and by that, I mean every *one* of you—Chosen Seekers. You will hold this title until such a time as all four Relics of Power have been found, either by our side or by the enemy. I warn you, however, this will not be an easy task, and it is entirely possible that you will fail more than once. We will experience more loss. I won't lie to you about that. The queen may yet locate another Relic—or she may acquire every one of those that still remain hidden. She will stop at nothing to gain the upper hand in this war. I ask only that you work together, and that you trust each other. Do you accept?"

As if we'd rehearsed it, every Seeker in the room spoke two words:

"*I do!*"

"Good. Oh, and there is one other thing." Merriwether eyed each of us in turn as he spoke. "I will be sending you to your respective homes today. You may think your time at the Academy has come to an end, but it has not. You all have a great deal yet to learn. Some of your lessons will take place in your hometowns. Others may take place in this very institution, though I cannot yet tell you when or how. With so many of you leaving the Otherwhere, the queen now has multiple moving targets—which gives us an advantage I hadn't foreseen. The queen's resources will be stretched thin. But know this: You will be watched. You will be hunted. And, when the time comes, you will be called upon to fight in the name of the Academy."

My stomach tied itself into a thick, painful knot as I recalled my various altercations in Fairhaven with the queen's minions before I'd come into my powers. Confronting a Waerg in a dark alley in my small hometown was bad enough. I could only imagine what she'd try now that she knew how determined I was.

"For now," Merriwether continued, "you are no longer Seeker *Candidates,* but simply *Seekers.* You are free to return to your homes in the other world. The instructors will guide you through the portals I have opened for you. The rest is up to fate." The Headmaster glanced around the Great Hall. "As for the rest of the Academy's students, you will be called upon as you are needed, whether in our land or in the other world. This is the time you've trained for. More than one battle is coming, and I need you to prepare yourselves."

The Headmaster waved a hand in the air, and the lights flickered back to a powerful, warm glow that immediately lightened any remnants of the dark mood that still lingered in the room.

"You are dismissed."

After everyone sat back down and the excited chattering had begun once again, I turned to Callum. But unlike every other student in the Great Hall, I couldn't bring myself to speak. Instead, I stared down to my interlocked hands, torn between happiness and a profound sense of loss.

"So, you're heading back to Fairhaven," he said. "I suppose you'll be leaving any minute now."

"Not quite yet," I replied, trying to push away the sadness burrowing its way deep into my chest. "I'm not even sure I *have* to leave today. I can't quite fathom it. I can't imagine leaving you behind. But I know it's what I have to do. We've known from the start that I'd have to head back sometime."

"Well, one thing is for sure," Callum said, reaching out to tuck my hair behind my ear.

"What's that?" I mumbled, still unable to look at him.

"You're not going anywhere without me, Vega Sloane."

My head jerked involuntarily so I was staring into his incredible blue eyes. "Don't tease me," I said when I saw the smile on his face.

"I'm not teasing at all. The thing is, I still have a job at the Novel Hovel. Besides, I've always wanted to know what the high school experience is like in your world. I was thinking I might enroll at Plymouth High, just for fun."

"Seriously? You're really coming to Fairhaven with me?" I asked, trying in vain to keep my voice down. "Tell me this isn't a joke."

"I mean, there will be complications. There's the dragon inside me, who's about to become a raging pain in my arse. So I'll have to be a little careful. But of *course* I'm going with you. I mean, if you'll have me."

I leaned over and threw my arms around his neck, and for once, I didn't care who saw me do it. After all, I was no longer a student, at least not in the traditional sense. I was free to move between worlds. Free to pursue whatever destiny awaited me.

I was going home, and Callum was coming with me.

"Of course I'll have you," I said, tears streaming down my face.

By now, the other Seekers had made their way over to our table and were politely waiting for my public display of affection to end so they could high-five me.

"Do you know how amazing this is? We'll all be able to hunt—err, seek—together," Desmond chirped.

"That might be a little tricky, Des," Oleana said, "given that we live on different continents and all."

"Well, Vega will find a way. Won't you? You can summon one of your doors, and we can all find our way to one another."

"Um…yes," I laughed at last. "I guess I can!"

"I can't believe you did this for us," Desmond gushed. "You would have been totally within your rights to hold onto the title, but you shared it. Who *does* that?"

"I can believe Vega did it," Meg said, grinning from ear to ear. "I've always known she was one of the good ones."

"I didn't mean she wasn't good…" Desmond stammered, red-faced. "I just meant…"

"It's okay," I laughed. "All I want to know is that you guys will have my back when the time comes. We have to find the Relics. That's the only thing that matters now."

"And we will," Oleana said, eyeing me before shooting Callum a shy look. "I mean, not all of us will have dragon shifters on our side, so we'll need your help, too."

"And you'll have it," I assured her. "I promise. I'll see you all in our world."

For the first time since I'd left Fairhaven, I couldn't wait to go back.

# FAREWELLS

WHEN WE'D FINISHED breakfast and said good-bye to the Seekers, Callum and I made our way to the Academy's infirmary to see Niala, who'd headed there to help the two Seekers who had been injured the previous night.

"How are they doing?" I asked her as she washed her hands in a sink some distance from the patients' beds.

"They're going to be fine," she replied. "The girl—Talia—her wounds were deeper than Crane's. One slash of the wolf's claws almost made it as far as her heart. But she was awake for a little while this morning, and in good spirits. Honestly, all they both wanted to do was join everyone for Merriwether's morning announcements."

"The nurse should've let them."

"I said that, too. But they couldn't even stand up, not without being in agony. I think their ambitions were stronger than their bodies. Anyhow, they need to rest. They have a long road ahead of them, if they're to help hunt the Relics."

"Well," I said, "you're a miracle worker. If you hadn't been there in that corridor last night, they'd be dead."

"If you hadn't been there, we'd *all* be dead," she replied, glancing at me then Callum. "We all owe you two a huge debt."

"I don't know about that. If I hadn't been stupid enough to lead us all into danger…"

Niala raised a defiant hand. "Raff was the one who led us, and we went willingly. We all thought we were doing something good. As I recall, you were the last person who agreed to go."

Callum, silent, laid a hand on my back as if to remind me what he'd said earlier.

*It's not your fault.*

"Listen," I said, eager to change the subject, "I—we—came to say goodbye. We're heading back to Fairhaven in a little while. Right after Cairn's service."

Neither Niala's face nor her voice showed any emotion, and Rourke, in his tabby cat form, simply sat on the floor, staring up at me. "Well, I hope you have a good trip."

I opened my mouth to respond but found myself throwing my arms around her neck instead. Hugging me back, she whispered, "I suspect we'll see each other very soon."

AFTER THE BRIEF but emotional funeral service in a small chapel at the Academy's north end, our next and final stop was Merriwether's office. He was seated behind his desk, staring contemplatively at the contents of a thick hardcover book.

"Ah, Vega. Are you ready for your next adventure?" he asked.

"As ready as I can be, I suppose. Though I do have a question." "Yes?"

"If we Seekers are all going home, how will we know what to do? I mean, how will we know where to look for the Relics?"

Merriwether let out a quiet laugh. "You ask me that, and yet just last night you found one and brought it here."

"I didn't find it. Raff gave me the clue in the prison, and…" I stopped talking when I saw the mischievous glint in my grandfather's eye. "You think it was fate," I said. "You think it was all meant to happen in exactly the way it did."

"I think there's a reason you left for Uldrach that night, that you ended up imprisoned in the queen's dungeon, and that you met the boy named Raff, yes. There is a reason he told you that verse. Perhaps he thought he was helping his own people by deceiving you, or by gaining your trust. But just as it was his destiny to convey the verse to you, it was yours to find the Relic."

"So the rest of the clues will just magically reveal themselves to us Seekers?" I asked. "When?"

"You're eager to find them," Merriwether said. "You want to get them before the queen can get her hands on them."

"Of course. I mean, sort of." I looked at Callum before glancing back at my grandfather. "Except…"

"Except for the fact that if you find them, your work in the Otherwhere will be done, and you may never see Mr. Drake again."

Callum reached out and took my hand as I nodded.

"If it makes you feel any better, Vega, your grandmother was a gifted Seeker. The best. And it took her over a year to find all the Relics. It may take you and your peers even longer."

"Really?"

Merriwether nodded. "They have a habit of keeping themselves concealed until they feel the time is right. The Sword of Viviane revealed itself, but who's to say when that time will be for the others? Either way, you have as good a chance of finding them as the queen's minions do. Better, I'd say, since they are relying on unconventional methods which may or may not serve their purpose."

"They don't have a Seeker to help them," I said. "That's good, right?"

"It is," Merriwether replied, but he looked concerned. "But don't forget, there are other Seekers out there."

I felt a frown crease my forehead. "I thought all the Seekers were invited to the Academy. I figured we were all accounted for."

"Not all who are invited choose to come. And some find themselves expelled for one reason or another. I'm sure you recall one such incident."

"Freya," I replied, remembering the girl who'd flung a giant rock at my head during one of my first ever sparring matches. A *Pathic*—a Seeker gifted with the ability to move objects with her mind. "You really think she'd help the other side?"

"There's no way to know. The important thing is that you and the others remain vigilant in your search."

"I can only imagine that my sister is seething with rage at the moment," Callum interjected. "She'll be chomping at the bit to find a way to beat us. If that means acquiring the help of a Seeker who's angry with the Academy, that's exactly what she'll do."

"True." Merriwether scratched at his silver stubble. "The queen—and her warlock husband—enjoy playing games, like cats with a mouse. I've seen the full extent of Lumus's power. I have some idea what he's capable of. If I were you, Vega, I would be wary when you return to Fairhaven. All may seem peaceful at first, but their side has spies everywhere. Trust no one, and trust nothing but your own instincts. Those who may seem friendly— even students at your own school—may work for the enemy."

"I'll be careful."

Merriwether laid a hand on Callum's shoulder. "Look after her, would you? She's extremely valuable—and valued."

"I wouldn't dream of letting her out of my sight."

"Good. Now go. Pack your things and head home. I'll see you again, perhaps sooner than you expect."

Without a word, I leapt over to my grandfather. And for the first time, I wrapped my arms around his neck, hugging him tight.

He tightened as though he wasn't sure what he was supposed

to do, but after a few seconds, I felt his arms tangle around me in a firm hug of his own.

"Be careful, Granddaughter," he said softly. "I don't want to lose you."

"You won't lose me. Not ever."

AN HOUR LATER, I finished assembling my few belongings into a satchel and was about to head over to knock on Callum's door when a fist thumped against my own.

"Come in," I called.

The door opened, and Callum walked in.

"You ready?" he asked with a bittersweet smile.

"I am. Are you?"

"I'm all packed," he said.

"That doesn't answer my question. I asked if you're *ready*."

"You mean emotionally."

I nodded. "It can't be easy for you to leave this place, with everything going on here. I know you feel protective of the Otherwhere."

"I do. But the best way to protect it is to stay close to you. And that's the easiest thing I can imagine."

Grinning, I grabbed my bag, reaching in to pull out my cell phone, which still glowed with the Academy's sigil. "I haven't looked at this thing in ages. So weird. I used to stare at it for hours on end, like it was my best friend in the world. Now I've practically forgotten it exists."

"Maybe when we're back in your world it'll become more important."

"Maybe."

As we headed down the tower's spiral staircase, I stopped and peered out a narrow window to the wild green terrain of the Otherwhere to the north of the Academy. "I'm going to miss this place. I feel like my time here isn't over yet, like I just got here yesterday. I could stay for years and still not learn enough."

"You've learned far more in a few short weeks than most Seekers learn in a lifetime, Vega. Besides, something tells me you'll be back here soon. In the meantime, I must admit I'm really looking forward to seeing Fairhaven again. I liked that place."

"Liv is going to lose her mind," I laughed. "When she finds out about us, I mean."

"Yeah, about that…what do you plan on telling her?"

"Oh, I have my story all plotted out," I said. "She'll take all the credit for setting us up, of course."

"Of course," he laughed. "She does sort of deserve it, after all. She *is* the one who introduced us."

"It's true."

It felt like years now since the morning of my seventeenth birthday when I'd first set eyes on Callum. So much had happened. So much had changed. I was no longer the same girl, and I could never be, not after everything I'd seen and done.

With a deep breath, I turned away from the window. "Ready?"

"Ready."

I took a deep breath and called for a door to take us home.

WE STEPPED through into my bedroom back in Fairhaven to find a cool late-summer breeze flitting through the silky white curtains.

"It feels like autumn," I said as I looked out the window. "So strange. By my calculations, it should still be around...August first?"

"Should it?"

"What are you suggesting?" I asked with a raised eyebrow.

"Check your phone."

I pulled my cell phone out of my bag and clicked it on. As always, its screen came to life despite the fact that I hadn't charged it in weeks. But the Academy's sigil was gone, and a photo of Will and me occupied the background behind a mind-numbing array of useless apps.

I pulled my eyes to the time and date.

"Holy crap!" I shouted. "Is this really right? It says it's August 20th!"

"Huh," said Callum. "Imagine that."

I cocked my head and stared at him. "Did you know?"

"Know what?" he asked with a shrug. "All I know is that the

relationship of time between our worlds has a funny tendency to accommodate Seekers. If you're meant to return to Fairhaven today, well, that's your fate."

"But if it's really August 20th, that means Will has been in California for weeks now. He'll be going crazy that I haven't called him once, or emailed, or…"

"Something tells me you should check your messages."

Panicked, I clicked on my text messages, only to see a massive assortment of notes passed back and forth between Will and myself.

"*So glad to hear you're planning to take a bit of a holiday,*" he'd written on August 2nd. "*I've been wanting that for you for a long time. Things here are good, but busy. I'll get back to you when I have more time, but stay safe, okay?*"

"Holiday?" I asked, looking up at Callum.

"Read on."

August 10th: "*The new guy in your life sounds great, V. Just make sure he treats you right. Glad you're having fun camping with your friends. Get in touch when you're back.*"

"Really? My brother thinks I went on a camping holiday? Doesn't he know that I don't actually *have* friends other than Liv?"

"Well, the camping thing's not entirely a lie, is it? I mean, if you think of the Academy as a really, really big tent made of stone."

"Yeah. Because stone tents are all the rage with teenage campers."

"Well, we *did* go hiking in the mountains," he added with a shrug. "Did some training, had some challenges. You even got to do some bird-watching…"

I laughed. "Wait. Did *you* write these messages?"

Callum shook his head. "No! I would never invade your privacy. Plus, I'm not a wizard or anything. It's not like I have the power to hack your phone with a magical spell."

"Merriwether," I said under my breath.

Not that I minded. He'd kept my brother from worrying about me during his first weeks in a new city, and that was all I cared about.

Now I'd have to figure out how to explain my absence to Liv, who would probably be livid that I hadn't texted her to let her know I wouldn't be in Fairhaven when her family's road trip ended.

"Well," I sighed, "I have to admit I'm a little disappointed that it's so late in the summer already. I was sort of hoping you and I could spend a few weeks lazing around together before school starts up again," I said. "But this is good, too, I suppose. I could use the distraction of normal high school life after the summer I've had."

"No doubt. Now, how about if you show me around your home, Sloane? I'm curious to see the house where I'll be staying."

"Staying?" My eyes went wide. "You mean you're going to stay here, with me?"

"Of course. It would hardly do to have you be here alone. What if the enemy were to threaten you?"

"You raise a very good point," I laughed. "I could definitely use your protection." I pushed myself up onto my toes and kissed him. "But more than that, I'm just glad to know you'll be sleeping in my bed."

"Ah, I see where your priorities lie." Callum was smiling, but his body tensed as he said the words.

"What's going through that extremely complicated mind of yours?" I asked. "I mean, we don't have to sleep in the same room if you don't want to."

"It's not about that, believe me. It's just...you know my time is coming. I don't want to be more of a danger to you than whatever might be lurking out *there.*"

"I know. But I'll be here for you. Besides, I think my presence calms you, at least when you're asleep."

"True."

But he didn't look convinced.

"I can feel him," he said softly. "Even now. Gathering strength. He's itching to fight. It's like there's a storm inside me, barreling toward...something I can't quite make out. But at least for now, I'm holding it back."

"Then we'll have to figure out how to make the storm our ally. It's as simple as that. Now come on, let's not start our time in Fairhaven with worrying and what-if scenarios. You've always told me to have faith in my brain. My strength. My abilities." I pulled him close and cupped his stubbled cheeks in my hands. "Now I want you to have faith in your own."

Callum stayed still for a long moment before exhaling. "Fair enough," he said with a smile that seemed genuinely relaxed. "So, what do we do now?"

I pulled away and smiled. "Now, I'm going to give you a tour of my house. Then we'll order pizza and watch bad movies until we both pass out. Because for a few hours, I need to be a normal teenager."

"That actually sounds...amazing."

CALLUM SLEPT in my bed that night, his arm draped protectively around my waist as usual. We stuck to our plan to remain well-behaved and respectful, each of us dressed in shorts and a t-shirt for good measure.

It was four in the morning when I popped awake, my mind reeling from a dream.

I couldn't remember the details, only that something was chasing me through the streets of Fairhaven—something beautiful but cruel. I kept crying out for help, but people simply walked by, unseeing, as though both my pursuer and I were invisible.

It was only when the entity caught me and dragged me backwards that I finally woke up, my t-shirt soaked in sweat.

I slipped out of bed and over to the open window, inhaling the damp night air to calm my raging heart. Callum was still asleep in the bed, his chest rising and falling slowly under the old, faded shirt that had once belonged to Will.

I was about to crawl back in beside him when something outside caught my eye.

A rabbit, hopping across the neighbor's lawn.

*So strange,* I thought. *I haven't seen a rabbit in ages…*

With its ears back and the white underside of its tail flashing in the dark, it almost made it to the other side of the street when something came charging at it in a frenzied blur of speed and power.

Before my eyes could register what had happened, the rabbit was gone.

I pressed my hands to the windowsill, freezing in place as I stared down at the huge animal that had consumed the poor creature in one quick bite.

Panting heavily, its eyes flickering unnaturally bright in the moonlight, an enormous wolf locked its silvery eyes onto mine.

# COMING SOON: SEEKER'S FATE

With Vega Sloane's return to Fairhaven comes the beginning of her senior year at Plymouth High. Which, of course, means friends, parties, and drama. Tensions arise with her best friend, Liv, who isn't exactly excited by Vega's new circle of friends...not to mention that keeping a constant eye out for mortal enemies can seriously eat into a girl's social life.

But a Seeker's work is never finished, and Vega has a crucial task ahead of her: to find the Lyre of Adair before the Usurper Queen's minions do.

*Seeker's Fate* is available for pre-order, and releases November 2nd, 2020!

# ALSO BY K. A. RILEY

## Seeker's Series

*Seeker's World*

*Seeker's Quest*

*Seeker's Fate (November 2020)*

*...and more, coming soon!*

## The Conspiracy Chronicles:

### *Resistance Trilogy*

*Recruitment*

*Render*

*Rebellion*

### *Emergents Trilogy*

*Survival*

*Sacrifice*

*Synthesis*

**Transcendent Trilogy**

*Travelers*

*Transfigured*

*Terminus*

**Athena's Law Series**

Book One: *Rise of the Inciters*

Book Two: *Into an Unholy Land*

Book Three: *No Man's Land*

If you're enjoying K. A. Riley's books, please consider leaving a review on Amazon or Goodreads to let your fellow book-lovers know about it. And be sure to sign up for my newsletter at www.karileywrites.org for news, quizzes, contests, behind-the-scenes peeks into the writing process, and advance info. about upcoming projects!

K.A. Riley's Bookbub Author Page

K.A. Riley on Amazon.com

K.A. Riley on Goodreads.com

Printed in Germany
by Amazon Distribution
GmbH, Leipzig

21096049R00188